Holly and Ivy

Books by Fern Michaels

Fancy Dancer
No Safe Secret
Wishes for Christmas
About Face
Perfect Match
A Family Affair
Forget Me Not
The Blossom Sisters
Balancing Act
Tuesday's Child
Betrayal
Southern Comfort
To Taste the Wine
Sins of the Flesh
Sins of Omission
Return to Sender
Mr. and Miss Anonymous
Up Close and Personal
Fool Me Once
Picture Perfect
The Future Scrolls
Kentucky Sunrise
Kentucky Heat
Kentucky Rich
Plain Jane
Charming Lily
What You Wish For
The Guest List
Listen to Your Heart
Celebration
Yesterday
Finders Keepers
Annie's Rainbow
Sara's Song

Vegas Sunrise
Vegas Heat
Vegas Rich
Whitefire
Wish List
Dear Emily
Christmas at Timberwoods

The Sisterhood Novels:

Crash and Burn
Point Blank
In Plain Sight
Eyes Only
Kiss and Tell
Blindsided
Gotcha!
Home Free
Déjà Vu
Cross Roads
Game Over
Deadly Deals
Vanishing Act
Razor Sharp
Under the Radar
Final Justice
Collateral Damage
Fast Track
Hokus Pokus
Hide and Seek
Free Fall
Lethal Justice
Sweet Revenge
The Jury

Books by Fern Michaels (Cont.)

Vendetta
Payback
Weekend Warriors

The Men of the Sisterhood Novels:

High Stakes
Fast and Loose
Double Down

The Godmothers Series:

Getaway (E-Novella Exclusive)
Spirited Away (E-Novella Exclusive)
Hideaway (E-Novella Exclusive)
Classified
Breaking News
Deadline
Late Edition
Exclusive
The Scoop

E-Book Exclusives:

Desperate Measures
Seasons of Her Life
To Have and To Hold
Serendipity

Captive Innocence
Captive Embraces
Captive Passions
Captive Secrets
Captive Splendors
Cinders to Satin
For All Their Lives
Texas Heat
Texas Rich
Texas Fury
Texas Sunrise

Anthologies:

Winter Wishes
The Most Wonderful Time
When the Snow Falls
Secret Santa
A Winter Wonderland
I'll Be Home for Christmas
Making Spirits Bright
Holiday Magic
Snow Angels
Silver Bells
Comfort and Joy
Sugar and Spice
Let it Snow
A Gift of Joy
Five Golden Rings
Deck the Halls
Jingle All the Way

FERN
MICHAELS

Holly and Ivy

KENSINGTON PUBLISHING CORP.
http://www.kensingtonbooks.com

KENSINGTON BOOKS are published by

Kensington Publishing Corp.
119 West 40th Street
New York, NY 10018

All Kensington titles, imprints and distributed lines are available at special quantity discounts for bulk purchases for sales promotion, premiums, fund-raising, educational or institutional use.

Special book excerpts or customized printings can also be created to fit specific needs. For details, write or phone the office of the Kensington Special Sales Manager: Kensington Publishing Corp., 119 West 40th Street, New York, NY, 10018. Attn. Special Sales Department. Phone: 1-800-221-2647.

Kensington and the K logo Reg. U.S. Pat. & TM Off.

Library of Congress Control Number: 2017944849

ISBN-13: 978-1-4967-0317-0
ISBN-10: 1-4967-0317-0
First Kensington Hardcover Edition: October 2017

eISBN-13: 978-1-4967-0316-3
eISBN-10: 1-4967-0316-2
First Kensington Electronic Edition: October 2017

10 9 8 7 6 5 4 3 2 1

Printed in the United States of America

The holly and the ivy,
When they are both full grown,
Of all the trees that are in the wood,
The holly bears the crown.
The rising of the sun
And the running of the deer,
The playing of the merry organ,
Sweet singing in the choir.

—"The Holly and the Ivy," traditional carol

Prologue

Pine City, North Carolina
December 2008

"We'll be just fine, Ivy. They were great on the flight to Charlotte, it's a quick one. We'll be home by the time you're having your first cup of coffee," John Fine explained to his wife of five years. "Of course this all depends if our flight arrives on time," he added.

Ivy smiled. "Dad would spit nails if he heard you say that." John had taken their twins, Elizabeth and James, for a three-day trip to Charlotte to visit his sister, who was home on a short leave from the military. Ivy's sister-in-law had never met her niece and nephew, and they had both decided this was a great time, since Piper was spending the few days in Charlotte with her and John's parents. They had flown courtesy of Macintosh Airlines, owned by Ivy's family, and most recently touted as the fastest-growing airline in the country. She had had a mandatory meeting she couldn't get out of, but felt sure John would do fine on his own. It was only for three days.

"Then make sure you don't tell him I said that," John teased.

"I won't. Don't forget to give Elizabeth Mr. Tibbles when you put her to bed tonight."

John had called her their first night away, explaining that Elizabeth refused to go to bed without Mr. Tibbles, a stuffed bear Elizabeth had become attached to when Ivy had moved her into her big-girl bedroom a month ago. Being a twin, her daughter was extremely attached to her older-by-three-minutes brother, James. It was at James's insistence that Ivy had decided they were old enough for rooms of their own. Added to that was the fact that her son made it very clear that he did not like girly dolls in his room. After all, he was three years old.

Ivy thought of her daughter's cherubic little face and smiled at the memory of her waving good-bye as they had boarded the plane. Now she was glad she'd remembered to tuck Mr. Tibbles in the suitcase at the last minute.

"Trust me, after last night's fiasco hunting for that bear, it'll be a long time before I ever forget Mr. Tibbles."

"I should have told you, I could've saved you a bedtime fit," Ivy said, a smile spreading across her face. John hadn't witnessed their bedtime ritual since they had put Elizabeth in a room of her own.

"We'll both put her to bed tomorrow," John added.

Ivy knew this was his way of telling her he was sorry he hadn't been at home to put the kids to bed lately, but she understood. He was her father's right-hand man at the airline and traveled frequently; though he tried to work his schedule around their family, it wasn't always possible. She worked for her father's airline as well, but since she'd had the kids, she had tried to keep her hours as close to nine to five as one could. Yesterday's meeting, however, had been mandatory, so John took the kids on his own. He was a great father, and Ivy hadn't given a second thought to his flying to Charlotte with the twins. His first time flying with the kids without her.

"I'll hold you to that. Now, let me tell them good night. They've got an early morning ahead of them."

She heard John call Elizabeth and James to the phone, their excited voices becoming louder as they neared the phone.

"Mommy, I want to kiss you," Elizabeth said. "Make the noise like Daddy does, okay?"

Ivy smiled. On the nights John wasn't home, whenever possible, he called them at bedtime, and he would make lip-puckering, sloppy-kiss noises over the phone. Both kids would giggle, asking him to repeat it over and over, and now, it seemed, it was her turn.

She did her best to replicate John's kisses, but Elizabeth told her she wasn't as noisy as Daddy, but it was okay. James, her little man, informed her he was too big for phone kisses, and said good night, he would see her tomorrow.

Ivy could hear John, Piper, and her in-laws laughing in the background. Poor James—at three, he was already an old soul.

"I'll say good night, and we'll see you in the morning," John said before hanging up.

Content with the evening's end, Ivy had decided earlier in the day to surprise John and the kids with a giant Christmas tree, which they could spend the day decorating. At lunchtime, she had gone to Baker's Tree Farm, one of the oldest family-owned tree farms in Pine City, and picked out a twelve-foot Fraser fir, making arrangements for it to be delivered to the house this afternoon. It was only ten days until Christmas, and they had never waited this long to put up their tree. With her bout of bronchitis turning into pneumonia, then both kids coming down with the chicken pox, it simply had not been any kind of priority.

Better late than never, she thought as she made herself a cup of hot tea before heading into the living room, where she'd had the tree set up. The hundreds of tiny white lights Kyle Baker had added made her job so much easier. While she loved decorating the tree, in the past she had been tangled up in too many strings of Christmas lights to really enjoy it, so Baker's effort had taken care of this for her.

She inhaled the fresh pine scent and sighed. This was her favorite time of year, and she never tired of dragging the dozens of boxes downstairs, one by one, removing the ornaments, each with its own special memory. She had placed the boxes next to the dark brown leather sofa. Placing her cup of tea on the coffee table, she carefully removed the tissue paper from the first ornament.

It was a small crystal angel etched in gold trim, which was now barely visible, its soft blue eyes had faded with time. It had a small chip on its left wing, and Ivy teared up every year when she removed this ornament from her special box. The angel was the last ornament given to her by her mother before she had died, when Ivy was just nine years old. She'd cherished it her entire life. There were only a few clear memories left of her mother, as the woman had been ill ever since Ivy was a baby, but she never failed to remember her mother's excitement during the Christmas holiday. She seemed to come alive just for the month of December; then, when the cold, stark month of January rolled around, she would return to her room upstairs and spend her days and nights being cared for by Lila, her nurse and the mother of one of Ivy's friends.

Her mother had given her the angel on their last Christmas together. Ivy would never forget her words when she'd presented the small ornament to her.

"Every time you hang this on the Christmas tree, know I am with you."

She hadn't really understood the significance at the time, but as she got older, she knew exactly what her mother's words meant. And each year, she would hang the ornament at the very top of the tree, knowing that her mother was looking down from heaven and was always with her. She carefully placed the angel aside, as this would be added to the tree later, when Elizabeth and James had their chance to decorate with their own three-year-old-appropriate ornaments. They were still little, and she didn't want to risk her special ornaments getting broken. Ivy understood three-year-old hands weren't as careful as her twenty-eight-year-old ones.

She spent the next two hours unpacking boxes of tiny sleighs, smiling snowmen, and dozens of bells in red and green. She left the colored balls in their boxes, but stacked them beside the tree, counting each box to make sure she had divided them evenly. Three boxes apiece should be enough. One for each year should just about cover their limited attention spans.

Ivy planned to spend the next week frantically shopping for the kids; then she and John would remain at home until after the New Year. They had talked briefly about taking the kids on a skiing vacation, but neither had committed just yet. Making last-minute plans was one of the perks of having a father who owned an airline. They never had to wait for discounted tickets, blackout dates were unheard of, and the long lines through security were avoided, since she, John, and the kids had applied and received TSA security clearance as soon as the service was available to the public.

They tried to keep their home life as routine as possible, but there were times when both she and John were called away. Her mother's former nurse, Lila, had a daughter, Rebecca, who was three years older than Ivy. They'd been friends since they were kids, and now Rebecca was as good as family. Elizabeth and James called her Aunt Becca, and Rebecca had saved Ivy on numerous occasions when she and John had to leave on urgent business trips. With luck, they could all stay home the next few weeks and simply enjoy being a family.

While Ivy missed her mother terribly, she had never felt as though she had missed things other girls her age had. Her father, an incredible man, had made it his life's mission to see that her needs were met in the same way that girls her age who had mothers were. He had encouraged her friendship with Rebecca, and even though at the time of her mother's death, the three-year age difference between them seemed enormous, they'd been as close as sisters and remained so. Her father took great pride in being a hands-on parent. Even though the airline often took him all over the world, she was never in any doubt that she was the most important person in his life. Ivy would accompany him sometimes, and these trips made her decide to follow in her father's footsteps. She had attended Duke University, received her master's degree in business, and to this day enjoyed every minute of the business her father had worked so hard to make a success. And it was a major success. Its main hub was in Charlotte, a short plane ride from Pine City, but most of her business could be conducted in the Pine City branch office. Ivy did her best to be a loving wife and mother, put her family first, and if the light in John's eyes and the joy she saw in her children's faces were any indication of her success, she thought she was doing a pretty darn good job at this *family thing*. She smiled, as that was John's favorite way of referring to her as a mother and himself as a father. Their *family thing*.

For the next hour, she added the ornaments that required a special connection to the strands of lights. When she finished, she viewed her handiwork. While she would never be the next Martha Stewart, so far the tree looked pretty festive and smelled divine. Once the kids added their decorations, it would be complete. She reached for her mug of tea, took a sip of its now-cold contents, made a face, and headed to the kitchen to make a cup of chamomile tea, hoping its calming effects would relax her enough so she could rest. She planned to get up before the kids arrived to make their favorite breakfast of chocolate chip pancakes and cheesy scrambled eggs. She filled her cup with water and heated it in the microwave. Normally, she would use her teakettle to heat the water, but she just wanted to take her cup upstairs and unwind with a hot bath.

Ten minutes later, she was soaking in a steaming tub of hot water, the master bathroom filled with the luscious-smelling gardenia-scented bath bombs she'd purchased at a local shop in Pine City, which had just opened last month. Ivy frequented as many local businesses as possible. Shopping in malls and chain stores was fine for the most part, but she had always preferred to shop locally. It was more personal, plus she had made a few good friends by doing so throughout the years. There was a new children's shop that had opened in the summer, and she hadn't had a chance to check it out. Rebecca told her it specialized in unique toys and handmade clothes. This might be the perfect place for her to get a jump start on her late holiday shopping.

She quickly rinsed off and stepped out of the tub. If she wanted to be up before John and the kids arrived, she'd best call it a night. Making fast work of combing out her long honey blond–colored hair, the exact shade as her mother's had been, she quickly worked through the tangles. She remembered as a child how her father would brush her mother's long hair, and her mother's smile, one of total bliss and just a hint of mischievousness. Or it may have been another kind of bliss, one that she was too young to acknowledge at the time. She gazed into the mirror and saw much of her mother in her reflection. Yet there was a great deal of her father, too. She had his *viridian*-colored eyes, John always said, and she would correct him stating that they were just *green*. James and Elizabeth did, too, yet they had John's toffee-colored hair, along with the curls she'd found so sexy the first time she spotted him lounging under a giant oak tree on Duke's campus one Saturday afternoon after she'd spent the morning in the Perkins Library researching a term paper. Their eyes locked, he smiled at her, and as they say, the rest is history.

She slipped into her pajamas, checked the alarm system, clicked the downstairs lights off, then returned to the master bedroom. After she had settled in bed, she tossed and turned, restless. Tired, but wound-up, she sat up in bed and reached over to switch on the lamp. The book she'd been reading lay open, waiting for her to finish it. She read for a few minutes, but the novel that had gripped her yesterday couldn't hold her interest tonight. Tossing the book to John's side of the bed, she found the TV remote and flicked the television onto a twenty-four-hour news station.

Focusing on the headlines long enough for the network to repeat itself over and over finally lulled her to a deep, dream-filled sleep.

Her father was surrounded by noise, loud mechanical sounds that came from the heavy equipment encircling him. Cranes, bulldozers, and excavators raced toward her father, and each time they were about to run him over, he would be lifted off the ground by a giant forklift, where he would be placed on top of a small rise in the flat land. Turning his back to the clashing, grinding, and shifting of hydraulics, as soon as he reached a large white door that appeared out of nowhere, the forklift, which saved him from being crushed by the construction equipment, picked him up and dropped him back in the center, where the machines rolled toward him again. Over and over, he was picked up, dropped on the small rise of land, his hand on the magical doorknob that again appeared instantaneously, the giant machines racing toward him. This time, the machines didn't stop.

The jarring ring of the telephone woke Ivy from her insane dream. As she shook her head, fragments of her dream clung to the edge of her mind, reminding her of her father's current construction project in Pine City—the new assisted-living facility he was planning to call The Upside. The land was currently being excavated for the project to begin. She rubbed her eyes and looked at the clock on the bedside table. Bright red numerals read 5:10 A.M. She grabbed the telephone. "Hello?" She spoke into the phone, her hoarse voice still heavy with sleep.

"Mrs. Fine?" a deep male voice asked.

"Yes. Who is this?" She switched the bedside light on and raked her hand through her hair. As she did so, she saw the cable news station that had lulled her to sleep hours ago was now blasting a giant ticker across the screen in bold red letters: BREAKING NEWS!

Ivy dropped the phone without bothering to disconnect. Her last coherent thought before the room began to spin, her vision nothing more than a pinpoint of light before turning completely black, was: Her entire family had just died in a plane crash.

Chapter 1

November 2016

"You're too young to be hanging around with a bunch of old ladies. You need to be with girls your own age," Daniel Greenwood explained to his eleven-year-old daughter, Holly.

"Well, you work around those 'old ladies,' and I think you need to be around women *your* own age. You will never find a girlfriend at The Upside, now, will you? And I do have friends my own age," Holly countered as she spread Skippy extra-crunchy peanut butter across a slice of bread. "I'm getting bored with peanut butter sandwiches, too. Can't you get some turkey or ham at the grocery store next time? Besides, Miss Carol asked me if I could help out with their Christmas musical production this year." Holly slipped that last bit in because she knew that her dad wasn't very hip with her participating in The Upside's Christmas *anything,* especially since it involved music. He was worse than Scrooge, and she'd told him that every time she thought she could get away with it.

"Holly, that's enough. The subject is closed. Finish making your lunch before you miss the bus. Again."

Tears welled up, but *no way, José,* was she going to cry in front of him. He would just tell her to toughen up and get over it. He was mean sometimes, and she wished she had someone she could talk to about her dad. She knew he loved her, but he wasn't a very nice dad the way her friends' dads were. All he did was work and come home, read the papers, throw something in the microwave for dinner, then shut himself up in his den for the rest of the night. He didn't even bother telling her good night on most nights. She tried her best to be cheerful and nice to her dad, but he would always come back with something snotty like, *"Don't you have homework or something to do?"*

"Get a move on, Holly. I don't have time to drive you to school today. And make sure you come home as soon as school is out. No stopping at The Upside." He gave her that dad look over his shoulder.

She rolled her eyes as soon as he looked away and stuffed her peanut butter sandwich and an apple in her lunch bag. Remembering that she'd forgotten something to drink yesterday, she grabbed a bottle of water and tossed it in her backpack.

Hoping he might be in a better mood this evening, she smiled, then said, "Sure, Dad, see you tonight. Have a good day at work." She had every intention of getting off at the bus stop three blocks from The Upside. She'd promised Miss Carol she would bring her a list of songs they could practice.

He waved her off without saying a word, his usual form of good-bye.

Holly slung her backpack over her shoulder and headed out the front door, making sure to slam it behind her. This was her way of letting her father know he had failed her again. She never said that to him, but it was exactly what she thought. She ran the two blocks to the bus stop, where Kayla and Roxie were waiting for her.

"We thought you were gonna miss the bus again," Roxie said, when Holly all but skidded to a stop.

She leaned over, her elbows on her knees, as she tried to catch her breath. "Almost, but I ran all the way. Dad's gonna kill me if I miss it again. That's, like, five times in three weeks."

Holly had been friends with Kayla and Roxie since kindergarten. They were always together at school, and this year, for the first time since first grade, they were all in the same classroom together. It was Ms. Anderson's fifth-grade class. When they had learned this at the beginning of the school year, they had made a pledge to never, ever let anyone come between them. They'd termed themselves *the three girl musketeers.*

The orange-yellow bus ground to a noisy stop. Holly was the first to hop on the bus, and she hurried to the much-coveted seat in the rear before anyone else noticed it was empty. She slid all the way over to the window, making room for Kayla and Roxie. They dropped their backpacks on the floor, using their feet to keep them from rolling forward when the bus took off.

"So," Roxie said after they were settled in their seats, "did you tell your dad about the Christmas musical?" Five-foot-four Roxie was the tallest of the trio. Holly thought that with Roxie's long blond hair, which reached all the way to her waist, and her clear blue eyes, Roxie was the prettiest girl in their fifth-grade class. Kayla, on the other hand, was a tiny little girl with short, curly black hair and eyes to match. Holly thought that both of her best friends were extremely pretty, and told them so often.

Holly was polite, friendly, helpful to anyone who asked her. She did her best to make good grades in school and succeeded pretty well except for math, where she barely managed a B minus. Ms. Anderson told her she would do better if she studied harder at home, and she'd even offered to come over to her house and tutor her, but her dad went into a rage when she told him what Ms. Anderson had offered. And she really tried, but math was never going to be her best subject.

Her dad was really good with numbers, and she'd asked him more than once to help her, but he'd told her no, she'd have to learn on her own or else she'd never get it. She wanted to tell Ms. Anderson that her father wouldn't help her with math no matter what, or any homework for that matter, but she didn't want to make her father look bad. He had never been really friendly to her, and she still didn't understand how her own dad could treat her like she was nothing more than a piece of yucky old furniture. So many times, she had wanted to tell Kayla and Roxie, but she suspected they knew that she didn't have the nicest dad in the world because they had been to her house lots of times, and her dad rarely acknowledged them when they were there. Sometimes she thought he was mad at her because of her mother, but she figured she was too young to understand that part of her dad. She wished her mother were still alive. It would make her dad happy again, she assumed, though she didn't actually have any real memory of his being happy. Every time she asked him about her mother, he would get so angry at her, so she had decided never to ask about her mother again. There was no one else to ask, either. Her dad had no brothers or sisters, no living parents. His parents had died when he was only a teenager. Holly's mom wasn't even thirty when she died. She kinda thought she remembered her mom, but she wasn't really sure. She had one picture of her mother that she'd sneaked from beneath her dad's pile of underwear when she was seven. If he missed it, he'd never said anything, and she wasn't going to tell him. Her mom was so pretty, with deep, reddish-gold auburn hair like hers. Her eyes were a clear gray, and Holly sometimes thought they kinda twinkled back at her whenever she took out her picture, even though she knew that pictures didn't smile or twinkle at people. It was wishful thinking, and she was smart enough to figure that out.

"I told him Miss Carol wanted me to help out with the music, but all he heard was The Upside and music, then told me I needed to hang out with girls my own age. I told him that I would come straight home after school." Holly hated dishonesty. "I crossed my fingers, you know, just so I could, well . . . lie." She smiled, and she knew that her best friends would get what she meant.

She had another secret that was ready to burst from her mouth, but she had promised Maxine she wouldn't tell a living soul. *Still, it is the coolest thing ever. If it really does happen.* She quickly pushed those thoughts aside before she revealed their secret.

"I don't see why it's such a big deal. It's not like you're hanging on the street corner with drug addicts," Roxie said with all the knowledge of a street-smart eleven-year-old.

"She's right," Kayla added. "Your dad should be glad we're such nerds."

They all laughed.

"I don't think he even knows what a nerd is," Holly said with a bit of sadness in her voice.

Roxie wrapped her right arm around Holly. "He knows, he's just mad at the world. At least that's what my mom says."

Holly jerked to attention. "How would your mom know? She hardly knows my father," Holly said.

Roxie seemed slightly uncomfortable. "I know, but she told me once that she knew your mother." She'd never said anything about this to Holly because she knew it would just raise more questions that she probably wouldn't have the answers to.

"How come you're just telling me this now?" Holly asked.

"I didn't want to hurt your feelings is all," Roxie said quietly.

Holly nodded. "Sure, I know. I'm sorry. I just . . . Well, I've never really talked about my mother. It just seems weird, you know? Maybe someday I could talk to your mom about her."

"Maybe," Roxie replied.

Kayla spoke up. "You guys are way too serious today."

"Sorry," they both said at the same time, and they all laughed.

"Two more stops," Roxie said, as though Holly and Kayla were suddenly clueless. They had been riding this same bus, the same route, with most of the same kids who'd lived in the same houses, since they were born.

Billy Craydell and Mandy Simpson hopped on the bus at the next-to-the-last stop, followed by Terri Walker, whom most of the fifth-grade boys called *Street* Walker. Holly felt very bad for her because she was a nice girl, just shy. She'd make a point to say hi to her today. Ms. Anderson once told the class that it took little effort to be nice; every Friday in class, she'd ask if anyone had had occasion to put her advice to use. Holly would this week.

The bus clanged to a stop in front of the two-story red-brick building that housed grades one through five. Kindergarten classes were held in the cafeteria, and Holly never really counted that as a real grade, though she supposed she should. Holly remembered attending kindergarten classes in the cafeteria and thinking she was so grown-up. If only she was an adult, she thought now as she waited to exit the bus.

Inside the school, the hallways were packed with kids lugging backpacks and lunch bags. Most of the older kids deposited their cell phones in their lockers. A new rule required that they not be carried. She had never given much thought to that rule, since neither she nor Kayla nor Roxie had one. She'd planned to ask her dad for one this year for Christmas. She knew he'd tell her no, but she thought it was still worth a try. Kayla and Roxie were asking for cell phones, too, though their parents would probably decide it was time for them to have cell phones, since both girls were about to turn twelve.

Holly spent the morning in Ms. Anderson's class, and at noon they broke for lunch. She found her table and saved places for Roxie and Kayla. She couldn't wait for this day to end. She had so many things to tell Miss Carol when she stopped at The Upside on her way home.

Just the thought brought a huge grin to her face.

Roxie plopped down beside her. "What's so funny?"

"Yeah," Kayla parroted, "why the humongous smile?"

Holly's eyes twinkled with mischief. "You'll just have to wait and see."

Chapter 2

Ivy did not bother answering the house telephone as she searched for her sneakers. It was a good day if she answered. Most of the time, she just let it ring until whoever called gave up. She'd just finished binge watching all the episodes of *Orange Is the New Black,* and needed to find something else on Netflix that would totally distract her from life. She scrolled through the selection, deciding on *Alias,* since there were several seasons. She set the timer to start so she'd be all set when it was time for the next round of binge watching. This series should take her at least a week to ten or eleven days to watch. In between, she'd do the same thing she'd been doing for the past eight years. She'd established a routine of sorts, and it worked for her.

She started her mornings around eleven o'clock with an entire pot of strong black coffee. Overly caffeinated with energy, she would spend the rest of the morning hiking the mountainous trails behind her house. She never had a path in mind when she headed out; instead, she just knew she had to burn off the excess energy she'd consumed from the coffee. After three or four hours, she would find her way back to the house, where she would shower in the downstairs guest bathroom. Really, she thought, as she found her sneakers in the guest bathroom, it was the only room in the house without the memories. The one room that had not been splashed with memories of a life she was no longer living. A life that was beginning to fade with the passing of time, a life she'd assumed was her God-given right as a woman, a life as a wife . . . and a *mother.* It hurt just thinking the word. She could not say it out loud without hot, angry tears streaming down her face. Right when she thought she had a handle on the life she no longer had, it would hit her full force: She was never going to have that life again. It was over. Done. Finished. And had she had the courage, she would have joined her family, but what little faith she had left kept her from joining them in death. Sometimes, though, she wondered if she had chosen to take the easy way out, how would she actually go about doing the evil deed?

She had numerous bottles of tranquilizers, sleeping pills, and several unopened bottles of antidepressants she had been prescribed over the years, but had never taken. Nothing would soften or blur the sadness she lived with daily. No, pills were too easy.

She had seen an episode of *True Crime* where a woman had poisoned two husbands with antifreeze by pouring it into a drink. Supposedly, it was sweet, and deadly. Ivy simply could not see herself running down to Pep Boys to purchase a jug of the stuff to bring home and add to her ice tea.

Though, really, weren't these thoughts of suicide overly dramatic, when she knew she would never have the courage to see them through to the end? She did not own a gun, and thought that method of taking one's life extremely thoughtless, since someone would have to clean up all the blood. She sometimes wondered if she could somehow magically put a bullet in her brain, then clean up after herself so that no one else had to deal with it, could she then bring herself to do it? But no, that would not be her way to end it all . . . if she ever decided to take herself out.

Knives were too scary, and she really did not like the sight of blood, so that, too, was out of the question. She supposed she could walk in front of a car, maybe go to the Blue Ridge Parkway, where tourists gawked at the scenery while driving, and hope she would get lucky and find the one car that realized when it was too late that they were about to hit a pedestrian. No, that was stupid, too, and why burden an innocent person with all that guilt? She certainly had enough to share, but it was all hers, and she would never wish her nightmarish life on her worst enemy. And she only had one enemy, and, fortunately for him, he was dead, too. He was the reason her family had died eight years ago in the crash, which had made national news for more than a year while the National Transportation Safety Board did its investigation. And when the NTSB concluded that the crash was due to pilot error, Ivy had wanted to kill the man who had taken her family and the other passengers: Captain Mark Dwight Murray. He had ruined the lives of so many who had lost their loved ones the way she had. The Boeing 747 had only been airborne for ten minutes when the captain's mistake cost 109 passengers and six crew members their lives.

No, she could not let her thoughts go down that path. Not again. She knew what would happen. She would get into her car and drive to Lucky's Liquors and come home with enough alcohol to keep her numb for weeks; then, when she had gone through her supply, she would do her best to stay sober, and would succeed until her thoughts once again took her down what she mentally referred to as *the dark path,* and she would trek back to the liquor store and restock her supply of booze.

Ivy hated that she was so weak that she could not be strong like her father, but she couldn't help it. Her life had been nearly perfect; then, *boom,* it was gone in a flash. She had never recovered and doubted that she ever would. One could not go on after such a tragedy . . . could they?

Her father had, but she wasn't as strong as he was. He'd lost his wife; as a single father, he raised his daughter; he ran a successful airline, and still headed it up to this very day. The great George Macintosh continued to thrive. And even though the airline had suffered a huge financial blow after the crash, it recovered and continued to fly high and flourish. When she walked down *the dark path,* her thoughts always questioned how her father could continue as CEO of Macintosh Air, knowing how many lives had been ruined by its mere existence. Then that little devil on her shoulder would remind her that because of her father's perseverance, she would never have to worry about money for the rest of her life. He'd continued to pay out as a death benefit what John would be making if he were still alive. There were even annual raises and bonuses. And even though she had been left with an enormous amount of money from John's life insurance, she was still on the payroll. And her father had never even mentioned the fact that she had not done a single day's work since the crash. Her father was just that kind of man, and she truly was grateful for his continued generosity, which enabled her to . . . to *what?* Wallow in self-pity? Drink herself into a stupor, day after day? Contemplate taking her own life? Was he unknowingly enabling her?

No, she thought. Her father was just being her father, taking care of her the way he had her entire life. Deep down, she knew she should make some attempt at a life, but she also knew that her heart just wasn't in it. As it was, it was all she could do to get from one day to the next.

Other than her morning hikes, the only times she left the house were for her trips to Lucky's or the grocery store. And these trips to Pine City were rare, as most of her basic needs could be ordered online and delivered to her house. She had just discovered that Amazon was delivering groceries and planned to utilize the service, and maybe she would join one of those meal delivery services, too. She ordered books, sneakers, and anything else she needed online, so why not food? If they sold booze, she would buy that online, too.

She made a mental note to do a Google search on alcohol sales via the Internet. There were wine clubs she could join, but she was not much of a wine drinker. No, she liked the hard stuff. Whiskey and vodka were her two best friends. Recently she had started to be a bit creative with her drinking, and had even purchased a book online for bartenders who wanted to go above and beyond the basics of alcohol consumption. She had ordered all kinds of mixers and found that she had actually begun to look forward to getting drunk at the end of the day. How pathetic was that?

Three hours later, after she had showered, she booted up her laptop and began her search for online booze delivery services. She got thousands of hits and opened a few before she hit pay dirt. An app called Saucey promised to deliver whatever your heart desired, alcohol-wise, in under an hour. She downloaded the app to her laptop and cell phone. No more trips to Lucky's. She knew that people in Pine City talked about her. More than once, she had heard people whispering, "loony bin" and "nut job." She had even overheard a woman telling another that she "walked the streets at night, searching for her lost family." The urge to slap the gossipy woman had been so strong, she had had to force herself to leave the grocery store, hence her latest desire to purchase her edibles online. Gone were the days of friendly chitchat in the checkout line at the grocery store. It was incidents like this that made her wish she lived in a larger city, simply for the anonymity it would offer. More than once, she had actually thought of moving, just to escape the memories. But she found that she could not, feeling this would be a form of abandonment. And she could never bring herself to leave behind what remained of her children. Her memories would always be with her, no matter where she lived; but every time she thought about moving away from Pine City, she found herself unable to justify leaving what little remained of them and felt disloyal even thinking about relocating. Their bedrooms. The rooms she had moved them into just weeks before the crash. Since waking up to the devastating news that her life as she had known it had come to a shattering end, she had never entered those rooms, and now, almost eight years after the fact, she did not dare do so for fear of her reaction. Someday, she supposed, she would have to, but she did not see that day coming anytime in the near future. Maybe she would never go inside their rooms. There was no reason to do so. Their toys, their clothes, all the possessions her three-year-olds had, were not going to ease her pain. Even after eight years, her grief was still so raw, she saw no reason to open up an even deeper wound, so she kept the doors to their bedrooms closed. When she had been tempted to enter, she had hired a local locksmith to install new locks and made him keep the keys. He'd thought she was crazy when she had asked this, but she paid him extra; to this day, she had never needed or wanted the keys.

She placed the laptop on the coffee table and went to the kitchen to find something to eat. It was dinnertime, according to her stomach, then cocktail hour. Heating something that resembled macaroni, she took three bites, then tossed the cardboard container in the garbage. Without another thought, she pulled a bottle of vodka from its shelf and poured herself a tumbler full of the odorless drink before adding ice and a splash of tonic water.

Today was going to end just like almost every other day had for the past few years.

She planned to drink herself to sleep.

Chapter 3

George Macintosh had come to a decision. Eight years ago, when he'd started construction on The Upside, he'd built his own retirement home on the grounds, too. His thoughts at the time were that he was not getting any younger and had still not remarried. After the crash, it appeared as if Ivy would remain grief-stricken forever, so he did what he had to do and arranged to live at the prestigious adult retirement community. Now, at age sixty-six, he was ready to retire from the airline business and enjoy the fruits of his labor, at least to some extent. He was in relatively good health and could have remained in the house that he'd built when he and Elizabeth were newly married, the house in which he had raised Ivy, but he wanted something new, something without the memories. He'd even considered asking Margaret, the woman he'd dated for the past thirteen years, ever since Ivy had married John Fine, to move in with him, but Ivy would completely disown him if he did. Not that she did not like Margaret, because she did.

However, George knew that his daughter, in a round-about way, blamed Margaret for the death of her family in that airplane crash. Margaret's son, Mark, had been the one piloting the plane whose tumble from the sky had ruined Ivy's life. Add the fact that the NTSB had ruled that the accident was the result of pilot error, and he could only imagine how Ivy would react if he asked Margaret to move in with him.

Ivy had told him numerous times that the only reason Macintosh Air had hired Mark was because of his connection with Margaret. Though George had not had anything to do with hiring Mark—any more than he played a role in hiring any of the pilots, copilots, flight attendants, mechanics, and the like—in Ivy's mind, he was responsible just by virtue of his connection to Margaret. Mark had been extremely well qualified, a fact that was splashed across the news for months after the crash. Some had speculated that he'd been drinking, as Mark was known to be a party animal when off duty. There had been no evidence to verify or disprove this accusation, and there was no evidence to suggest that he had been partying before he was scheduled to pilot the plane. George chose to believe that something horrible had happened in the cockpit, something that Mark and his copilot, Gary Frudell, had not been able to control.

Personally, he'd never ruled out an act of terrorism; though, again, none of the known terror groups claimed responsibility. But the thought had always lingered in the back of his mind. Three days before the crash, four members on the terrorist watch list had been spied at Charlotte Douglas International Airport. Two were arrested on various charges, and the other two remained unaccounted for, to this day. He believed they were on the flight that killed his son-in-law and grandchildren. No remains were found, so this theory, like the others, could never be proved, but it's what he truly believed.

He had tried telling this to Ivy, but she would not listen. Once the NTSB labeled it *pilot error,* she had never considered another possibility. He understood that she needed someone or something to blame. She had lost everything, and while he understood the loss of a spouse, he could not in his wildest dreams imagine what it would be like to lose a child. And Ivy had lost two children, as well as her husband.

Though he knew better than most that there was no time limit on grief, he also knew one had to go on, move forward, and do one's best to make the most of the life one had left. He'd tried; and on most days, he thought he'd been fairly successful. But now, he felt lower than low because he was about to issue Ivy an ultimatum. He did not want to, did not relish the idea of causing any unnecessary hurt to his daughter, but as her father, he had to do this. If she turned against him, he would find some way to deal with that, too, but he had to start sometime. He thought of the old saying: *There is no time like the present.*

He reached for his cell phone and dialed Ivy's cell number because she rarely, if ever, answered her landline. He looked at the clock. Half past seven, so she should still be awake.

She answered on the sixth ring. Her words were slurred. "Hal . . . oh?"

"Ivy? Are you all right?"

Silence.

"Ivy?" He raised his voice several octaves.

"What?" she finally responded, though her words were sluggish.

George realized that Ivy had been drinking again, so he'd have to postpone what he'd planned to tell her. He'd have to visit her, and it broke his heart every time he saw her, saw how she had let herself go.

"I'm coming over in the morning, Ivy. Something has come up, and we need to discuss it ASAP, and I will not take no for an answer."

"Really?" she singsonged in her drunken voice.

Even though she was no longer a child, but rather a thirty-six–year-old woman, he still felt responsible for her. You never stopped being a parent just because your child reached adulthood. If anything, being the parent of an adult child was tougher because you had no real control.

"And I wish you would lay off the alcohol, Ivy. *Really.*" He put extra emphasis on the last word.

Another period of silence.

"I'm going to hang up now. I'll see you first thing tomorrow morning. It's important." He hung up and did not wait for her reply.

He had to help her see that her life was not over. Yes, she had suffered one of the worst blows life could deliver, but she could not spend the rest of her life holed up in her house drowning her sorrows in booze and self-pity.

With renewed determination to help Ivy want to live again, he decided he really would give her an ultimatum. Come back to work or not. And if all worked as he'd like, she would take over the airline that had destroyed her life. If not, then his plan to sell it would proceed. They both needed a change.

Chapter 4

Ivy knew she had had too much to drink, but she hadn't cared until after she hung up the phone and thought about the conversation with her father. Surely, he knew she had a good reason for getting smashed? She was not a candidate for rehab. Was this the reason for his early-morning visit tomorrow? Was he going to stage some sort of intervention? She hoped not, because she didn't really have an issue with alcohol. It just numbed her for a while, allowed her to block out memories of the tragedy she had suffered, and, most of all, allowed her to sleep. Or pass out. Either way, it worked for her.

She eyed the clock beside the bed. Eight o'clock was much too early to call it a night, so she reached for the remote and turned the TV to a news station. She listened for a few minutes, then switched over to a travel channel. She was a few minutes into a program when a commercial for Macintosh Air splashed across the screen. She turned the TV off, tossing the remote to the floor. Would the nightmare never end? Would she be reminded every single minute of every single day of what had happened eight years ago? Yes, she thought as she rolled over to the edge of the bed. This was her life, and unless she decided to end it, which she was too cowardly to do, she had better accept it. She wanted to move on, knew she should, but could not. Or maybe the truth was that she *would* not. For if she did, what would that say about her? As a wife? As a mother? She could not even begin to imagine where to start, even had she wanted to. There was absolutely nothing that could draw her away from the life she had made for herself. It might not be for most, but so far, it had worked for her, and she did not see herself changing anytime in the near future.

The future, *her future,* terrified her. Deep down, a part of her knew she could not go on this way forever, but where to start? How? When her thoughts turned to the slightest possibility of a real future, her mind would shut down. This was a betrayal in every way, she tried to rationalize with herself. It was not fair to her children or John. Then the nagging voice of reality would edge its way in: They're dead, and she had best move on.

She sat up in bed and looked, really looked, at her surroundings. Closed draperies, chest and night tables layered with a thick film of dust, clothes tossed on the floor. She could not remember the last time she had actually changed the linens. A month ago? Or dusted the furniture or vacuumed the floors? This neglect of basic cleanliness seemed to have a sobering effect on her the way nothing else had. Without overthinking the situation, she immediately got out of bed.

She removed the sheets and tossed them in a ball on the floor. Inside her closet, she grabbed a laundry basket, filled it with the clothes strewn about the floor, then added the sheets on top.

In the laundry room, she filled the machine with hot water, detergent, and bleach, and placed the dingy sheets inside. She sorted the rest of her laundry in small piles according to color. Darks, lights, and whites. When she finished, she went to the kitchen and removed garbage bags, a can of furniture polish, and a bottle of window cleaner from under the kitchen sink. Before she could even begin to question her sudden urge to clean, she made fast work of dusting her entire bedroom. When she had finished, the dresser sparkled and smelled of lemons, and the night tables glistened.

She opened the heavy drapes, then pulled the sheer drapes aside. She shook her head. Grabbing a wad of paper towels, she wiped several dead insects from the windowsill. Unlocking the window, she yanked hard before she was able to slide the window up. The screen was covered with dirt and bugs. She took a deep breath, wanting to close the window, but decided to leave it open. The evening air was cool and refreshing, with a slight pine scent in the air. She had no intention of washing windows, but she knew at some point that they'd have to be cleaned. Until then, she did what she could. She sprayed window cleaner on the sill and wiped away the dirt. Next she vacuumed the carpet, then added the attachment used for cleaning fabric. She ran it up and down the length of the draperies until the dust was no longer visible to the human eye.

She sniffed the room and was satisfied with her work. She looked at the clock. It was half past ten. By now, she was usually seated in front of the television, with her drink of choice next to her, but tonight she just could not. She reasoned with herself that she had to get her act together for her father's visit in the morning. Then again, that little nagging voice of reason reminded her that her father was not going to look in her bedroom. She would be lucky if he stayed long enough to sit down. Though he had been to her house numerous times in the eight years since the accident, she had never felt the urge to clean. She kept the downstairs area presentable, but knew that if one looked closely, they'd see the dust and dirt accumulating in the corners and throughout. She always kept the drapes closed, but she knew where the dirt was. Before she changed her mind, she ran upstairs for the vacuum and the dusting polish. Two hours later, the living room shone like a star, the floors were free from dust, and she had even vacuumed those drapes as well. She polished the kitchen cabinets, removed some unknown gunk from inside the refrigerator, then scrubbed it clean. She scrubbed the countertops until there was not a single crumb to be found. She put the sheets in the dryer, then did a load of whites, pouring too much bleach on the clothes, but she did not care. She needed clean right now. Clothes and all.

An hour later, when the buzzing of the dryer sounded, she almost jumped out of her skin. The house was always so quiet, minus the low voices on the downstairs television, that she could not remember the last time she had actually heard the dryer's alarm go off. Normally, she would toss in what few items she actually washed in the machine at night; then she would put them in the dryer before leaving for her morning hike. She was never inside when the buzzing sounded.

"Damn it!" she said out loud. Tears sprang up in her eyes, and she plopped down on the sofa, tired from cleaning. She was . . . She did not know what she was. Lonely? Angry? Sad?

All of the above, that nagging voice of reason reminded her. She needed a drink, but something prevented her from pouring one. Her father would be here in a few hours. She needed to be in her right mind when he arrived, as she did not want to give him more reason than she had already for thinking she was out of her mind. Being drunk now was not going to help her situation one little bit. Later, maybe, but not now.

Before she changed her mind, she forced herself upstairs and took a shower in the master bath. While it had not been totally off-limits, she could not remember the last time she had actually showered in here. Mostly, it was used for late-night visits when she was too tired or too drunk to go to the downstairs guest bathroom.

Fifteen minutes after showering, Ivy had remade the bed with the freshly washed and dried sheets; then she crawled into bed, exhausted. She fell into a deep sleep and dreamed of a little girl who cried every time she heard music playing.

Chapter 5

Daniel spent the morning regretting life. Regretting the way it had turned out. But most of all, he deeply regretted the way he continued to treat his daughter. Plain and simple, the problem was that she reminded him of Laura. She had the exact same shade of hair, with streaks of gold throughout. Her clear gray-blue eyes were an exact replica of her mother's. Mostly, Holly was everything he was not. She was kind. She was giving. She was patient. She was smart. She was mature beyond her years. And though he had never brought the topic up, she had the voice of an angel.

He'd heard her singing in her bedroom more than once; yet he never complimented her, never told her how beautiful and unique her voice was. And he'd never told her that she had inherited her love of music from her mother. He never told her this because he'd forbidden any form of music in their house. For that matter, he made a point never to discuss her mother and her mother's love of singing. It was because of Laura's singing that he was widowed and Holly motherless. If only she had not had to go on that audition. He remembered how excited she had been when she received a callback from Paul Larson, the famous musical director of numerous Broadway hits. She had been so excited, running around the house, kissing Holly, lifting her high in the air, and whirling about. He could not help but get caught up in her excitement. She had sparkled and glittered that day. Her dream of a career onstage in a major musical was most likely about to come to fruition. Laura had even talked of relocating to New York City, and Daniel had agreed that if she were to get a role in a musical, and if there was promise of a real future, they would leave the house his parents had left him and move to the city. With a bachelor's degree in horticulture from UNC State in Asheville, a job in the profession he loved might not be as easy to find, but he'd been willing to do whatever it took to make his wife happy.

And then she had died. Life stopped that day, and he'd never really cared about anything much since. Had it not been for Holly, who knows what he would have done? Traveled the world, though that was just a dream. He didn't have the money for that kind of lifestyle. He could have chosen another profession, but his heart had always been in the land. He'd been as passionate about horticulture as Laura had been with her music. He understood passion; but now, he knew that passion could kill you. So, here he was, almost forty years old, working as horticultural director for The Upside. He really loved his work, though he did not care too much for the managerial side. Still, it provided a hefty income. He was still able to get his hands dirty, oversee the development of their nursery, and, when time allowed, managed to crossbreed a few seedlings, which gave him great pleasure.

There were times when he huddled up in the large greenhouse, watching his seedlings take shape in the form of brilliant-colored flowers. When he saw the seedlings blossoming throughout the flower beds of The Upside, he felt such an incredible sense of pride. But at the same time, he always felt guilty for feeling any kind of pleasure. Look what pleasure had cost him. Was it worth it?

Some days, he wasn't sure. Then there was Holly. It always came down to his daughter. She had no real memory of her mother, or if she did, he'd refused to allow her to talk about it with him the few times she had tried. The hurt was still there, and though not as strong as it had been, it still bothered him to talk about Laura and how she had passed away. He'd never told Holly how her mother died, only that it was unexpected, and that there was no need to discuss it. Laura was gone, and that was the end. But now that Holly was getting older, he knew the day would come when he would no longer be able to silence her questions with a stern look. She had already rebelled against his wishes by sneaking to The Upside to hang out with that group of old women who seemed to think she was family.

It had all started when she was eight years old.

Pipes in the sprinkler system had gone haywire one night. He'd been called in by the night manager. He'd had no choice but to pack up Holly and bring her with him. An older woman named Carol, whom he'd chatted with a time or two, lived at The Upside. She had taken Holly to her home that night to watch her while he and the night crew repaired the system. Holly had been so excited about making a new friend, he'd taken her to visit Carol a few times after that night. Holly told him that Miss Carol was the grandmother she never had. He had not seen any harm in letting Holly visit her or her group of lady friends until she had started singing. She had the voice of an angel. Miss Carol had encouraged this, and Holly wanted to spend more time with her, as the old broad was quite the musician. They could make beautiful music together if he allowed Holly to continue down her current path. And now, she was talking about a Christmas musical, one that he knew was open to the public.

It was not going to happen. No way, no how. He had his limits. It was bad enough he'd lost Laura during the holiday season. He sure as heck was not going to let his daughter pursue a career in music, as he'd overheard her telling her friend Roxie the last time she had been over. Music was forbidden in his house, and that was that. He'd made that rule very clear as soon as Holly had been old enough to understand. She had asked him a zillion times why he hated music, and he'd always given her his stock answer—it was nothing more than background noise, and he despised unnecessary noise. And it was true. He liked the quiet. The silence. He wore earplugs as much as possible while he worked just so he would have silence. One of his coworkers asked him once if he had musical anhedonia, and he'd been shocked, not that he'd asked, but that there was an actual name for what he felt. However, Daniel knew his dislike of music had much more to do with the loss it had generated rather than simple dislike or some sort of psychological problem.

As far as he was concerned, music was noise. Nothing good ever came of it, and its consequences could be devastating. So he would do whatever he could to keep his daughter from a career that would most likely end in sorrow, anger, or frustration when success was not the outcome. She would thank him for this when she was old enough to understand life. He was sure of that.

He'd stop at Ollie's on his way home and get a pizza to take home for dinner tonight. Holly loved pepperoni pizza with black olives and extra cheese. He'd even splurge and buy a liter of Sprite, her favorite soft drink, something he rarely allowed. This would make her happy, and he'd have one more successful night at home with his daughter.

Parenting was not that hard. Give the kid what she wants and get over it. Holly was a good girl. She knew not to expect all the bells and whistles she saw on television; that was not real. He hoped she would always remember that the arts, and music, and acting, were silly, self-centered, conceited activities. Maybe he would talk to her about becoming a doctor or an attorney—anything but music. Though she was not that good with numbers, she could learn if she tried hard enough. Her teacher had enraged him when she had offered to come to their house and tutor Holly. Did she think he was incapable of helping his daughter with her homework? Maybe she thought he wasn't that bright. Whatever—it didn't matter. Holly was smart; she would do fine in math as long as she studied hard.

He'd make sure she spent extra time on her math tonight, and every night, until she brought her B minus up to an A. He would not take no for an answer, either. She should be spending more time studying than singing. While he would not acknowledge the singing, he had no problem with enforcing good study habits.

Tonight, over pizza, he would make his request known.

Chapter 6

Just as she had told Roxie and Kayla, Holly got off the school bus at the stop closest to The Upside. Her best friends had promised not to tell anyone where she was going. She would be home long before her father arrived; just this once, she figured: *What he does not know is not going to hurt him.*

She had made that excuse for disobeying him way too many times, but she just could not help herself. And she really could not see how what she was doing was harmful, dangerous, or otherwise objectionable. The time she spent with Miss Carol and her three best friends, Helen, Maxine, and Barbara, was the most fun she ever had . . . well, except for the time she spent with Roxie and Kayla.

She rang the doorbell, excited at the song list she had come up with. Miss Carol was an awesome pianist, and Holly did not care if her father liked music or not. He didn't have to listen to it. But she planned to make music and singing her career and had already started searching for colleges where she could pursue a major in music. She knew she was way too young to be doing this, but it was something that she could not stop. It was almost as if music was a part of her soul. She thought about singing all the time, and at home, when she was alone in her room, she sang softly, so only she could hear. Her father definitely did not approve of her interest in music. In fact, he did not seem to approve of anything she did outside of school.

If she became famous someday, then maybe he would listen to her sing. Then again, maybe not.

"Oh, Holly, come in," Miss Carol said cheerfully, opening the door, then grabbing her in a big, loving hug.

Holly returned the hug, and it actually felt so nice to feel the love of another human, an adult. Instantly tears filled her eyes. She couldn't help it. She eased out of the hug and turned her head to the side, so Miss Carol would not see her tears. She was a big baby. What would Roxie and Kayla think if they saw her blubbering like this? They'd probably hug her, too, just like Miss Carol did.

She rotated so that her back was to Miss Carol. She placed her backpack on the bench. Sniffing and knuckling her eyes, she plastered a smile on her face. "You're really gonna like the music I've picked out. At least I hope so. It's just so awesome." Her voice sounded whiny, like a little kid's, but she could not help it.

Miss Carol was in her late seventies but looked a whole lot younger. She reminded Holly of that cool woman in the James Bond movies she liked to watch with Kayla and Roxie. Judi something or other.

"Sweetheart, something is wrong. Do you want to talk about it over a plate of warm chocolate chip cookies and a Coke?"

Holly cleared her throat. "That sounds awesome, thanks," she said, and followed Miss Carol to her large, cheery yellow kitchen that overlooked the giant aqua-blue swimming pool in her backyard.

Miss Carol had the biggest and the coolest house at The Upside. Lots of Holly's friends referred to the place as *the old fogey's playground,* but Holly knew it was much more than that. They had condos for the elderly people who were not able to live on their own; and if residents were really sick, there were doctors and nurses to take care of them. Holly felt really bad for them, but most of the residents at The Upside lived in private homes. Her dad called it *a gated community.* Whatever it was, she liked being here a lot more than she liked being at home.

Holly followed Miss Carol to the kitchen, where Holly pulled a bar stool out and sat down at the island in the center. Miss Carol's back was to her as she pulled a sheet of freshly baked cookies from the oven. She placed them on the granite counter, then took a plate from the cabinet. She piled the cookies onto the plate, took two cans of Coke out of the refrigerator, filled two glasses with ice, and placed them in front of her.

"Now tell me what's going on, kiddo. *Really.*" She emphasized her last word like she meant business, and Holly knew that her friend would not fall for just any old story, so she decided she had to go with the truth.

She took a sip of her fizzy Coke, then began. "It's just that my dad doesn't ever hug me, and, well, it felt kinda nice when you hugged me, you know?" She felt her eyes tear up again, and this time, instead of trying to hide them, she let them fall as she went on. "He's a good guy, but he's not a good dad. No, wait . . . I don't mean that." She stopped, then focused on her words. She did not want Miss Carol to think her dad was a bad person. "He's just so quiet all the time."

Miss Carol took a hefty swig of her Coke, then bit into a cookie. She nodded, but did not utter a single word. Holly took this as a sign that she should continue.

"It's always kinda sad being around him, like he's just going through the motions, but he's not really there." Holly had heard that line in a movie—she could not remember the name—but it was a perfect depiction of her father. "It's like he's there, but not really. Does that make sense?" Holly asked, then took a giant bite of her cookie.

Carol nodded in agreement. "Being a grown-up is hard sometimes. When you're older, you'll understand. Your father had a tremendous loss, Holly. I have lost a spouse, too. It was tough for a few years. Though I never had children, I can imagine being a single parent is not very easy."

"But it's been, like, eight years! I just do not get it," Holly said, then finished her cookie. She reached for another. "Isn't that a long time to grieve?"

"Sweetie, grief has no time limit."

"Why not?"

She took a deep breath, then another drink of soda. "I wish I knew. My guess is that people are just different emotionally, so grieving is unique for everyone. When Houston passed away, I was very sad. He'd been sick for a very long time, and part of me was relieved that he was not suffering anymore, but, boy, did I ever miss him. I moved on because I had to, and he would have wanted me to. That's when I decided to move to The Upside. My life has been on an uphill trajectory ever since." She smiled, then added, "And you, young lady, are a big part of that."

Holly grinned. "Thanks, Miss Carol. I feel the same way, too. Now, about that Christmas music." She had tucked a piece of notebook paper in her back pocket. She pulled it out and handed it to her friend.

Miss Carol scanned the list and whistled. "Young lady, you have some mighty fine taste in music. I'm sure I have the sheet music for most of this, and if I do not, I'll hit up the music store so we can start practicing right away. Christmas is right around the corner."

"Are we going to practice today?" Holly asked, her sadness gone. It was hard to be unhappy around Miss Carol.

"No, sweetie, not today. I have a board meeting scheduled for four o'clock. As much as I'd rather stay here with you, the meeting is important for the residents. Can you come by tomorrow after school? I'll make sure to have all the music you want." She eyed the paper on which Holly had scribbled her suggestions.

"I'll be here," Holly said, then tossed back more of her soda. Her dad would get mad if he knew that she had had a Coke. She wasn't sure why he disliked soda, either. He disliked a lot of cool stuff, and she wished she knew why. Then, maybe she could help him. She truly loved her dad, but her home life was not much fun. She preferred spending time with Miss Carol and her own two BFFs.

"You want to take some of these cookies home for your dad?"

"No! I mean . . . no thanks. Dad's not much for junk food." She really should tell Miss Carol that her father did not know about most of her visits. What if he was in a car wreck, and no one knew how to find her? She could think of a million reasons why she should tell her father about her trips, but she knew that if she did, there would be no more of them, or, at the very least, any there were would be on his terms, which meant an hour or two a week. They had to practice as much as possible. Though she had kept her promise to Maxine, she knew that if she did not perform in The Upside's annual Christmas musical, she would be missing the opportunity of a lifetime.

She wiped her mouth, finished the last of her Coke, then stood. "Thanks for the cookies, Miss Carol."

"You're most welcome. Why don't you let me give you a ride home? It's on my way."

Holly's eyes practically bugged out of her head. "No, I'm okay walking. It's not that far." It was just a few short blocks, and though she would have liked to spend the extra time with Miss Carol, on the off chance her father was home and saw her getting out of the car, she did not even want to think about what would happen.

"Tomorrow, then," Miss Carol said.

"I'll be here," Holly said, then headed for the front door. "Bye, Miss Carol," she called as she opened it. She wanted to add *I love you,* but did not. She was pretty sure Miss Carol already knew that Holly loved her. Grabbing her backpack, she hefted it over her shoulder and hurried toward home. Her dad would have a heart attack if he caught her sneaking again.

And if he knew what Maxine had planned for her, he would lock her up until she turned fifty. He would find out, she knew that much, but she had to make sure it was under the right circumstances, and she knew exactly when that would happen. She crossed her fingers and offered up a little prayer. Just in case.

Chapter 7

Holly's eyes were red from crying so much. She could not sleep, and her stomach ached from eating too much pizza. Normally, she would have had two or three slices, but this evening, she had eaten six slices while her father read her the riot act.

"You will bring that B minus up to an A next semester, or you will be grounded until the school year ends. Is this clear?" he'd ordered.

So stunned by his words, she simply nodded and continued to stuff herself with pizza until she thought she was going to be sick. She had drunk too much soda, and now she was suffering. She had cried her eyes out when her father dismissed her from the table, and she was not even sure why. He had not found out about her trip to Miss Carol's that afternoon. If he had, she felt sure he would have said so. She had not failed any tests, she had cleaned her room, done her homework when she was told, and never talked back to him. Why the sudden, renewed meanness? She did not know. She only knew she could not wait until morning, so she could leave this house. It was so depressing. Holly wished she had relatives she could live with.

By the time she was old enough to move out, she feared she would be as hateful as her father was now. Though in all fairness, he had not really been hateful when he spoke to her. He'd just been very *adamant*. She had learned that word last week in her spelling class. Her dad was *adamant* about everything he said to her; there was no wiggle room. Everything was really cut-and-dried with him. She rolled over in bed and saw that she still had hours before it was time to get up and get ready for school. She wished she had an iPad or a laptop. She could watch a movie, or read a book, listen to music, anything to occupy her mind while she waited for morning to come. She was not even allowed a small bedside light to read by. But again, it all came down to what her dad allowed her to do. Other than school, homework, and the occasional sleepover with Roxie and Kayla, this was it. She knew she was only eleven, but she also knew she was smart and acted older than a lot of kids her age. Minus Roxie and Kayla. They all could easily pass for eighth graders, or at least that's what they'd concluded during their last sleepover. A lot of girls her age were allowed to go to the mall on weekends, go to the movies, and engage in tons of other activities that her father refused to allow her to do. She could stand that, but the one activity she really wanted his support in was her singing. But he flat out refused to talk about music or anything remotely connected to the subject. She wanted to find out why. She would ask Miss Carol tomorrow, and if she did not have any answers, then she would ask Roxie's mom. She wondered why Mrs. Pellegrino had never mentioned that she had known Holly's mother. Holly would have liked to ask her father about it, but she was afraid he would just get upset like he always did when Holly tried to talk about her mother. She eyed the clock again and saw that only an hour had passed since the last time she had looked at it. She squeezed her eyes shut and focused on happy things.

Songs. Music. Miss Carol. Roxie. Kayla.

She lay there and had finally dozed off, when the blare of her alarm clock jolted her out of a state of semisleep. She sat up in bed, regretting that she had spent most of the night wishing for the sun to come up. Now she wished she had just slept and worried about her problems later.

"Holly," her father called, then banged loudly on her door. "Are you up?"

They went through this every morning. She always set her alarm clock, no matter what; yet he still felt he had to knock on her door to wake her, like she was a little kid.

"I'm up, Dad. Be out as soon as I'm dressed." She rolled her eyes, stuck out her tongue, and smiled. If he ever saw her doing these things, she would be in more trouble than she was already in, even though she hadn't really done anything wrong. Well, actually, she had, but she had not been caught. Not yet. She would have to cancel her trip to Miss Carol's today. She would call her and explain about her math grade.

Holly made her bed, then dressed in a pair of jeans and a pink sweatshirt that read MUSIC ROCKS ME TO SLEEP AT NIGHT, a birthday gift from Roxie last year. It was her favorite thing to wear when it was chilly outdoors. She brushed her teeth, twisted her long hair into a French braid, then grabbed her backpack and jeans jacket and headed to the kitchen. Her dad's back faced the entrance; normally, she would have added her jacket so he would not see her wearing this shirt, which she knew he disapproved of, but today she was feeling gutsy. The worst he could do was ask her to change into something else. She tied her jacket around her waist.

"Morning, Dad," she said as she took a box of cereal from the cupboard. She took her bowl and a spoon from the dish drainer, the same bowl and spoon she had used yesterday and every day before that. Removing the milk from the refrigerator, she fixed her cereal in silence. Just as she did almost every morning.

"You make sure you come directly home from school today. I want you spending at least three hours on your math. No questions. Understood?"

Holly's heart raced. Did he know about her trip to Miss Carol's yesterday? She swallowed, and the puffed rice got caught in her throat. She nodded.

"Did you hear me?"

Again she nodded, but this time she raced over to the sink for a glass of water. She took a drink and continued to cough and gasp.

A hard slap on her back caused her to lose her breath. Her eyes watered as she tried to take in air. She coughed until the cereal dislodged itself from her throat; then she turned to her dad. She could barely speak, but she managed. "I was choking!" She spit the words out, her voice low and hoarse.

Her father did not say a single word. Instead, he filled his thermos with coffee, grabbed a package of turkey from the refrigerator, and proceeded to make sandwiches. Holly watched in stunned silence, waiting for him to comment. When he did not, she grabbed her bowl of cereal and tossed it in the sink without bothering to wash it and place it in the dish drainer, as she did every single day. She grabbed her backpack and, without another word, walked out of the kitchen to the front door and purposely slammed it as hard as she could. Before her dad could race out the door and tell her what a horrible daughter she was, she ran as fast as she could to the bus stop.

Kayla and Roxie were not there when she arrived. It was still early, but she did not care. A bit of alone time was what she needed. She sniffed, wiped her tears on her shirtsleeve, then dug through her backpack for a tissue. She blew her nose, then wished she had some eyedrops because her eyes were red from last night's crying jag, and they were worse now that she had cried all the way to the bus stop. She was totally ticked off at her dad. He was really a mean man. She did not care if her thoughts were hateful. Maybe if her father had a dose of his own medicine, he might realize that she was not his enemy. She was his daughter, and Holly could not remember the last time he'd hugged her or said a truly kind, encouraging word to her. He acted like she was just there, someone he had to tolerate. Was that a type of abuse? Ms. Anderson had talked about abuse in class and said that it came in many forms. Maybe she should talk to her today? Explain what really went on behind the closed doors of the house she lived in. Maybe a phone call or a visit from the school counselor might nudge her dad in the right direction.

She disliked these thoughts. Maybe it would only cause her father to distance himself even more if she called in a third party. Wishing there were someone other than Roxie and Kayla she could talk to, she reconsidered sneaking by Miss Carol's house this afternoon. Maybe she could advise her. It was all so very confusing. If her mother had lived, she knew her life would have been so much better. She would talk to Roxie's mom the next time they had a sleepover at Roxie's. She had barely caught her breath when her two BFFs rounded the corner, both waving excitedly when they saw her, as she was usually the last to arrive.

Kayla immediately spoke when she saw Holly. "What's wrong, Holly? You've been crying," she said, stating the obvious.

Holly gave a halfhearted smile and swiped her eyes again with her shirtsleeve. "Just the same old stuff. Dad. Griping about every single thing I do."

"What's new?" Roxie asked. "What's he griping about this time?"

They dropped their book bags on the concrete and sat on top of them. Crouching on the bags was serious business, as they usually had their lunches in them. But a smashed peanut butter and jelly sandwich was a small price to pay in the name of friendship.

"He said I have to study math three hours every day, and if I do not bring my math grade up to an A, he's going to ground me for the rest of the school year." Her eyes filled with tears again. "He's such an . . . *ass*." She said the last word in a whisper. She did not normally use swear words, but she felt that her situation called for one because it made her feel better for some weird reason. She would ask for forgiveness tonight when she said her prayers.

"No, he's not an *ass*. He's a *bastard*," Roxie joined in, putting a great deal of emphasis on her last word.

"We shouldn't swear," Kayla said.

"No one is here to tattle on us," Roxie informed her.

Kayla, chastised, just nodded.

"So what are you going to do about it?" Roxie asked Holly.

Holly scrunched up her shoulders and shook her head. "I don't know yet. I have to practice with Miss Carol, but if he finds out that I am sneaking over there every chance I get, who knows what he will do? I can't miss the Christmas musical this year." She wanted to add that her future depended on it, but she had promised to keep Maxine's secret, and she rarely, if ever, broke a promise. "I guess I'm going to have to study hard, but I can't do it for three hours a day. I'd go bonkers. I hate math." And she sort of hated her dad, too, but she would not say that, either.

"I'll help you," Kayla offered. Of the three, she was the most gifted math student. "I can ask my mom if I can come over after school and tutor you. I'm sure she'll say yes."

"Thanks, but what about going to Miss Carol's? I absolutely *have* to practice. I have a lot riding on this." She knew she sounded like a drama queen, like she was a famous singer already, but one day, she hoped to be. Roxie and Kayla knew how important her singing was to her. It was part of her, like words were to a writer or colors to an artist. She had to sing, and Miss Carol had promised to teach her to play the piano this summer. She had such a bright future, but her dad could not seem to accept this. He was a total downer.

"Kayla, do her homework. Let her look at your paper when we have a test. We can switch seats in class—that way, for sure, she'll get an A," Roxie said.

"No! I can't add *cheating* to the list. I already feel bad enough about lying to my dad about going to Miss Carol's. I do not want Kayla to get in trouble, too. I'll figure something out."

Kayla spoke up. "I'll tutor you if you want. Really, it's okay."

"Thanks. I just need to get through this day. I have to . . . *contemplate.*" Another spelling word she had learned last week. Ms. Anderson was a great teacher, but Holly could not seem to grasp math as well as she did her other subjects.

"Finals are coming up, you know? You're gonna have to decide which is more important. If your dad forces you to study three hours a night, you won't have time to practice. Just sayin','" Roxie said with the wisdom of a girl twice her age.

Thankfully, the bus arrived then, with the usual grinding gears and squeaky brakes, and prevented Holly from answering. They got on, found their seats in the rear of the bus, and all were silent, each deeply immersed in thought.

Chapter 8

Just as he'd promised, Ivy's father arrived bright and early. He came bearing gifts: Starbucks coffee and bagels from Pine City's only bakery, aptly known as The Bakery. Pine City's business establishments were nothing if not ground-breakingly original.

"I still know how to make coffee," she said when she opened the front door for him. She was not one for breakfast, but whatever he had in the brown paper bag smelled yeasty and divine.

"I'm sure you do," he said, bypassing her and heading for the kitchen. He wore khaki slacks and a perfectly ironed chambray shirt. His reddish-brown hair had not thinned at all or contained a single strand of gray or silver. Ivy thought that he appeared much younger than his sixty-six years.

Making himself at home, he took two plates and two coffee mugs from the cupboard, then located a bread knife and a butter knife in the drawer where she kept the kitchen utensils. He sliced both bagels and dropped them in the toaster. All this, and he had yet to say exactly why he was here. Ivy remained silent as she sat at the kitchen bar, watching him. He was quite efficient, she thought, as she observed his neat, capable movements. When the bagels were done to his satisfaction, he put one on each plate, then took the mini containers of cream cheese from the paper bag the bagels had come in, expertly slathering the cream cheese on top. He placed both cups of coffee in the microwave and punched the buttons. When the microwave gave its usual *beep beep beep,* he removed them and filled both mugs with the strong-smelling brew.

She so wanted to ask him what he was up to, but did not. It was his idea to visit, so she would let him take the lead at his own pace.

He set a mug of coffee and a bagel in front of her, then sat on the bar stool across from her. "So I guess you're wondering why I'm here," he announced after taking a sip from his mug.

Ivy also took a drink of coffee. "Well, now it is obvious why. To make sure I have breakfast?" she replied, her tone sarcastic.

Her father took a deep breath and slowly released it. "Please do not insult me, Ivy. You're perfectly capable of feeding yourself."

"Yes, I suppose that at thirty-six I'm quite capable of feeding myself, among other things." She was in no mood for this, but she would play his guessing game. They had played this when she was a child. And, to be sure, it had been fun thirty years ago. Now it was simply irritating.

A shadow of what she knew to be annoyance crossed his face. She knew her father quite well.

"After what I have to say, I'm not so sure about that."

Ivy furrowed her brows and took another sip of coffee before answering. "What's that supposed to mean?"

He took a deep breath, brushed invisible crumbs from his chambray shirt. "It's been eight years, Ivy—"

"Do not even go—"

"Hear me out." He paused, holding out his palm while

he spoke. "Do not interrupt me. Please, just give me a minute."

She nodded.

"As I was saying, it's been eight years. I cannot even put into words the hurt we, *you,* have experienced. I can only equate it with losing your mother. While that was one of the worst times in my life, it does not compare to your losing Elizabeth, James, and John. I cannot even begin to imagine your loss. It's just not in the natural order of life. I rarely wake up a day when I do not think about the enormity of your loss . . . what you lost, what the world lost."

Tears streamed down his face. He brushed them away with his thumb. "But it's time for you to live again. Would John want you to give up on life? You have got so much to offer the world." He met her gaze.

Ivy did not know what to say. While she had expected something along these lines, she had not counted on his being so direct. "I do not have anything without my family, Dad." And this was true. The day their lives ended, hers had, too. "What do you want me to say? To do?" Her eyes filled with tears, too.

"Just live, Ivy. Move on with your life. You're still a vibrant woman. You're still young." He stared at her. "You could have a family again."

Ivy jumped up so fast, she knocked over the stool she had been sitting on. "How can you be so cruel? Do you think I can replace my family like . . . like the airplanes you replace? Just build another? A bigger and better model? I hope to God that is not what you're implying. Because if it is, you're not the man I think you are. Or the father." She stomped away, heading to the living room.

"Ivy, stop!"

She dropped down onto the sofa, tears blurring her vision. "What do you want from me?"

He sat beside her, taking her hand in his. "In no way am I suggesting you can replace your family. You know me better than that. Frankly, I'm surprised those words came from your mouth. Think how much you love Elizabeth and James. I have those same feelings for you, and as I have said before, it does not matter if you're six years old or thirty-six. One child can never replace one that is gone, Ivy. For God's sake, that's such an awful thought!"

He took a deep breath, squeezed her hand, then let it go. "I'm stunned you would even say that."

"Then why are you here? I know you did not come here to tell me I need to live my life. I have heard that from you dozens of times. What is so different today? I know you, Dad. There is a reason for your early-morning visit."

He sighed, and nodded. "You're right, there is. I have just decided now is not the time, so let's just forget this. Can we?"

Ivy looked at her father. He was hurting. She knew him well. "Is it my drinking?"

"No. Though I wish you'd stop drowning your loss in alcohol before it becomes a real problem. You have enough to deal with as it is."

She silently agreed, but would not give him the satisfaction of verbalizing this. "Whatever it is you came here to say, go ahead. Really, I'm okay with whatever it is." At least she hoped she was.

"No, I do not think you are, and I have just realized one of the issues I wanted to talk to you about is not the right thing to do. It was silly of me to give it a second thought, and the timing is not right. Maybe it will never be right."

"Dad, do not do this to me."

He looked down, then met her gaze. "All right. I was going to tell you I'm retiring. I thought about asking you to take over the reins, but I just now realized that's never going to happen." He did not mention the financial ultimatum, which was really useless when he thought about it. Ivy was on more than solid financial ground.

"You're right about that. It's not going to happen. Ever."

"Then I'm putting Macintosh Air up for sale."

Ivy's face paled. "You're serious?"

"I have never been more serious in my life. Like any entrepreneur, it has always been my hope that you would take over the business someday, but I understand why you do not want that."

"You of all people should," Ivy said.

It was the last profession on Earth she wanted to work in. An airline company. Managing those silver instruments of death. The nuts and bolts, the wires, the cables that had ruined her life, taken the lives of her family. She had not flown since and doubted that she ever would again. Just the thought of boarding an airplane made her nauseous. This should not be a problem, since she never planned to travel far from North Carolina ever again. And if she chose to travel, she had a perfectly good vehicle to take her anywhere she decided to go. But she opted to stay home, and that was that.

"I suppose you're right, but you know the story, Ivy. I guess there is not anything I can say to convince you to change your mind. However, as sole owner of the airline, if I sell, there will no longer be a guaranteed income for you in the future. I could not add that into the terms of the sale."

"You know I don't care about your money. Besides, I have enough of my own. I guess I'm pretty darned lucky in the dollar department. John took out a hefty life insurance policy on both of us right after the twins were born. You know that."

She remembered the trip to Asheville when they'd met with their insurance agent. The twins were only three months old at the time. She had left them with Rebecca and could not wait to return to Pine City, as that was the first time she had been away from them since they were born. She had signed the required documents and agreed to whatever John and the agent discussed. She remembered thinking how she did not give a hoot about term life, whole life, and a laundry list of other policies. She just wanted to get home to her babies. And now, all these years later, his sound financial planning, as well as her father's generous continuation of her salary and a death benefit for John, allowed her to do exactly as she pleased. Which was absolutely nothing. At least nothing of value, but she pushed this thought aside, trying to focus on her father's words.

"I guess I'm on another level, Ivy. I had always hoped to keep the company in the family. I guess I'm just a foolish old man, huh?" He offered up a halfhearted smile.

Sighing, she shook her head. "You're not foolish. We both know that's not true. If you're trying to make me feel sorry for you by implying that you're old and feeble, it's not going to work." Ivy gave a slight smile.

Her father caught her eye, winked at her, then said, "And I could say the same for you, minus the *old* and *feeble* part."

"So I'm foolish, and you think I want you to feel sorry for me?" Ivy drew in a deep breath, blowing it out so fast her hair flew away from the sides of her face.

"Let's just stop this. We're not accomplishing anything, Ivy. I'm not calling you anything, and, certainly, if anyone is deserving of sympathy, it's you. I'm not trying to make light of this disaster that your life has become. I just want you to be happy. If staying here all alone, all day, every single day of the week, letting the months and the years pass by, makes you happy, then I believe it's time I kept my thoughts to myself. When you're ready, you'll make a change on your own without any prompting from me."

He stood up and crammed his hands in his pockets, jin-

gling his keys as he'd been doing for as long as she could remember. He headed for the door, then stopped and turned.
"Just so you know, I'm going to sell the house. I hope you're
okay with that?" he asked.

Ivy managed a small, tentative smile. "Of course I'm
fine with that. It's not my house."

"No, it is not, but it was your childhood home. If you
want me to hang on to it, I will." His smile held a touch of
sadness that she had only witnessed a few times in her life.
"There's really no reason to sell the place. It's not like I
need the money."

The gloom was getting to her. "I think it would be a
great place to start a new life. Some lucky family might figure out how to turn the place into a real home." She gazed
up at him. "Again."

A corner of his mouth twisted upward. "Thanks, Ivy.
For the *again*. I think we were pretty happy, once we got
used to your mother's death. Don't you?"

Ivy hated emotions, especially this early in the day, and
did not want to talk about anything connected to her
mother. She was sad about her childhood home and knew
all she had to do was say the word, and it would remain as
it was forever, but her dad needed to enjoy his golden
years. Besides, the place was too big for one person. All
the land, the apple trees, the leaves in the fall. It took a lot
of work to maintain a house that size.

"Dad, I think you need to sell the house. We were both
happy there. Those times are gone, of course, so there's no
point in hanging on to a piece of property because you
have an emotional attachment to it."

He raised his brows. *"Really?"* A trace of his old humor
could be heard in that one single word.

Ivy suddenly realized what she had implied. "Do not
say a word."

"I do not believe it's necessary. Now I have places to go

and things to do." He walked outside, then turned around to stare back at her before getting into his car. "The Upside is having their Christmas musical again this year. I'd love it if you'd be my guest."

Ivy rolled her eyes. This was the third year in a row he'd invited her. She hated anything remotely connected to the upcoming holidays, but for some reason, she felt compelled to say, "I'll think about it."

Chapter 9

Holly focused on the royal-blue numbers Ms. Anderson had written on the whiteboard at the front of the classroom. She neatly copied each equation on her paper, ten in all. A surprise pop quiz. They were studying fractions, and she absolutely hated them, but she had to do her best. She needed an A, and she was going to get one. She had decided this on the bus ride to school that day. And she would do it without any help or copying off Kayla's paper, which would have been impossible, even if she had wanted to cheat. Focusing on her math, she worked and reworked the problems on her scratch sheet, drawing the pie and dividing it into sections just like Kayla had explained on the way to school.

When Ms. Anderson rang her little bell, letting them know time was up, Holly surprised herself as she had completed all ten equations. Though she was not sure she had figured them out correctly, she had at least done her best and was satisfied with her effort.

Roxie, who sat in the seat behind her, tugged on her braid. This was their signal. Slowly Holly moved in her seat so that it appeared as if she were simply rearranging herself into a different position. She glanced at Roxie, who mouthed, "Think you passed?"

Holly shrugged, but grinned. Roxie knew this to be a good sign and gave her a thumbs-up in return.

"Has everyone completed the test?" Ms. Anderson asked as she stood in front of the class. Like they had a choice.

As the students grunted and groaned, and even let out a few snickers, the teacher collected all their papers. "This test is half of your semester grade. I hope you have all been listening and paying attention." She stacked the papers on her desk. "I'll grade these over the weekend and give you your results Monday."

Half of our semester grade? She must be joking!

Holly felt a hurtful tug on her braid. "What?" she whispered as she turned to face Roxie, not caring if she got in trouble.

"Half?" Roxie whispered in return.

Holly just nodded and looked over at Kayla, who sat three rows over from them. She grinned. Of course Kayla did not have anything to worry about. Math was her best subject. Roxie stuck her tongue out at Kayla. Holly turned to face the front of the class, thinking that anything positive would work in her favor. She would start by paying complete attention to her teacher instead of sending signals to her two best friends.

For the next ten minutes, Ms. Anderson asked the class if they'd done a good deed that they would be willing to share. Holly raised her hand, then quickly jerked it down to her side. She was going to tell the class about Terri Walker, but before she was called on, the lunch bell rang, so the opportunity slid by.

In the hallway, muffled voices and high-pitched squeals of laughter echoed, lockers banged, books were dropped, and groups formed a line by the entrance to the cafeteria. It was noisy.

"Peanut butter again," Roxie stated while they waited in line. She held her brown paper bag in her hand.

"No. I did not bring lunch today. I was so mad at Dad when I left, I just forgot. I'll buy today, I have money." Holly actually liked eating the lunches prepared by the sweet little ladies in the cafeteria. They kinda reminded her of Miss Carol and her friends. She really liked older people.

The line slowly moved forward. By the time Holly paid for her lunch and sat down at their usual table, her stomach had begun to growl, reminding her that she had not eaten anything but a few bites of cereal this morning. She dug into the lasagna with gusto. The garlic bread and iceberg lettuce salad were so good, she wanted to get another plate, but she did not because she would feel silly.

"Is the lasagna that good?" Kayla asked, breaking the silence. They'd dived into their lunches as if they were starving.

"It's the best I've ever had," Holly answered. "My dad doesn't cook much." In point of fact, he never cooked. He just heated stuff up, she thought.

"Your dad is weird," Roxie said. "I think he needs to see a shrink or something. My mom thinks so, too."

Holly looked at Roxie as though she had just announced she was going to Mars or some other planet. "Did she really say that, or is this something you're making up?"

Roxie was prone to exaggeration.

"Kind of, but not really. She just said your dad needed to talk to a professional, maybe a grief counselor or some kind of nut doctor. She said he was a major hunk and did not even realize that half the women in Pine City would do just about anything to get a date with him."

Holly was sure she had misunderstood Roxie.

"Say that again, and tell it to me exactly the way your mother told you. Seriously," Holly said. She placed her fork

on her tray and pushed it aside. She was not hungry anymore.

"Her dad is very handsome. Isn't that what you're saying, Roxie?" Kayla explained in her sweet, ladylike way.

"Yep, it is. Gross as it sounds, that pretty much sums it
up in a nutshell." Roxie grinned. "No pun intended on the
nutshell part."

Holly had never thought of her dad as anything but a
dad, and, yes, a nutcase. She had never really thought too
much about his lack of dates. She had teased him a few
times, but he seemed to be okay being a bachelor. It was
totally weird when she came to think about it.

Holly sheepishly asked her friends, "Do *you* think he's . . .
well, you know, good-looking or whatever?" She was embarrassed just asking, but she needed to know this. Maybe she
could help her dad in some way if she understood more
about him. Never having given his appearance much
thought, now that she thought about it, he really was a
nice-looking man. She did not look like him much, maybe
her nose, but a nose was a nose.

"*Gawd!* Why are we wasting time talking about your
dad? Yeah, most of the single women in town would give
their left tit to have a date with your dad. There. Does that
answer your question?"

All three were silent; then they burst out laughing.

"You are so nasty, Roxie. I think I'm going to tell your
mom," Holly spurted out, but she was still laughing at
Roxie.

"I am just repeating what she said."

Curious, Kayla asked, "Does your mom really tell you
this stuff?"

"Yes. Well, not actually face-to-face. I hear her talking
to her friends. She's pretty open with them. I heard her say
that Ms. Anderson had a crush on your dad, and she wants

to invite him to Thanksgiving dinner at her house this year."

Holly's heart raced. "I swear to God, Roxie, if you are making this stuff up just to get my mind off that math quiz, I am going to fill your backpack with frogs." Roxie was terrified of frogs. "Those giant, ugly bullfrogs you really do not like."

"I am telling the truth. I swear it. I was eavesdropping on her, kind of. She talks on her cell phone all the time. It's hard *not* to listen in. So maybe if you could get Ms. Anderson to cozy up to your dad, she'll give you an easy A, then you can focus on the musical." Roxie's expression stilled and grew serious. "You need to do whatever you can to let Ms. Anderson know that you know that she thinks your dad is hot."

Holly grew silent. An idea began to take shape in her mind, but she needed to think about it before sharing it with her two best friends.

"What's going on in that head of yours? I know you too well," Roxie demanded authoritatively.

"Yeah, you look very weird, Holly. In a mysterious way. Not like ugly, just odd," Kayla noted. "Hurry up, because we have only got five minutes until the bell rings."

"Ms. Anderson called my dad once and asked him if she could tutor me after class, the math stuff, and all. He was not very happy, and I think he told her he did not need her help, but what if she insisted? What if I asked her to come to my house and tutor me? They'd be together, and maybe they'll hit it off, and I'll study hard, then maybe, and this is a big *maybe*, Dad might take an interest in her and I can get back to sneaking over to Miss Carol's to practice. Do you think this is possible? You know, my dad is not the friendliest person in the world, or even in Pine City. Actually, he's mostly quiet and keeps to himself. I simply do not know what to do."

Holly had to make this work for herself and her dad. More than anything, she had to figure out a way to meet with Miss Carol and practice until her lungs burst. She was not going to miss the opportunity to sing in front of Paul Larson.

The bell rang.

"We'll discuss this on the bus, Holly. Do not worry, we'll come up with something if we put our minds together."

Holly picked up her lunch tray and took it to the window where the trays and utensils were stacked. Roxie and Kayla tossed their brown bags in the garbage can. They headed back to Ms. Anderson's class with a new plan, and it did not involve any sort of mathematical equation.

Chapter 10

After her father left, Ivy spent the morning folding laundry and scrubbing the bathrooms. Why this sudden desire to clean had overtaken her, she had no clue, but she was active, burning off this newfound energy. These were mindless tasks. She used to have a housekeeper when she worked, but now that she had to do the chores herself, she realized their therapeutic value. It was as if she were trying to wipe away all the negativity in her mind; by scrubbing her house, she felt something odd overtaking her. She had not even bothered to take her morning hike or turn on the television. She was actually doing what most normal people did. She felt good about herself for the first time since . . . since her family had died. Maybe her father was onto something. Eight years was a long time. She would never stop grieving for her family, but maybe she could start cleaning up her act. And scrubbing the house from top to bottom was a good place to start.

Upstairs, she walked past Elizabeth's and James's locked bedrooms. Tears sprang to her eyes, but they were not really tears of grief. They were tears of a new beginning. Her dad's visit this morning had unlocked something inside her, and it felt as though a floodgate had opened, drowning her with held-back emotions. Not sure that what she was about to do wouldn't bring her grief back in full force, she knew it was time. She had been putting this off far too long.

Ivy went downstairs to the kitchen and began her search. After digging through four drawers filled with a variety of junk, she found what she was looking for.

The business card for Andy's, the name of the locksmith who still had the keys to the locks she had had installed on Elizabeth's and James's bedroom doors. She held the card out in front of her, saw that her hands were trembling, and was about to toss the card back into the drawer. But something made her stop. She would make the call. *One step at a time.* Just because she had the keys did not mean she had to enter the rooms. So she picked up the phone and dialed the number on the card.

Ten minutes later, she grabbed her purse and her car keys and headed downtown to pick up the keys to the children's bedrooms. She did not bother with her hair or makeup; she hadn't in years and decided that a trip to the locksmith was no time to start. Surely, all the cosmetics in the house had expired, anyway, and were useless now. It did not matter, and why the random thought had even occurred to her seemed odd, given the way she had been living for the past eight years. She could not recall the last time she had fixed her hair or worn makeup.

Putting her strange thoughts aside, she pulled into the parking lot at Andy's and went inside. It smelled musty, and oily, but this was a locksmith's, not Macy's, where she used to shop for perfume.

A man in his midfifties, with a big belly and a bald head, sat in an old, faded green recliner behind a glass counter, which was at least ten feet long. Inside the glass case, there was a variety of locks and keys.

"Can I help you?" he asked in a pleasant voice as he slowly pushed himself out of the chair.

"I called about picking up the key to my locks." She was sure this was the man she had spoken with earlier. She looked at the name sewn in dark blue letters on his shirt. ANDY. She was also sure that this was the man who'd installed the locks, but he'd aged and put on a few pounds.

"Yes, I know. I remember installing those locks myself. You are ready for the keys, I'm guessing."

Was she?

She sighed. "I don't really know yet, but I think it's time I have them."

"I understand, Mrs. Fine. I lost my son three years ago in Baghdad in a terrorist bombing. He was twenty-eight, loved serving his country. He was a Green Beret, best of the best. Susan, his wife, was pregnant with their first child when he was killed. But you gotta keep on living. She's a great mom, and she remarried about three months ago. Next to Andrew, Richard is the greatest. Loves little Andy like his own son. You ever remarry?"

She just wanted the keys to the locks. Her personal life was none of his business. He was just making conversation, but she wasn't quite ready to talk about her past. So she said, "No, it's just me. I . . . well, I have things that keep me busy." Lame as ever, but she was not about to tell Andy that she spent the mornings in bed, drank coffee like an addict, and spent her afternoons traipsing the trails behind her house, then boozed it up in the evenings. No, that truly was not his business, either. "If you'll just get the key, please. I'm in a bit of a hurry." She wasn't, not really, but she did not want to stand here and discuss life and death. That's all she ever thought about, day and night.

"Sure, sorry. I get carried away. Be right back." He opened a door behind the counter, which led to some kind of storage area. He returned with a small manila envelope. "Here you are. If the locks give you any trouble, spray a little WD-40 on the key and the lock. Should slide right in."

Her only thought was she did not have any WD-40, but she had yet to make the decision to unlock the doors. *One step at a time.* "Uh, sure, I'll keep that in mind. Thanks for keeping the keys for me. I'm sorry about your son." She knew what it felt like to lose a child.

"You have any troubles, just call me," Andy said as she made her way to the door.

Ivy waved good-bye, and once she was back in her car, she took several deep breaths. Her heart was pounding like a Gatling gun. *One step at a time.* This would be her new motto. Wasn't that what alcoholics said to get through the day? She had heard it somewhere, probably on TV or the Internet. She backed out of the parking lot and thought about driving to Dad's house, but he was probably working, making preparations to sell his house and the airline, so he could start his new life. Somehow she did not see him fully retiring. He was not the kind of man who could sit around and do nothing, or play golf all day.

He'd worked so hard to make Macintosh Air a success. Could she really just walk away from the family business? She had already, but she knew how passionate her father was, knew all the blood, sweat, and tears he'd poured into the airline to make it as successful as it was today, in spite of the crash. They'd had a perfect record before that crash and one ever since. She read the papers online, so she was not totally out of the loop, though Ivy would never tell this to her father.

She thought about it as she drove along Main Street. Many family-owned shops lined the street. Some had already started putting up Christmas lights; giant pine wreaths and pots of bright red poinsettias flanked their doors. Pine City was such a simple little town, just an hour from

Asheville, and she had always loved living here. Every year, Main Street was decorated to the nines for Christmas. She could never leave her hometown, that much she knew. She had too many good memories here.

What the heck was she thinking, anyway? She was not going anywhere. Her dad's visit, it seemed, had affected her more than she wanted to admit. He'd made her think about her future. *One step at a time.* That was the best she could do for now.

With all the positivity flowing through her, she suddenly knew what she had to do. She had only been there once. It was the second worst moment of her life. It had been a cold, dreary day. Temperatures had plummeted into the teens, the wind sharp and cutting, whipping at the dark wool skirt Rebecca had given her. She had been in such a state of shock, she had not been able to focus on Father Angelo's words.

It was like a bad dream. She remembered thinking she would wake up, and they would finish decorating the tree. But standing in the bitter cold, listening to words that offered no comfort, the cold wind biting at her bare legs, her father at her side, Ivy had wanted to crawl into the ground, into one of the three empty graves with caskets that held nothing but the mementos Rebecca had picked out just so there would be something placed in the two small white coffins and John's larger one.

She did not remember much after that. She had lived in a complete and total fog for months after their deaths. Every time Ivy tried to imagine the last few minutes of her family's life, she had to drink to block out the horrifying images that plagued her every waking moment. The alcohol became her best friend. It helped to blur the vile images, to still the screams she imagined the passengers uttered as they felt the plane hurled toward the ground.

To this very day, the true cause of Macintosh Air's fatal crash was a mystery, since the nature of the supposed error had never been revealed. The media had tossed out everything from a drunk pilot to a fight in the cockpit. Her father had other ideas, but she refused to listen to them. In her mind, Mark had somehow made the deadly error and killed over one hundred people.

She made a right turn, then a left, where the road narrowed to two lanes, and merged into one at the cemetery's entrance. Giant black gates reminded her of two black widow spiders, their fuzzy tips coming together to form a barricade. Clearing the insane image from her head, she pulled up to the gates and pressed a button to open them.

There were no special codes, no mechanical voice coming from the small speaker and asking her questions. The gates slowly opened. Ivy could hear the mechanical grinding as they slid aside, allowing entrance to grief-stricken mourners and others. Before she changed her mind, she tapped the accelerator a bit too hard, sending little bits of dust whirling behind her. The gates closed as soon as she had entered, and for a minute, she was not sure she should be there. Her heart pounded and her hands clutched the steering wheel in a death grip, fear and nerves causing her hands to feel damp and slippery. Taking a deep breath, she pulled her car off to the side, where two other cars were parked. *Probably belong to people who work here,* she thought. She forced herself to focus on her surroundings, anything to keep her on this path, literally, or she was going to run back to her car and leave this horrible place, where memories of her babies were buried.

A small cry came from her lips when the sidewalk curved to the left and she saw the small rise in the earth. A giant oak tree, its leaves all but gone, shadowed the three headstones that memorialized all that she had lost. The graves were well tended. Her father, she thought. Artificial fall leaves were placed in special vases on the ground above each grave.

The trees whirled around her, and the bluish-gray sky began spinning like a globe. Reaching for something, anything but the headstone to steady her, Ivy screamed when a hand touched her on the shoulder.

"Are you all right?" a masculine voice asked. "You look a bit . . . unsteady."

Drawing in a deep breath, Ivy realized she had been on the verge of fainting. To the best of her knowledge, she had never fainted in her entire life. Her hands shook, and her heart raced, but she was okay. Ivy nodded to the stranger, then pushed herself up. "Yes, I'm . . . okay."

"Are you sure?"

Ivy closed her eyes, hoping to block out the engraved words she had just read on her family's headstone, but the image was now branded on her brain, and she knew it would never leave her. It had been a bad idea to come to the cemetery.

"Ma'am?" the male voice came again.

Ivy shook her head, as if she were clearing away a cobweb, and turned around so she could see who was there.

He was very tall, and his shoulders were so wide, they looked as though they were about to pop the seams on the yellow windbreaker he wore. Pale blue denim encased long, muscular legs. Dark hair curled around his collar as Ivy looked into a pair of clear blue eyes. *What calming eyes,* she thought as she tried to gather her thoughts. "I'm sorry. It's my first . . ."

"Your first visit?" he finished for her.

She nodded. "Yes," she said, her voice a mere whisper, tears filling her eyes and clouding her vision.

"I can help you to your car," he offered.

"No, no, I'm fine, really." She raked a hand through her hair, used the sleeve of her shirt to wipe her eyes. "I'm going to go now. Thanks." Before he could say another comforting word, Ivy turned and walked back to her car as fast as she could. When she reached her car, she cranked the engine over, turning the heat on as high as it would go. She was so cold, her teeth chattered.

Unsure of the temperature, Ivy knew that her shivering was more of a nervous reaction rather than a response to the cold. It was cool outside, but not so cold that it would have brought on a case of the shivers. No, she was simply overwhelmed. This trip to the cemetery was not a good idea at all.

She sat there with the engine running, the vents blowing hot air in her face. Feeling the warmth, she huddled even closer to the vents, so the air could warm her face. What made her think she was ready for this, she did not know. Her father's visit, she supposed. When she felt warmer, and in control, she backed out of the parking space and turned the car toward the closed gates. She pulled her car as close to the metal box as possible and pushed the button that opened the gates. As soon as they were open, she raced away from the cemetery as fast as possible. Her hands still shook, but she was able to drive safely.

After such a harrowing experience, all Ivy wanted to do was go home and pour herself a drink.

Chapter 11

"All you have to do is tell your dad that Ms. Anderson insists on tutoring you, Holly," Roxie explained as they boarded the bus. "She said she would tutor you. It's simple, really. She can give you an hour in the afternoons, you focus on every single thing she says, show your dad how hard you're trying. Then, if you're lucky, he'll leave you alone, and you can sneak to Miss Carol's and do your thing while he is busy planning a dinner date with Ms. Anderson."

"You make it sound so easy," Holly said. But she knew her father better than anyone. No way was he going to allow Ms. Anderson to come to the house every day just so Holly could bring up her math grade. He'd already told her she had to study her math on her own. And the dating part, that was a total joke. She decided she would either beg or throw a temper tantrum; she would play it by ear. She had to have a few hours each week in order to secure her future, but she could not tell him that. One thing at a time.

Once they were in their usual seats at the back of the bus, they continued to discuss ways for Holly to meet with Miss Carol so she could practice.

"Why don't you just tell your father how important this musical is to you? Surely, he'll understand." Kayla, ever the sweetest and most upbeat of the three, always seemed to have a simple solution for everything.

"I don't think it would matter. You know how he hates music and anything to do with it. I just might as well forget the whole idea, it's just too much trouble. Believe it or not, I do not like lying and sneaking around," Holly said. Saddened at the thought of missing the opportunity of a lifetime, she just had to come up with a solution. Most dads would be thrilled if their daughter had this kind of opportunity, but he didn't know she even *had* an opportunity like this. Her two best friends did not even know. Maxine said it was best to keep this between them in case it did not work out, since then she would not have to explain if he did not show up.

Her dad was nothing but a total bummer, and that was becoming more so with each passing day. He did this every year around the holidays, so it wasn't like she didn't know what to expect. He hated Christmas, he hated music, and Holly wondered if he hated her, too.

"You are not giving up! We'll come up with a plan, trust me," Roxie said. "Why don't you come home with me today? You can talk to my mom. About your mom and dad. She might be willing to help us, but you can't tell her what I said about women giving their right tit. I'd be in big trouble!"

"*Left tit,*" Holly corrected. They all laughed. "I'm not sure it's a good idea. Dad was in a supercrappy mood when I left. If he stops by the house to check on me, and I'm not there, I'll be in a lot more trouble."

For once, Roxie was quiet. Kayla and Holly both stared out of the window as the bus stopped and started. Uphill, downhill, the streets were as familiar to Holly as her own house. Ranch-style houses, big front yards with trees still clinging to the last few colorful leaves of fall, Holly loved Pine City and could not imagine living anyplace else. At least not until she started college, and that was a superlong time away. She had traveled to Asheville with her father, and to a few other small towns throughout the state, but that was it. Why was she even having these kinds of thoughts? She was eleven—well, she would be until the last day in December—a horrible day for a birthday as far as she was concerned. While the rest of the world prepared to bring in the New Year, she would get to pick out a movie to rent, and her dad allowed her to stay up as late as she wanted, which was totally cool, but it was time her dad allowed her to have more freedom.

"I'll go home with you," Holly said, "but your mom will have to call my dad. I do not like the way I feel when I tell lies." Holly did not like it at all and knew that neither Roxie nor Kayla did, either, unless it was absolutely necessary.

"Okay. Kayla, can you stay, too? Maybe I can talk Mom into ordering a pizza or subs from Ollie's."

"Sure, but I'll need to call my mom, too. I don't want to worry her, you know how she is." If Kayla was one minute late from anything, her mother freaked out, but that was because Kayla was an only child, and her mother and father were a lot older than some of the other parents. But she was the sweetest mom ever, and Holly loved it when she spent the night at Kayla's house. Kayla's mom would always make sure to have all kinds of snacks on hand, good and bad, and anything Kayla wanted to do was fine with her mother as long as it was age-appropriate. They were even allowed to watch horror movies, which they all loved, especially the Freddy Krueger ones. Holly was not sure if her father cared if she watched these kinds of movies because the topic never came up. When she did go to the Redbox by Walgreens with him to rent a movie, she always tried to pick out a movie he would enjoy, too, just in case he wanted to watch it with her.

He usually spent most of his time in his den when he was home. She had no clue what he did, but he seemed to spend a lot of time in there. He had tons of horticultural books and read a lot. He did not have a computer, and Holly thought that was odd, but she was used to her father's strange ways.

When the trio stepped off the bus, the afternoon air was chilly, and they all shivered as they walked up the long drive to Roxie's house. Of the three houses, Roxie's was the biggest and the prettiest. It was three stories tall, with lots of wood, and the big glass windows faced the mountains. There was an Olympic-sized pool in the backyard surrounded by lots of tables and lounge chairs. There was even an outdoor kitchen. It was the coolest place to hang out in the summer.

Roxie's dad was some kind of insurance executive and made gobs of money, but Roxie was not spoiled at all. Like Holly and Kayla, Roxie did not have all the gizmos that many other kids their age had. They'd once said they had each other, and that was enough for them.

As soon as they entered the house, Roxie called out, "Mom, I'm home. Holly and Kayla are here, too."

Jen Pellegrino was an older version of Roxie, or vice versa. She had beautiful, silky, long blond hair and hazel-colored eyes that sparkled with mischief. Her long, tan legs were so pretty, Holly thought she could have been a model, had she wanted to be.

"Hey, girls, great to see you. I bet you're all starved," Jen said. "Let's go to the kitchen and see what I can come up with."

"Mom, Holly's dad doesn't know she's here. Could you call him for her? He's kinda mad at her."

"Oh, Holly, I'm so sorry, sweetie. Did you two have a fight or something?"

Holly set her backpack down by the table. "No. He's just upset over my math grade." There was more to it than that, but it was all she needed to say. Jen knew that Holly's home life was rather strange. Not really bad, just different.

"Then let me call him now. I do not want him worrying about you."

"Thanks," Holly said.

"Can we order something from Ollie's?" Roxie called to her mom, who was already on the phone with Holly's dad. She nodded yes, and Roxie gave Holly a big high five.

Jen put the phone down. "Your dad said it's fine if you want to stay for dinner, as long as I can drive you home, which I can. You girls want that pizza now, or do you want to wait?"

"Now," Roxie said. "I'm starving."

Holly shot Roxie a questioning look. Lunch had not been that long ago. Roxie shook her head, and this was yet another signal between them. It meant to go along with whatever she said.

"Me too," Holly added.

"I'm *famished* as well," Kayla said, and they all laughed.

"Such a big word for such a young girl," Jen said teasingly.

"She's the lady in our group," Roxie said to her mother.

"You're all young ladies, each unique in your own special way."

Roxie giggled. "You sound just like the camp counselor I had last summer. Promise me I don't have to go back next summer? I want to stay home this year."

"You can stay here, Rox, if that's what you really want to do. But I thought you liked camp."

"I did, but I'm too old for that now. I'd rather stay home and hang around with my friends."

"Then I'll make it happen. Maybe we can host a pool party this summer, and you can invite your entire class."

"Mom! Please do not start planning stuff already," Roxie pleaded. "No way would I ever invite my entire class." She crossed her eyes and stuck out her tongue. They all giggled, including Roxie's mom.

Holly thought Roxie was lucky to have such a fun, cool mom who really cared about her. Again she thought of her mother, and how her life would have been different if her mom had lived. She did have Miss Carol, who was like a grandmother to her, and she totally loved spending time with her, but still, Miss Carol was not her mother.

Jen called Ollie's and ordered a pizza, submarine sandwiches, and a giant chocolate chip cookie pizza for dessert. Holly was not even remotely hungry, but no way would she pass on this feast.

"Let's go upstairs," Roxie said. "Mom, let us know when the pizza arrives."

"Sure thing, kiddo," Jen said.

Once they were safely inside Roxie's room, Holly spoke up. "I know you have something up your sleeve, so you'd better tell me now."

"You are going to eat, then Kayla and I are gonna help you with your math, and we do not want to be disturbed. Because your grades are terrible."

"But—" Holly said.

"Listen. But instead of your studying here in my room, you can sneak over to Miss Carol's for at least an hour and practice." Roxie plopped down on her bed, her eyes sparkling with mischief.

"What if your mom decides to come looking for me? Worse, what if my dad does? I'd be toast, for sure," Holly said.

"It's the best I can come up with. What about it, Kayla?" Roxie asked. "Do you think it's a good idea?"

"It's better than anything I can come up with," Kayla said.

"So, we have pizza, race back upstairs, and I sneak over to Miss Carol's." Holly said this to Roxie just to make sure she was on the same page.

"Yes, and I'll make sure we're not disturbed. If Mom comes upstairs, I'll just tell her you're in the bathroom. It's simple. You can take the back trails, and no one will see you."

"I do not want you to get in trouble, either. I don't like lying to your mom. And I do not like your telling lies to your mom, either."

"It's your choice, I'm just trying to help," Roxie said. "I know how important this Christmas musical is to you. Plus, think about all the years our parents lied to us, telling us Santa Claus crawled down the chimney to deliver our presents."

Holly was seated on the bed next to Roxie and flopped over onto her side, since she was laughing so hard. Kayla caught on, and the three laughed until their sides hurt.

"I think that's okay for parents," Kayla said when she stopped laughing.

"It's called a *double standard*," Roxie said. "At least I think it is."

There was a tap on the door, and they quickly pulled out books and notepads. "Girls, the pizza is here," Jen said through the crack in the door. "Come get it while it's hot."

"Be right down, Mom," Roxie called. "All we have to do is cram a slice of pizza in our mouths, then we'll come back to my room to study. She knows I'd never pass up a cookie pizza, so I'll just bring each of us a slice, and Mom will have no reason to bother us. So what do you think?" Roxie asked Holly.

"I think if my dad catches me, I'm grounded for life," Holly said. "I'm not sure if this is worth all this sneaking around. The musical will be open to the public. The Upside plasters announcements about it everywhere. It's going to be hard to practice, but once the musical starts, he'll know and ground me, but it will be worth it."

Chapter 12

Ivy did not even bother taking the keys out of the ignition when she pulled into her driveway. All she wanted was a drink to blot out the images of those three cold marble headstones etched with a date she would never forget.

Inside, she partly filled a glass with ice and tonic water. She pulled a fresh bottle of ice-cold vodka from the freezer, then grabbed a lime from the large bowl of citrus fruits she kept next to the sink. She filled the rest of the tall glass with vodka, then squeezed half a lime into the chilled glass. She did not even bother with her usual routine of television and relaxing on the sofa before she took her first drink of the day. She stood at the sink and downed it as fast as she could. Her throat burned, and her eyes watered, but it was not from the liquor. It was from holding back the tears that she had been forced to keep at bay in order to drive home without getting into an accident. Now, with her tears blinding her, she didn't try to hold back the tortured sobs that practically choked her.

Ivy sobbed until her eyes were red and swollen, and she could barely breathe because her nose was so stuffed up. Taking a deep breath, she turned the water on and splashed it over her face until it was numb from the cold. She used a tea towel to dry her face. She wanted another drink, but something was holding her back. It wasn't a physical craving; it was the emotional numbness that she craved. Out of the blue, Ivy had an epiphany. By drowning her sorrows in alcohol, she had committed a great disservice to her family's memory.

Why had she never thought of this before? Had the situation been reversed, John would not have cut himself off from the world. He would not have worked diligently to chase away all their good memories with a bottle. Yes, he would have been devastated, but he would not have given up on life. And he certainly would not want to see her this way.

She got all that, but what about her precious children? It was so hard even after all this time. They'd been practically babies. Had they lived, they would be eleven years old now.

"God, what have I done?" she cried out.

Knowing she had to find answers for herself in order to move forward, and before she second-guessed herself, she emptied the entire bottle of vodka in the sink. Knowing there were several more bottles of vodka and whiskey in the pantry, she gathered them up and brought them to the kitchen, where she proceeded to empty each one down the drain. When she finished, she squirted liquid dish detergent in the sink and let the hot water clear the cloying scent of the whiskey from the kitchen. She grabbed a large garbage bag from beneath the sink and stuffed it full with the empty bottles. She turned off the water, then grabbed the bag so she could stuff it in the garbage can outside.

She crammed the bag inside the bin and saw that there were at least five other bags filled with mostly vodka and whiskey bottles. Glad there was no one around to witness her shame, she closed the bin and went back inside.

She did not know what to do with herself. She had established a routine and stuck to it for so long, she felt disjointed, out of sorts. She gazed around the living room, searching for her jacket. Draped over the back of the chair, she put it on, grabbed a bottle of water, and went outside, heading for the trails behind her house. She had been doing this for so long, she was familiar with the scent of the wild honeysuckle, the kudzu vines that grew wildly on the banks, weaving around the tree trunks. Sugar maples and giant oak trees canopied her usual route, almost like a nature-made tunnel. She remembered when she was a child, hiking the trails with her dad. He'd taught her the names of many wild plants, but in her grief, while she recognized many, their names were long forgotten. Would she have taught her children the names of North Carolina's native plants and trees? Never once since she had lost her family had she consciously contemplated what their lives would have been like if they had lived?

Would she have continued to work? Would she have been the kind of mother to volunteer for school functions? Would she and John have chosen to send them to public or private schools? There were so many moments she would never have, and she knew this, even accepted it, but it was so very sad now. They would be in their last year of elementary school, had they lived. She wanted to scream, shout, and beg to be given that day back because she would never have allowed her family to leave.

John's sister, Piper, called at least once a month to check on her. Since the accident that destroyed Ivy's family, Piper had finished her last tour in Afghanistan and had gotten married. The last Ivy heard, Piper was pregnant. Her in-laws had moved to The Villages in Florida and sent a postcard now and then. She had pushed them away, too. They reminded her of John and all that she had lost.

And why today? she wondered as she walked up a steep trail behind her house. Had her father's talk of retirement, selling both the airline and her childhood home, triggered her back to reality? Ivy did not know, maybe would never know, but she was darn well going to do everything in her power to *try* to make some kind of life for herself.

No matter what, however, she simply could not go back to work for Macintosh Air, much less take it over. That was out of the question. She had had eight long years to think about her future, and she had not thought about anything other than her family. But the one thing she knew was that whatever the future would bring, it would not include Macintosh Air. No way!

She stopped when she reached the top of a small incline, her usual resting spot. Mother Nature's hand had removed several of the giant pines that had once encircled the area. Ivy liked the openness; she could see the mountaintops; the Carolina skies were so blue, it almost hurt to look at them. A flat rock that had been here since she and John purchased the house was her resting place. She took a deep breath, inhaling the cool, crisp, autumn air. The Blue Ridge Mountains surrounding her glistened like a chest of sacred jewels; the many shades of deep oranges, reds, and yellows were a sight to behold.

Her father used to tell her that autumn in the mountains was God's way of allowing one an inside glimpse into his treasure chest before he closed it for the winter. She had not really understood then, but looking around her, she did now. The colors were not man-made, of that she was sure. How had she allowed herself to overlook such beauty? She told herself it was okay, since she had spent most of her days in a stupor and could not have appreciated the beauty even if she had wanted to. Come what may, it was not like she could take back the last eight years. Though she would have given her soul to do so, it clearly was not in the plan, God's plan. So many nights she had prayed for just one more day with her family, even an hour, just five minutes, so she could tell each of them how much she loved them.

Of course she could not turn back the hands of time, but one could wish. She opened her water and took a drink, stood up, and decided she would check out some newer trails, or ones she was not quite as familiar with. Though she had chugged the vodka and tonic down like water, she felt no effects. It took at least four drinks for her to even begin to feel a bit woozy.

"I'm not going to take another drink of alcohol, ever," she said, glad there was no one around to hear her. And she wouldn't. She would do whatever she had to do to detox, and when all of the alcohol was out of her system, she promised herself she would start to live again.

Standing up, she stretched her legs, did a few squats, then headed back to the house, as the days were getting shorter, and darkness coming much earlier. The last thing she needed was getting lost in the dark, though she was pretty sure she would find her way home. However, with all that had happened today, she was not willing to take the risk.

Chapter 13

Holly ate so fast, her stomach hurt, but she had to do this. As soon as she finished eating, she slipped out the back door, promising she would run as fast as she could. Holly stopped once to check the map Roxie had drawn for her. Miss Carol's was not that far, but she already felt like she had been running for miles. She had to catch her breath or she would be totally useless when she arrived. Sure that she was on the right path, and having caught her breath, she started to sing. Quietly at first, then she figured that since no one was around, she might as well give it her all. This would count as practice, too. So she raised her voice and began to sing a bit louder. As she wound her way up and down the paths, she continued to sing her song. When she had finished her favorite pop song, she began to sing "Ave Maria," softly, as she had heard it on YouTube when she had used the school library's computer last week. Excited, she had added this song to the list she had made for Miss Carol. Most of the songs she had planned to sing were traditional Christmas carols, but Holly wanted to sing something significant, something meaningful for the Christmas season. Sure that Miss Carol could help her choose an appropriate song, she saw the deep curve on the map and ran the rest of the way. When she appeared in Miss Carol's backyard, she waited a few seconds, then walked around to the front door.

She lifted her hand to knock, but the door opened before her hand touched the wood. "I was starting to worry about you," Miss Carol said. She stepped aside and motioned for Holly to come in.

"I stopped by Roxie's for pizza." At least that much was true.

"Pizza is always good. Ollie's?" Miss Carol asked.

"Yes, of course," Holly said. "It is the best pizza ever, but, then again, the only pizza I have ever had is Ollie's."

"Then you'll always know good pizza. You do not have to go to Chicago or New York for a good slice of pie. Believe me about that."

"Is that what they call pizza up North?" Holly asked as she followed Miss Carol to the music room at the very back of the house.

"Some folks do. I think it probably depends on what part of the country you're from. Us Southern folks just call it pizza, and Ollie's is the best around Pine City, no doubt about that."

Miss Carol's music room was totally the coolest room ever. One entire wall was covered in framed sheet music signed by its creator. Shelving on the wall opposite held two violins, three different styles of guitars, and, in the corner, a set of drums. But the real showpiece was the Steinway grand piano that sat in the center of the room. There had never been a time when Holly entered Miss Carol's music room that she had not been overwhelmed. Today wasn't any different.

The room literally took her breath away. There were all sorts of instruments casually lying about. Holly knew this was intended to make the room more appealing, and all, but she also knew that Miss Carol could play all of the instruments, and she did so better than anyone Holly knew. Add in the fact Miss Carol was a retired music teacher and her very best friend, at this exact moment, Holly was 100 percent totally happy. She pushed all thoughts of half-truths and lies aside and focused on the here and now.

"I have all the sheet music we need, after all. Now, young lady, do you want to go through a few vocal exercises before we get started?"

"Sure," Holly replied. Even though she had warmed up on the walk over, a little extra work never hurt.

Miss Carol sat down on the piano bench and hit a middle note, as she knew these were sometimes the toughest notes to carry through. Holly went through the required *eh eh eh eh eh*, then continued with higher and lower notes. After half an hour, her throat started to close up and feel tight. She knew this was time to rest.

"I think I have had enough," she said.

"That's excellent, Holly. Most vocalists do not know when to stop. You do, and that's the true mark of a professional." She closed the lid over the ivory keyboard, then tucked the sheets of music inside the piano bench.

"How about a cup of hot chocolate? It'll warm those vocal cords."

Holly would love to have a cup of hot chocolate, but she had to make it back to Roxie's before Jen realized she was missing. "Thanks, but I have to go home and study. Dad says if I don't bring my math grade up, he'll ground me for the rest of the year."

"Now, surely, he would not do that, especially knowing how hard you're going to practice these next few weeks."

It is now or never, Holly thought as she considered her response. "Dad doesn't want me to sing in the musical."

There, she had said it.

Miss Carol tilted her head to the side. "Are you sure of this? Absolutely sure? I cannot imagine why not." She sounded as perplexed as Holly did when anything related to music was raised in connection with her father. "Of course he wants you to keep your grades up, but you surely have misunderstood him about singing in the musical?"

She shook her head. "No. He hates music. I'm never allowed to sing in the house or play music. I don't even own a radio or any device that plays music. Dad just says it's noise, and he hates noise." Holly felt such embarrassment at this admission.

Miss Carol looked as if she had been hit by a giant bulldozer. She shook her head. "Then how did you learn to sing so well? Where? Who?"

Holly bunched up her shoulders. "I don't know. I listen to music when I can at school. Roxie and Kayla have MP3 players. We watch music videos a lot." It was weird admitting this now. She had known Miss Carol since she was little and just assumed she knew . . . She did not know what she assumed about Miss Carol. She knew her father from The Upside, knew her mom had died when she was very small.

But she suddenly realized that Miss Carol only knew the singing Holly, the happy Holly, the humble Holly. She did not know the girl who lay in bed at night wishing for a long-lost relative to come and whisk her away to a life that was more loving, where music was not considered something bad, and when she wanted to belt out Rhianna's current hit, she could do so without the fear of being told to stop. Though in all fairness, her father had not exactly told her she could not sing. But he didn't have to. She just knew.

"I see," Miss Carol commented.

Holly knew there were a million questions to be asked and answered, but right now all she could focus on was how long it would take her to get to Roxie's if she ran all the way. She had been gone almost an hour, more than enough time to finish their cookie pizza and study. She did not want her two best friends to get in trouble because of her.

"I better go" was all Holly could say. "I really need to study. I'll try to come back tomorrow. Same time. If that's okay?" she asked as she inched her way down the hall toward the front door.

Tomorrow was Saturday. No way would she be able to return, but she did not say this. She would come up with an excuse on Monday. Her dad was always holed up in his den on weekends. No way could she sneak out because, as soon as she did, that's when he'd come looking for her.

"Yes, yes. Anytime. I'm here all day. We'll rehearse tomorrow."

Holly wanted to give Miss Carol a hug, but she felt awkward and gangly all of a sudden. "Bye, see you later," she called out before racing around to the backyard, which led to the trail back to Roxie's. If she ran as fast as she could, she would just make it.

She glanced at the map once more to make sure she knew exactly where the path branched off into three separate paths. Stuffing the map in her jeans pocket, she took a deep breath, then ran as fast as she could. Uphill, downhill around the deep curve where the trees shaded the trail from the late-afternoon sun. It was practically dark out, she noticed as she scrunched under a couple of low-hanging branches. She hadn't paid attention to the trees on the run over. The sun was blazingly blue and bright when she had left Roxie's, and she had not felt as closed in as she did now. She stopped to catch her breath and pulled the map out for a second look. Sure she was heading in the right direction, she picked up her pace, with thoughts of joining the track team when she was in high school. Running and jumping over tree branches was fun, though she did not remember seeing this many trees on the run over to Miss Carol's. Or this many fallen branches. But she had not really paid attention. She was trying to get to Miss Carol's and back in an hour, she told herself. Of course she had not been paying attention. She stopped again; though this time, a faint trickle of fear eased its way up her spine and settled in the pit of her stomach. Glancing around her, she saw nothing that looked even remotely familiar. As directionally challenged as she was, she knew she had not gone this way before.

For the third time, she pulled out her hand-drawn map. Cloud-covered skies did not allow for much sun to peek through the tall pine trees.

She gazed up, searching for a bit of blue sky, but saw nothing but fast-moving grayish-blue rain clouds. "Crap," she said out loud. It always rained in the fall here, but she hadn't counted on that when she took off way more than an hour ago. Frightened that she would be alone in the deep woods all night, she started to sing, as singing always calmed her, soothed her soul.

"Ave Maria" seemed very appropriate. She hummed and inched her way slowly back the way she had come, and she would ask Miss Carol to drive her to Roxie's house. She could tell her she got lost, at least that much was the truth, for once. When she got home, she would worry about her dad's finding out what she had been doing. Right now, her main concern was returning to Roxie's before they were found out, too. Her friends were risking a lot for her to be in this musical. Holly would find some way to pay them back for all they were doing to help her. She might even tell them about the secret she and Maxine shared.

At least fifteen minutes went by, and Holly was still searching for the path to Miss Carol's or Roxie's. At this point, she did not care, she just wanted to get out of the woods. It was getting dark, and she felt totally creeped out. Not that she was afraid of the dark, she just did not like that she was in the middle of the woods in the dark.

She wished she had a penlight, or matches, anything to provide light. She squinted at the map again, but she was totally confused. The sun was down, and she was not sure if Roxie's house was east or west, and the same for Miss Carol's. She had never been in a situation where she personally had to know which way was north, south, east, or west.

From now on, she would pay more attention in geography class. They'd studied maps last year, but she had had a map in the light of her classroom full of her classmates, and her teacher to guide her on their imaginary trips to her imaginary destination. Actually, it was fun, pretending to map out a route as if she were the adult in charge. This, however, was not fun, not fun at all.

She felt her eyes tear up and was glad no one was around to see what a big baby she was. If this got out at school, she would be the laughingstock of the class for the rest of the year. She wiped her eyes with her knuckles and sat down on the damp dirt. She looked to the left, then to the right.

Nothing, not even a hint of light. She whirled around and looked behind her, hoping she would see a random light somewhere. It no longer mattered whose house it was; she just needed to find a light she could focus on. But there was nothing but darkness, and the outline of the trees, whose limbs looked similar to skeleton-like hands reaching out, trying to grab her.

It suddenly occurred to her that by now, Roxie would have told her mother she was missing. They would come searching for her. A huge sigh of relief filled her. Of course she would be grounded until she graduated from college. Right now, being grounded was preferable to being here in the woods alone at night. She guessed it had to be at least seven, which was not particularly late, but her dad would be home by now, wondering why she was not home yet. Though the way he went straight to his den, never bothering to check in on her at night, he might believe she was safely in her room, studying her math. That was a big possibility, and it just might work to her advantage. So, until someone found her, she was going to remain here, wherever *here* was.

She was glad that she had brought her denim jacket and had on her sweatshirt, so at least she was not freezing. She sang a few Christmas carols; then she tried a few Taylor Swift tunes. Next it was Carrie Underwood. She had been sitting here for at least an hour. The skies had gone pitch-black, and not even a single star was visible. She was incredibly frightened now. Was it possible that Roxie thought Miss Carol had driven her home? Maybe, but she had left her backpack behind at Roxie's. Roxie being Roxie, she would just bring it over or keep it until Monday.

Shivering now, more out of fear than the chilly evening air, Holly slowly turned in a circle, and this time she spied a light. "Yes!" She raised her fist high in the air. Unsure exactly where the light would lead her, at this point, she did not really care. She just wanted to get out of these dark woods.

She focused on the light, and only now and then did she look down at the terrain. Twice she almost fell, but she managed to steady herself. She was close enough to the light now to see that it was one of those spotlights that lit up the entire area. She did not recognize the house, but she did not care. Pine City was a safe place, and she hoped that whoever lived here would allow her to make a phone call.

Holly slowly walked around to the front of the house. She stopped a couple of times to make sure the homeowners had not let a dog or a cat out. When she did not hear any barking or meowing, she walked up a steep set of steps and rang the doorbell. The house was very fancy, more so than even Roxie's. She did not remember seeing this house around, but lots of houses were built deep into wooded areas for privacy.

She waited another minute, then rang the doorbell again. Her dad would surely ground her for life now. Or if she were lucky, just until she turned sixty-five.

Chapter 14

Ivy had just finished taking a hot shower and was about to make herself a cup of tea when she heard the doorbell ring. Glancing at the clock on the stove, she saw it was a little past eight. Most likely, it was her father stopping by on his way home. Or maybe Rebecca, who owed her a visit.

Ivy unlocked the door and was about to open it, when she remembered to turn on the light on the front porch. When she opened the door, she fully expected to see her father or Rebecca. Anything but what she saw. For several seconds, she thought she was imagining the small, tear-stained girl standing on the other side of the door.

"I'm sorry," the little girl said. "I mean, I am sorry to bother you, but I'm lost, and I just need to use your telephone."

A few more seconds passed before Ivy was able to move. "Of course, please come in." She opened the door, and the little girl took a few steps into the entryway and looked down.

"It's okay, come on inside."

Holly knew that her sneakers were muddy, and did not

want to ruin the woman's floors. "My shoes," she said, looking down. "They're muddy."

Ivy took a deep breath and smiled at the girl. "A little mud never hurt a thing. Now come inside so you can call your parents. I'm sure they're very concerned about you."

This meeting was the last thing Ivy expected. And today of all days. Ivy's hands shook, and she would have liked a tall drink right about now, but she had made a promise to stop the alcohol, and stop drinking she would.

After she turned off the light on the porch, Ivy said, "I have a phone in the kitchen. Follow me, please." This child's parents must be worried sick. What in the world was she doing out at night, alone?

Without waiting for the girl to say anything, Ivy headed back to the kitchen. Thankful there were no empty booze bottles lying about, and even more thankful that she had cleaned the place, Ivy found the phone and handed it to the girl. She almost dropped it when she saw her in the bright light of the kitchen. Her hair had golden streaks throughout. Her heart-shaped face was beautiful. Her eyes shone with unshed tears. Ivy was so overwhelmed, she wanted to wrap this child in her arms and never let go. But the poor girl would think her out of her mind if she did.

"Would you like a cup of hot tea before you make your call? It will warm you up while you wait."

Holly had never had hot tea before. She smiled and nodded. "Thanks, but I need to call my house first."

"Sure, I'll be right back." Ivy stepped into the living room so the little girl could have some privacy. She gave her a few minutes; then, as she was about to return to the kitchen, the little girl found her and held out the phone. "My dad needs your address."

"Oh, sure."

She took the phone from the little girl, prepared to hear an angry parent, but what she heard was the complete opposite. "It's 6190 Huckleberry Way. Of course she can." Ivy gave the phone back to the girl, who did not look happy.

"Okay, Dad," she said, then hung up without bothering to say good-bye.

"Dad mad at you?" Ivy asked as she motioned for the girl to follow her to the kitchen. She filled the kettle with water from the sink and placed it on the stove.

She took two bright yellow cups and set them side by side on the counter. "What flavor would you like?"

"I don't know. Just regular, I guess."

"I take it you're not a big tea drinker? It's okay, I'm just starting myself. I'm a coffee drinker, mostly, but tea is supposed to be good for you. I was going to make myself a cup of green tea. Would you like to try some?"

"Please," the girl said.

It suddenly occurred to Ivy that this little girl must think she was incredibly rude, as she had never introduced herself. "My name is Ivy. What's yours?"

"Holly," she said, and Ivy turned around to see she was smiling.

"Ivy and Holly, like the vines, that's . . . Well, I do not know what you'd call it, but Holly is a beautiful name."

"Thanks. So is Ivy."

Ivy turned her back to Holly while she placed tea bags in the mugs. "So, Holly, tell me about yourself."

"There isn't much to tell, really. I'm eleven. In fifth grade. I don't like math at all, which is why I'm here."

Ivy slowly poured hot water over the tea bags. Elizabeth and James would be eleven. Her hands began to shake, and she placed the teakettle down for a minute. She took two spoons from the drawer and placed them in the mugs.

She did not want to frighten Holly if she saw how badly her hands were shaking. It was not from lack of alcohol. It was the day. The entire day had been unlike any in so many years, but Ivy found that she was quite comfortable with this child. She had made a point to avoid being around children whenever possible, for they brought back too many memories, but not this child. It was odd, as though she were drawn to her in some way.

"Not a math person, huh?" Ivy said to let Holly know she had heard her.

"No. I like spelling and English, but math is just too hard."

"Well, sometimes people are born with an aptitude for math, while others have an aptitude for English, or science, even foreign languages. I majored in business, so math was pretty easy for me, but I had a terrible time with spelling." Ivy had no clue why she was telling Holly all of this. She had not spoken of her college years in so long, she had thought they were nothing but distant memories.

"Dad says I have to study harder, and I'll figure it out, but it's hard for me on my own. My friend offered to tutor me, but I can't let her."

Ivy heard a trace of something in Holly's voice, but she did not know her well enough to know exactly what Holly had said that bothered her. "So why can't you let your friend tutor you?" Maybe this was being a bit nosy, but Ivy was very curious about the girl, that's all.

"Dad says I won't ever get it unless I learn it on my own."

Ivy was not so sure about that, but it was not her place to voice an opinion. "I bet you're a hands-on kind of learner. Maybe if your dad showed you how to work out your numbers, you'd understand better." It probably was not the best response she could have made, but it was her first thought.

"Sometimes in class, if the teacher shows me a few times, I get it, but then I freak out when it's time for a test and forget everything. That's why I'm barely making a B minus."

"That's not a bad grade at all," Ivy said. "I carried a few B's in college."

"I make straight A's in all my other classes. I just can't seem to get math. My best friend Kayla is a real brain in math. She offered to help me, but I do not think Dad will allow it."

Even though it wasn't any of her business—after all, she did not know this child or her family, but she couldn't help herself—she had to ask, "Why not?"

Holly blew on her cup of tea; then she took a sip. "This is good."

Was that Holly's way of avoiding her question? She certainly had every right to keep her family issues private.

Ivy took a drink of her tea, too. She waited a couple seconds, then spoke. "You really like the tea? If you don't, it's okay with me. I think it needs a pound of sugar, what about you?"

"I like it, really. It's good. Sugar might make it better, though," Holly agreed.

Ivy rifled through the cupboards until she located some packets of sugar. She had not bought a bag of sugar since . . . since she and her kids had bought the makings for sugar cookies just a few days before they died.

She took a deep breath. *I'm fine,* she told herself. And if she wasn't, she had to be, at least until Holly's father took the girl home. She would not have a meltdown in front of this little girl, who seemed wise beyond her years. Still, there was something else, but Ivy could not decide what it was about the child that nagged at her. It didn't matter, she supposed. Once Holly was safe at home, she would likely forget all about Ivy.

"Here you go," Ivy said, and handed her three packets of pure sugar. She dumped five packets in her tea, took a sip, then added another.

"You like sweet stuff?"

"I do in green tea," Ivy said, and laughed. She actually *laughed*! And it felt nice. She would not overanalyze this. Not now.

Holly added one packet of sugar to her tea, stirred it with her spoon, then took a sip. "It's really good with a bit of sugar." She took another drink, and Ivy hoped she wasn't just drinking the tea to be polite. It wasn't going to be her favorite, that Holly knew, but she would finish her cup.

"Dad thinks if I study hard, alone, I'll grasp math better, but I have tried, and I just don't understand fractions. I would rather wash dishes."

Ivy smiled. She remembered feeling that way when she was about her age, only it was spelling. She hated it, but her father spent as much time as she had needed to go over the words with her, teaching her ways to remember the correct spelling of each word. She would never forget in second grade learning to spell *together*. Her father had made it very simple when he'd told her to remember it by breaking it down: *to get her*. She would never forget that word. And she learned that *dessert* was always spelled with two *S*'s because it was twice as nice as the *desert* sand. Silly when she thought about it now, but it had worked because her father made the effort to help her.

"What about your mom?" Ivy asked.

"I don't have a mom," Holly answered.

Ivy's heart flip-flopped. *Poor kid . . . that's it,* she thought as she took another sip of tea. She had made a connection with Holly, and that had to be it. She was a young girl without a mother. Just like she had been at her age.

"I'm sorry," Ivy said. She was not sure what had happened, so the typical *I'm sorry* would have to suffice.

"It's okay, really. She died when I was really little. I don't even remember her all that much. I have a picture, though. Dad says I look just like her."

"Then your mother was a beautiful woman," Ivy replied. She must have been because this child was unusually pretty. "I'm sorry you lost her." She was about to tell her she had lost her mother, too, when the doorbell rang.

"That's probably your dad," Ivy said, stating the obvious.

Holly quickly jumped off the bar stool and took her cup of tea with her, placing it in the sink. "Dad doesn't allow me to have much sugar or caffeine," she explained.

Ivy ran her finger across her mouth as if she were zipping it shut. "It's our secret." *Poor kid, she's deprived.* Green tea was an antioxidant. Of course she would not know that, but still. A kid and sugar were meant for one another, in the appropriate amounts, of course.

"Why don't you wait here while I answer the door. Maybe your dad can stay for a cup of tea." Ivy said this because she wanted to see what kind of man would not allow his daughter to have help with math and would forbid sweets. Holly had not actually said sweets were forbidden, just that she was not allowed much. Maybe she had health issues? Either way, she wanted to meet the man who allowed his eleven-year-old daughter to get lost in the woods at night.

Filled with dislike before she even opened the door, Ivy remembered to turn the porch light on first; then she opened the door.

She stared at a tall man with hair that was too long, shoulders that were too broad, and eyes that were too sad. She was staring at the man who'd tried to help her at the cemetery today.

Chapter 15

Stunned when he saw the woman, Daniel was speechless for a moment. Recovering quickly, he'd told her he was there to pick up his daughter. She invited him inside, but he refused.

Once he and Holly had thanked the woman for her help, and they were inside his truck, he let loose. "You are not to take the bus home. I will pick you up or send someone to get you, is that understood?"

Holly cowered in the backseat like a frightened animal. "Yes."

He drove slowly because he wanted to talk to her. "You will not go to Miss Carol's or Roxie's, is that understood?"

"Yes," she said.

"Is that all you have to say?" He was very angry.

"Yes," she said again, only this time she added just a tinge of snottiness to her one-word answer.

"That woman probably thought you were crazy, or, at the very least, thinks I'm crazy, a rotten father. Don't you ever think before you act?" He held his right hand in the air and kept his left hand tightly on the steering wheel.

"Of course you don't, or I wouldn't have to hunt you down like some wild-ass animal."

"I'm not an *animal*! But you treat me like one!" Holly shouted. Since she was in trouble, she might as well make the most of it.

"What did you say?" Daniel Greenwood asked in a low, menacing tone.

"You said I acted like an animal, and I said you treat me like one, all caged up! I cannot believe how mean you are! I wish you had died instead of Mom!" Holly screamed as loudly as she could. And then she began to cry loudly, and she did not care. At that moment, she hated her dad with all of her heart and soul, and he probably hated her, too.

Daniel took a calming breath. He wanted to teach her a lesson, but this was not the right way. It was never the right way with this kid. "As soon as you get home, I want you to shower and go to bed. I do not want to hear the slightest sound out of you. Do you understand that, Holly? You're almost twelve years old, and I think it's time you grew up a bit. Tomorrow you will spend the entire day studying your math."

In the backseat, Holly continued to cry, but she nodded that she had understood him. It was times like this that he almost hated Laura for leaving him behind with this responsibility.

As soon as he pulled into the driveway, he'd barely come to a complete stop before Holly jumped out of the car. She raced in through the front door, which he'd left unlocked. Careless, but there was not much crime in Pine City. Still, he should have known better. He pulled his truck into the garage.

Inside, he could hear the shower running in Holly's bathroom. At least she was following his orders. Not sure how long that would last, he grabbed a beer out of the refrigerator and headed for his den. He'd spent the day going over a new set of plans for the second phase of the new condos that were scheduled for groundbreaking next spring. While his part would not happen until the building was almost complete, the design, ordering, and general planning on such a large scale took time. They were calling the new condos The Bright Side. He liked it, and it made sense, given that most of the residents were at least fifty-five. He had his eye on a condo, but he did not meet the age requirement yet. He liked The Upside, liked the people he worked with, and was happiest when he was working. Home was totally different.

Every day, Holly looked more and more like her mother. She was thin like Laura. Her gold hair hung down to her waist, just like her mother's had. She was a good kid, and he knew he was hard on her, but he had his reasons. When she was older, she would thank him, he had convinced himself. For now, he'd be lucky if she even spoke to him.

Did she really wish he'd died instead of her mother? He knew she was upset and did not really mean that, but it hurt to think that she even had the thought. He knew he'd been harsh with her, but it's what fathers do. How else would she learn to get by in the world? Look what had happened to her mother. One minute she was on the brink of an exciting career; then, without warning, she died a very tragic death.

Daniel would do everything in his power to prevent his daughter from making the same mistake. No matter how mistaken or misguided he might be, he was doing the best he could, but sometimes, he thought, it was not good enough.

He'd allowed her to have dinner with Roxie, and she had taken advantage of not only her friends, but him, too. She had to learn that actions have consequences. He would make sure she spent the entire weekend studying. In the kitchen, where he could keep an eye on her. If left alone in her room, who knew what she would try?

Holly was lucky the woman had been nice enough to let her use the telephone. Crime was pretty nonexistent in the area, but still, he had to teach Holly to be cautious and not take unnecessary chances. Otherwise she would end up just like her mother. In spite of what Holly thought, she was his daughter, and he truly wanted what was best for her.

Tomorrow he'd call Miss Carol and explain whatever involvement Holly had in The Upside's annual Christmas musical was not going to happen. She was a kid, she could sing pretty well, but he felt sure they would find some other talent to take its place. Holly knew how he felt about Christmas, and about music, and she had gone behind his back, anyway. He really should ground her for the remainder of the school year. He could keep an eye on her then. She could read and watch TV and study her math. He wanted straight A's next semester, would accept nothing less.

As soon as he heard her turn off the water, he tossed back the rest of his beer and turned the lights out. He would stop by her room before she went to sleep.

He saw the light beneath her door and knocked. He waited for her reply, but did not get one. "Holly?" he asked, and tapped on the door again.

"Come in."

He pushed the door aside and saw she was curled up in the fetal position on her twin bed, her back to the wall. Her eyes were red-rimmed from crying. She rolled over so that her back faced him.

"Holly, turn around and look at me when I speak to you." He took a deep breath. He was tired and did not feel like playing games.

"Holly," he said again, this time in his sternest voice.

She rolled over, but refused to look at him.

Daniel sat down on the edge of her bed. She pulled her knees closer to her chest. "I'm not going to hurt you, so stop acting like this." He pointed to the way she was curled up and shoved against the wall, so she was as far away from him as she could get without actually leaving the room.

She sighed, but didn't say anything. He could not force her to talk, but he could force her to listen. "Look at me when I speak to you," he said again.

Holly opened her eyes, and he saw they were brimming with tears.

"You cannot go behind my back and do whatever you want. Do you get that?"

She nodded.

"Then explain tonight. I was humiliated going to a stranger's house to find you there, acting like I was the bad guy. I allowed you to miss the study time I'd mandated the night before. I know you like to hang out with Roxie and Kayla, and I gave you permission to stay for pizza and to study. Jen Pellegrino was worried sick when she could not find you. Not only are you in trouble, but your friends are grounded, too. Do you get what I'm saying?"

He was frustrated. She stared right through him, and he was not sure if even a single word was getting through to her. "Answer me, Holly."

She pushed herself into a sitting position, pulling the blankets up to her chin. "Yes, I get it. I am not stupid, like you think. I am sorry, okay?"

Daniel shook his head and stood up. "I'm responsible for you, Holly. You have to follow the rules. Life is full of rules, and if you are not taught when you're young, you'll never amount to a hill of beans. It's important that you do exactly as I say. Do you think you can follow the rules? Do I have to hire a babysitter to stay with you when I'm gone?"

"I would love a babysitter. At least I'd have someone to talk to. Living in a house with only you is like living in a house with no one else. *Dad.*"

"I can arrange it, if that is what you want."

"Do whatever you want, I don't care anymore. You don't care what I want, so why should I bother to care what you want?" Holly said, her voice thick with unshed tears.

"You had better get some sleep. Study time comes early," Daniel said as he stood up and stretched.

"Tomorrow is Saturday."

"I'm quite aware of that. Now get some rest. I'll see you first thing in the morning. Set your alarm just like it's a school day." And on that note, totally oblivious to the effect his bullheadedness was having on his daughter, he walked out of the room, closing the door behind him.

He felt like the meanest man alive, and he was sure Holly thought he was, too. But she was all he had. If something happened to her, he would simply go mad.

Chapter 16

Ivy could not get the image out of her mind of Holly following her father to his truck. She had given up on the soothing tea and made a pot of strong coffee. She was sure he was the same man she had seen at the cemetery this morning. Why he was there, she could only guess; most likely, he was employed there, given the way he was dressed.

She had never seen him in any of the shops downtown, but that did not mean a thing. He might work in Asheville, for all she knew. She had been out of the social scene for eight years, so who knew? She tried to remember if Holly had given her last name, or if the father had, but if either did, she could not recall what it was. If she had a last name, she could do a local Google search. She could call Rebecca, but it was already too late, as Thomas and Jacob were in elementary school. Thomas was in fifth grade, the same grade Holly was in. Maybe tomorrow she would poke around, see what she could find out about the girl.

The girl had been so sweet, but she had also been frightened. Was she afraid of her father? If Ivy gave it her best guess, she would say that she was, but she did not want to jump to conclusions. Kids at that age were very emotional and just beginning to mature, and it was especially tough for girls. She knew, as she had been a handful herself when she had not gotten her way. She smiled, remembering how her father would always talk with her, and he would discuss her punishment and why he had to do what he did. He'd never laid a hand on her, but she had been grounded more than once, and had had her car taken away the summer before her senior year for sneaking to Orlando, Florida, with a group of friends. She had very much deserved to have her car taken away.

Years later, she told her dad how bad she had felt sneaking off and causing him to worry, but she had had too much fun to care at the time. *A lesson learned,* she thought. She had been seventeen years old. At eleven, she could not imagine not being close with her father, and her mother, too, when she was alive. Holly said she was very young when her mother died. She spoke very casually about her, as though she were simply an acquaintance from the past.

Ivy had her own issues, and getting involved in someone else's problems was not her style. Still, she could not help but feel bad for Holly. She was an exceptionally beautiful young girl, and Ivy wondered what Elizabeth would have looked like if she had lived. Tears filled her eyes, and she let them fall. For the first time since the accident, she felt that her tears were cleansing, as though this was a final cycle to cleanse the last bit of sadness from her soul.

Her dad was right, as usual. She needed to start living again. While her heart would be forever broken for the family she loved and lost, she knew that if she was to have any kind of future, she would have to do a complete about-face.

Today had been a sad day, a very sad day, but it was also a good start. She had had that one drink, tossed all the booze down the drain, and deleted the Saucey app from her phone and her computer. Pathetic, but necessary at the time. And she would have to struggle to keep a positive attitude, but she would give it her best shot. When she put her heart and soul into something, she did not back down. Prior to the accident, she had never been a quitter. And she did not intend to go back to the way she had been the last eight years.

Was she finished grieving for her family? Never! Could she begin to move forward? Yes, but *one step at a time.* She would start by visiting her father tomorrow. He'd been through hell and back, too, first losing his wife after a long illness, then having his two grandchildren snatched away in the blink of an eye; yet she had only thought of her loss and how badly she was hurting. It was time to take her father's advice and start living again. It might not be pretty at times, she was willing to accept that, but she would try nonetheless.

For John, for Elizabeth, and for James.

Chapter 17

"Tell me you're joking?" Carol said. She usually did not talk on her cell phone when she was driving, but this news was so stunning, she had made an exception to her own rule. "Why in the world would you keep this a secret?"

Carol Bishop and Maxine Hammond had been best friends for the past few years. Both widows, and both having had careers in the field of music, they'd hit it off instantly when they'd met at an association meeting right after they'd bought their homes at The Upside.

"I wanted it to be a surprise, but if her father isn't going to allow her to sing, what's the point?" Maxine asked. "Paul is doing this as a personal favor, you know?"

Carol rolled her eyes. Every male in the world either owed Maxine a favor or wanted a favor. "Of course, and it will be worth his time, we both know that," Carol said. "I think she's much better than Jackie Evancho, don't you?"

"Absolutely. And a nice girl, to boot. I would hate to see her become a success and have it ruin her as it has so many young people. Elvis, for one. I still can't believe he's gone. Every time I visit Graceland, I expect him to be lurking around a corner."

Carol chuckled into the phone. "I'd advise you to keep those thoughts to yourself before someone thinks you're a candidate for the loony bin."

"You know what a fan I am. I saw him three times in concert. To this day, I have never heard anyone who can top him," Maxine crooned, her love for the dead icon more than obvious.

"There is always someone better out there. It's not like it used to be. There are a lot of opportunities for singers now. *America's Got Talent. The Voice.* I bet if Elvis had a chance like that, we would have heard him belting his songs out a lot sooner. I'm driving now, so I need to pay attention. I'll make a few phone calls when I get home. Do not cancel Paul . . . just yet."

"I won't, but work fast—will you?—as you know how busy he is," Maxine added. "I'll wait to hear from you."

Carol ended the call and focused on her driving. She wasn't all that fond of driving, let alone talking on the phone while she did so. Too dangerous, especially in the mountains, but fortunately, she was not on the Blue Ridge Parkway.

Ten minutes later, she drove through the gatehouse and waved at the attendant. She weaved around three round-abouts before turning onto her street. As soon as she parked her car, she hurried inside. She had to find out exactly why Daniel was not going to let Holly participate in the musical this year. She had thought something was off yesterday when Holly showed up, warmed up, then seemed in such a hurry to leave. While she could not force Daniel to let his daughter perform, she could at least give it a try.

In the kitchen, she found her address book and looked up his phone number. She dialed his number and crossed her fingers. After the sixth ring, she hung up. It was Saturday. Maybe he and Holly were running errands. Whatever the case, she would continue to try to get him on the phone. To her way of thinking, this business with Holly was too important just to ignore. The girl had a phenomenal talent, one that had to be nurtured. And Holly simply loved to sing. To take away her singing would be like cutting off an arm or a leg.

If asked, Carol would guess that Daniel thought Holly was too young to expose her talent just yet. Maybe he wanted to wait until she was older. What a talent the world would miss if he did not allow Holly to use and develop her gift.

But he was her father, and Carol respected that. If he felt Holly was not ready, then maybe next year or the year after. However, having Paul Larson in the audience was truly a once-in-a-lifetime opportunity.

Maxine was right. He wouldn't bother if it were a waste of time. Carol suspected Maxine and Paul had been an item back in the day, and this was the main reason he was traveling all the way from New York City. Maybe there was a rekindling romance in the air? Maxine usually told her these things. Maxine was still quite a looker, with her shiny red hair and green eyes. She still had the figure of a forty-year-old, too. Possibly Helen or Barbara would know. Quickly she dialed Helen's number.

Helen picked up on the first ring.

"It's me, listen. I have a question and do not interrupt me." Carol did not bother with a *hello*. They were way past that now.

"All right," Helen said. "Shoot."

"Has Maxine mentioned anything about a boyfriend? We all know she's always on the hunt, but she usually tells us."

"Not one word. Why?" Helen asked. "Do you have someone in mind? Remember, she is not the only one available."

Carol laughed into the phone. In their seventies, and all widowed, they were still looking for the perfect man. In fact, all four of them—herself, Maxine, Helen, and Barbara—were known throughout their gated community as The Matchmakers. They just had not found the perfect men for themselves.

"How could I possibly forget? It's all we've talked about lately," Carol said. "She's invited a friend from New York to the Christmas musical. I was just curious, given that it is a *male* friend."

"Not a word to me, but if she even hints at the possibility, I'll let you know. After that, we can grill her over lunch. I think it's my turn to host this week," Helen said.

Every week, they had lunch on Wednesday. For the first year after they'd met, they'd gone to all the local eateries, usually one of the three restaurants at The Upside, but sometimes they would all travel to Asheville, but none of them cared for the drive. When Helen suggested they take turns hosting their luncheons, they'd all jumped at the idea. And they'd made it fun. Each week, they would pick a theme out of the box they used to collect suggestions in, and whoever's turn it was that week would draw a suggestion from the box and start working. And they went the full Monty, too. Not only were their luncheons' food themed, they were also decorated to fit the theme, and at the end of each month, they would vote on who did the best job, and that lucky person got to skip a week if they chose to do so. So far, none of them had ever skipped her turn. It was fun, and it gave them all something to look forward to in the middle of the week, when a lot of the planned activities at The Upside were ones they chose not to participate in. There were many to choose from: rumba classes, aerobics, and yoga. They'd tried the aroma-therapy class, and all agreed it gave them a headache. There was also Latin dancing the first Saturday of the month, which they all attended because The Silver Foxes, a group of single men, also attended, and all were excellent dancers. They were all friends, but nothing had happened in the romance department.

Carol had even tried a glassblowing class once. But after walking away with several burns, she had decided that was not her thing, either. There were several dozen other activities planned by The Upside, and Carol loved living here, but she did not want to spend every single day booked with an activity that required a commitment. After all, she was retired. Her biggest activity was planning the annual Christmas musical, and she adored doing it. It was quite the undertaking, and add in the music part, Carol was in heaven. After Houston had died, she had not known what to do with her life. Deciding to move to The Upside had been the best decision of her life.

"We'll pick her apart then," Carol said, before saying her good-byes.

Boy, would she ever.

Chapter 18

"I'm calling so early because I have a question," Ivy explained to Rebecca. Never mind it was half past seven. Rebecca had kids. She never slept in, and Ivy never called her this early.

"Hang on a sec," she said.

Ivy could hear the boys and Rufus, their 130-pound black Labrador, in the background. She grinned, knowing the chaos Rebecca lived through on a daily basis. Her best friend loved every minute of it, too.

"Okay, I'm back. Jacob was trying to put Thomas's dirty socks in Rufus's mouth," Rebecca explained. "Never a dull moment around here. So why the early-morning call? Is George okay?"

"Dad is fine, he stopped by yesterday. He said he's retiring and plans to sell the airline."

"You're kidding?" Rebecca asked. "I cannot see him retiring and playing golf all day."

"Me either, but he says he wants to call it quits." Ivy paused, then added, "He asked me if I wanted to come back to work."

Another pause.

"And?" Rebecca coaxed.

"I said no. I can't, Rebecca."

"Of course you can't. I wouldn't even think of it."

Ivy rarely discussed this with Rebecca or anyone else, for that matter. She had been so immersed in her grief, both were touchy when the topic of the airlines came up.

"But that's not why I called. I know this is going to make you ask a dozen questions, and I'll answer them later, but could you ask Thomas if he knows a girl named Holly? She's in fifth grade, too. Has long gold hair. A beautiful child." Since there was only one elementary school in Pine City, odds were good that he would at least know of her.

"Okayyy, I'll ask him. Hang on." Rebecca placed her hand over the phone's mouthpiece.

Ivy heard muffled voices, then Rufus's loud barks. She could not help but smile. It was a real genuine smile, too. Her heart felt light for the first time in eight years.

"Yes, he knows her. They're both in Sarah Anderson's class. So what do you want me to ask him?"

"*The* Sarah Anderson?"

"The one and only," Rebecca confirmed.

She and Sarah Anderson had been friends in high school. In fact, it was Sarah herself who had planned their infamous Orlando, Florida, trip. She laughed. Sarah had moved away after her senior year, and after that, they'd never stayed in much contact, a Christmas card now and then, then nothing.

"Small world, for sure," Ivy said.

Here goes, she thought. She was putting her nose where it did not belong, but she could not help herself. It was as if she were being pulled in some way by this little girl's visit, and she just could not get the image of her out of her mind.

"Ask if he knows her last name."

"Hang on." Rebecca did not bother putting her hand over the mouthpiece this time.

Ivy held the phone away from her ear.

"It's Greenwood. *G-R-E-E-N-W-O-O-D*. You know, the same as a forest that is green with foliage," Rebecca said.

Ivy knew what *greenwood* was. And she actually thought she had heard the name before, but she could not figure out in what context.

"Okay, thanks. I'll call you later," she said, and hung up before Rebecca could ask her why the sudden interest in one of Thomas's classmates.

The minute she hung up the phone, she brewed her second pot of coffee, then went upstairs to get her laptop. She booted it up and poured herself a cup of coffee while she waited. She needed to update her computer. It would be considered a dinosaur by today's standards. Her father had given it to her four years ago, for her thirty-second birthday.

As soon as her homepage came up, she went to Google to begin her search.

She typed *Greenwood, Pine City, North Carolina* in the search engine, then hit the search button. Thousands of hits came up.

"Dang," she said out loud as she scanned the links. Everything from forestry products to pine trees. She had to be more specific with her search parameters. She tried to remember if Holly had told her what her father's name was. Ivy was sure she would have remembered if she had.

She tried another search, only this time she typed in the search engine: *Holly Greenwood, Pine City Elementary School, Pine City, North Carolina.*

Scanning through the hits, she stopped when Pine City Elementary came up in a link. She clicked the blue line to open the link and scanned the article: *Holly Greenwood, Ashley Baines, and Jeffrey Laird received the Presidential Award for the third year. . . .*

"Smart girl," Ivy said. The short article in the *Pine City Banner* read that Holly Greenwood had also received an award for perfect attendance. "Disciplined too."

Was this odd for a girl who, she suspected, might be abused in some way by her father? She Googled, *Patterns of child abuse in eleven-year-old females.*

Thousands of links. She hit the first one, read the signs of abuse. She read five more articles before concluding that Holly fit the profile of an abused child. Acting on her gut instinct, she used the computer to look up Sarah Anderson's phone number.

She scribbled down the number. Ivy knew she was stepping way out of line, and she also knew that anyone who discovered what she was up to would believe she was obsessed with Holly because of what had happened to her own children, but she would deal with that if and when. If anyone would know if a child was suffering abuse, it would be her schoolteacher.

She dialed Sarah's number.

"Hello?" immediately came a pleasant-sounding voice.

"Sarah?" Ivy asked. She had remembered Sarah's distinct Southern accent. This Sarah sounded as neutral as could be.

"Yes, this is Sarah."

"Is this the Sarah Anderson who sneaked to Orlando with Ivy Macintosh the summer before their senior year?" She figured she might as well spit it out. There was no point if this was not *the* Sarah Anderson.

A little giggle, and Ivy recognized it immediately.

"The one and only," she said.

"It's Ivy." Surely, she would remember her? It had not been *that* long.

"I remember you! How could I ever forget Orlando? What in the world are you up to? It's been forever." Sarah seemed genuinely excited by her call.

Ivy did not want to go into all the horrid details about her past. Maybe Sarah knew, maybe not. However, she knew she could not just blurt out the reason for her phone call. There had to be a bit of reacquainting first.

"It sure has. So I understand you're a fifth-grade teacher now? Who would have ever thought that you, of all people, would want to teach school? I remember how we both could not wait to finish high school."

"I know. Weird, right? I think I grew up a bit when I went away to college. Berkeley was a real eye-opener for a Southern girl," Sarah said, then went on, "I majored in mathematics—can you believe that? I taught in San Francisco for a while, then my mom got sick, and I decided to come home. I teach at the elementary school now," she finished.

She had to ask. "How did you lose the Southern twang?"

Sarah laughed. "It was bad, huh? Actually, I studied acting while living in California. I thought it might be fun. It was not my thing. People there are totally different from Southerners. Lot of people thought that because I had a Southern accent, I was not the brightest star in the sky. I took elocution classes for a year, learned what they call Standard American Dialect, and it stuck. I thought about becoming a news anchor after that, just to show those hippies, but I found I loved working with children, and here I am."

"What about you? I know you studied at Duke, but you weren't sure what you wanted to do back then? I remember you said you wanted to work for your father, but then changed your mind," Sarah said.

She'd always had one heck of a memory. "I went to Duke, received my master's in business, and I did work with Dad for a while." She took a deep breath. It was very difficult to talk about her past in such a casual way.

"I know about your family, Ivy. I am so very sorry," Sarah added, her voice soft and comforting.

Tears filled Ivy's eyes and stopped in the back of her throat. "Thank you. It's been . . . rough."

She *so had not* wanted to talk about the crash, but it had made national headlines. It was naive of her to think Sarah wouldn't ask questions or mention it, as her and her father's loss had been headlines for weeks.

"I would imagine so," Sarah said.

"Yes, it was. Still is." She could not put into words what her loss was like, so she was not even going to try. What she could do was change the subject. She needed to come up with a reason other than asking about Holly for her call. "I'm trying to move forward. That's why I called. I thought maybe we could have lunch or dinner sometime." And she really wanted to, she realized after the lie flew out of her mouth. She would ask her face-to-face about Holly.

"I'd love to. I'm free just about anytime except school hours during the week."

Taking a deep breath, Ivy plunged right in. "What about lunch today? We could meet at The Red Barn." The place was practically an institution. If you lived within twenty miles of Pine City, you knew The Red Barn. It was owned by a local family and famous for its Southern-style food. They'd even been featured on the Food Network as one of the top ten places to dine in North Carolina.

"We'd never get in without a reservation," Sarah said. "But there's a new diner on the corner of Main Street, where the All-Day Dry Cleaners used to be. It's called The Blackberry Café, and it just opened a few months ago. I have been wanting to give them a try. I hear their food is excellent."

"That would be great. How about we meet at noon?" Ivy asked, feeling excited for the first time in eight years. She had planned on going to see her father, but she would go later or on another day. It would be fun catching up with Sarah.

"I'll see you there. I'm glad you called," Sarah said before they hung up.

Okay, she had actually made plans for the day. Suddenly, just like in high school, she wondered what in the world she was going to wear?

Chapter 19

The phone had been ringing off the hook all morning long, and her father refused to answer it. Holly was about to go cuckoo from listening to it ring and staring at her math book, which Mrs. Pellegrino had brought over this morning.

It was the twenty-first century, and they did not even have a computer or the Internet. She would be able to search online for math help if they did, but her dad insisted they could get by just fine without having a computer or the Internet. He was so incredibly mean. In high school, she knew for a fact that the students used computers and the Internet. What would be his excuse then? He'd probably have her homeschooled when it was time for high school. He treated her just like she was a baby, and there was no one she could talk to about it. Miss Carol would listen, but she did not want to ruin her friendship if Miss Carol decided to talk to her father. She knew him well. He would stop *all* contact with her if she thought Holly was telling family stuff to her.

Her dad was the most private person. She did not get him. He did not have any friends that she knew of. He never went out on dates or anything. Maybe her dad was a

criminal hiding from his past? But that could not be true
because he worked at The Upside, and he'd gone to college, too. And he had married her mom.

Maybe he was responsible for her mom's death. He had
never told her exactly *how* she had died, other than it was
very sudden and tragic. When she tried to talk to him
about her mother, he always got angry and said the topic
was not open for discussion.

She really needed to talk to Jen Pellegrino. She wondered if Mrs. Pellegrino knew how her mother had really
died? First thing Monday morning, she was going to write
a note for Roxie to take home to her mom, and she hoped
her mom would answer her back, so Roxie could bring the
note to school on Tuesday. Since she was grounded, she
was not allowed to talk on the phone. But she was listening for her father's truck to pull out of the driveway, just in
case he decided to leave. He was holed up in his den, as
usual, only coming out to get something to drink. He already had a bathroom in there. Holly figured he should
add one of those minirefrigerators and a microwave oven.
Then he'd only have to come out when he went to work.

If he did decide to leave, for whatever reason, she
planned to call Roxie's house and ask to speak to Mrs. Pel-
legrino.Then she wouldn't have to send a note to her.
Roxie was probably grounded, too, at least that is what
her dad said. She was sorry her friends were in trouble.
Holly would bet her allowance he did not even know if
Roxie and Kayla were in trouble, that he probably told her
that so she would feel bad. They did not force her to go to
Miss Carol's house in the sneaky way that she did. It was
her father who did. If he weren't such a . . . an ass, he
would let her have a little more freedom.

And what would he do if Ms. Anderson invited them to
her house for Thanksgiving dinner? He would say no; of

that, she was sure. They would do the same old thing they did every year on Thanksgiving.

He would serve that stinky pressed turkey with instant mashed potatoes, bottled gravy, canned green beans, and that nasty jellied cranberry stuff. She considered herself lucky if he bought a frozen pumpkin pie. Then he would tell her to wash the dishes, and he would spend the rest of the day watching football games. She tried watching them with him, but every time she said something, he would tell her to be quiet so he could hear what the announcer was saying.

The man was so totally mean to her. Sometimes she wondered if maybe he was not her real dad, but only her stepdad, and he had gotten stuck with her after her mother died. She planned to find out about her mother, and she was going to tell Ms. Anderson that her dad was an abuser. He was, really. He'd never hit her, or anything, but he ignored her. She knew for a fact that Kayla's and Roxie's fathers took them places. Once, Roxie's dad, Joseph Pellegrino, had taken all of them to the movies in Asheville, and they'd gone to a supercool restaurant called the Mellow Mushroom after the movie. He was fun, and he acted like he truly cared if they were having a good time.

And what did her dad do? Her dad took her to Ollie's for pizza, and that was it. More often than not, he would bring the pizza home. He was totally cruel to her.

She heard a noise from the back of the house and quickly acted like she was studying her math. He had made her study at the kitchen table so he could "keep an eye on her," he'd said. If he allowed her to study in her bedroom, he knew that she would not. At least he knew that much about her, which she guessed was something. She was reading *Deathly Hallows,* the last book in the Harry Potter series, and it was due back at the library this week. If she had to study every waking hour, she would not be able to finish the book before returning it. She had already checked the book out four times. Five times was the limit on popular books, and the school library didn't have any of the Harry Potter books. So, most likely, she would not get to read the ending. What kind of dad denied his children a final Harry Potter ending? A mean dad, just like hers.

"Holly, I'm going to the grocery store. Would you like to go with me?" Her father stood in the doorway. He was a big man, she thought. A big *mean* man.

"No, I'll just stay here and study," she said, suddenly thrilled that he was leaving her alone. She could call Roxie and ask to speak to her mother.

"All right, I'll be back in an hour."

"Have fun," she called out. She hoped he slipped on a banana peel and broke a leg or an arm. Then he would be at *her* mercy. No, she really did not mean that. Kind of, sort of. She crossed her fingers and took it back.

He went out the back door. She listened for his truck to back down the drive. As soon as she heard him pull onto the street, she raced down the hall to where the phone was. They only had one phone, and it was not even portable. When she saw that the little alcove where the phone was located was empty, she wanted to scream! The phone book was there, the scratch pad and pencil, and the chair, but no phone.

He had taken the phone with him! He truly was an abuser and the meanest man who ever lived. What if she needed to call 911? What if he was in a wreck and the police tried to call her?

What if? What if? What if?

She could not believe he would stoop so low. It was more than obvious he didn't trust her, but to take the phone out of the house? But wait, she thought, she hadn't actually *seen* the phone in his hands. It was probably hidden around here somewhere. All she had to do was find it.

Before she changed her mind, she opened the door to his bedroom. He did not like for her to go into his room. He said she must respect his privacy. Well, since he did not respect hers, she did not feel the least bit guilty when she opened the closet and began her search. She opened a couple of shoe boxes, which were filled with important-looking papers. No phone. She moved a stack of sweaters on a shelf, thinking the phone would fit perfectly behind the clothes. No luck there.

She opened his dresser drawers, lifted up his white T-shirts, looked under his perfectly folded rows of socks. Who folded socks like this, anyway? She was lucky if she found a matching pair in her drawers. Of course, she did her own laundry and rarely bothered folding *socks*. More and more, she realized just how much her dad was a true weirdo. Men do not fold socks unless they're . . . weird. There was a name for superneat people like him, but she could not remember what it was. She would have to ask Roxie. If she didn't know, she would make a point to find out for her.

She had gone through all the drawers and still no phone. She got down on all fours and looked beneath the bed. Nothing. Not even a dust bunny. More evidence her father was a weirdo. Who didn't cram stuff under their bed?

She would have to search the den and be quick about it. He'd already been gone twenty minutes, so she did not have a lot of time left. His den was as neat as the rest of the house, excluding her room. Her room was clean, but not nearly as clean as the rest of the house. She opened the large filing cabinet against the wall behind his desk. Nothing in there. She moved to his desk, sitting in his chair, which was super comfy. No wonder he spent so much time in here. It was cozy, with the fireplace and all. She tried the bottom right drawer, but it was locked. Then the left, and it, too, was locked. The long middle drawer was not deep enough for their old-fashioned phone, so she scanned the bookshelves and saw nothing but his old yard-work books.

Maybe he'd hidden it in the garage? He probably took it out through the back door, hid it, then came in to tell her he was leaving. She looked at the clock on her father's desk. It was old-fashioned, too. She had twenty-three minutes left. Before she could overthink the situation, she raced out the back door to the garage.

"Crap," she said to herself. If the phone was here, no way would she have enough time to search all the possible hiding places. And if she found it, by the time she brought it back inside, plugged it in, and called Roxie, her dad would be home.

Defeated, she went back inside and had no more than sat back down at the table than she heard her father's truck pulling into the garage. She had barely made it and decided she would have to settle for writing Mrs. Pellegrino a note. She would start now, before she forgot all the things she wanted to ask her.

In her big loopy handwriting she began:

> Dear Mrs. Pellegrino:
> I need to find out what happened to my mother. Dad does not allow me to talk about her. I am very afraid that he might have done something to her. Like killed her and put her body somewhere. Roxie said you knew my mom. Could you please write me back and give the note to Roxie to bring back to school Tuesday. He will not let me use the phone. I am trapped in this house. Just in case something happens to me.
> Sincerely,
> Holly Greenwood

Quickly she folded the note and stuffed it in her back pocket. Her dad would kill her if he found it. She heard the back door open and took a breath. Her heart was beating very fast. She focused on the fractions.

"Holly, come and help carry this stuff inside!" he called.

She should add slavery to her long list of complaints, too.

"Be right there," she said. She turned her math book over on its spine so that he would not be able to see that she was still on the same page. In fact, it would be a good thing if he did, because she would tell him how hard it was and it would take her years to get through the book. She changed her mind, then, and flipped it back over.

She stepped out the back door. Her dad had three grocery bags in one hand and the telephone in the other.

Ass, she thought. "Why do you have the phone out here?" She would act like she was surprised. He knew she would have used the phone the second he left, that was obvious, but she wanted to call his bluff, so she acted surprised. She took one of the large paper bags from him.

"Guess," he said as he opened the back door. He stood to the side so she could enter first. She looked over her shoulder. She did not trust him at all. He could have a hatchet or something, ready to smash her skull in.

Inside, she hurried to the kitchen and placed the heavy bag on the counter. He placed his bags next to hers. "Want to help me put this stuff away?"

Like I have a choice. "Sure." She began to empty the bag. Just the usual stuff. Frozen dinners. A bagged premade salad. Some apples. Milk. Cereal. *Nothing worth eating.*

"I thought we could go out for lunch today," he said, surprising her.

Holly almost fell to the floor. "Why?"

He had never taken her out to lunch, at least not that she could remember. "Because I know what it's like being grounded, and having your parent forcing you to study when you'd rather be talking on the phone." He glanced at the phone he'd placed on the counter. "Or reading. I thought you might enjoy getting out of the house, but if you'd rather not, I can make us a sandwich."

"No, I mean, yes, that would be fun. I'll put my math book away and go brush my teeth."

"Be ready in ten minutes," her dad called out.

Maybe he wasn't such a mean ass, after all.

Chapter 20

Ivy could not remember the last time she had eaten in a restaurant with a friend. She occasionally went to dinner with her father, but that was it. Socializing made her feel guilty. Lots of things, in fact, made her feel guilty. *Survivor's guilt,* the shrinks called it. She agreed with them, but she was turning over a new leaf. So, again, *one step at a time.*

She found The Blackberry Café and parked in the parking lot at the rear. She hoped she would recognize Sarah when she saw her. Certainly, she did not sound the same. She entered the café, scanned the few tables, and stopped when she spied Sarah looking over the menu. She had not changed even one little bit. Ivy walked over to the table and pulled out the chair. "Hey, there," she said, grinning from ear to ear.

"Oh, my God, you look exactly like you did in high school!" Sarah exclaimed. She stood up and gave Ivy a big hug.

"Thanks, you do, too," Ivy said, feeling a bit bashful all of a sudden.

They both sat down.

"Isn't this the cutest place ever? I remember my mom picking up her dry cleaning here," Sarah said. "It smelled so bad, I'd always get a headache when she would send me inside to pick up the clothes."

Ivy nodded. "It's perfect, though I would never in a million years have thought someone could turn the old cleaners into such a quaint little spot." Ivy took in her surroundings. The walls were painted a pale lavender, and paintings of blackberry bushes covered one wall. Shelves displaying cookbooks for sale, along with jams and jellies and aprons, gave off an air of hominess. A large glass case opposite them held all kinds of cakes, pies, and cookies. The tables were white wicker with blackberry-colored cushions. Definitely nicer than the dry cleaners. There were three other tables occupied besides theirs. Not too busy for Saturday afternoon, and that was fine with her.

"I'm so glad you looked me up. I wanted to call you . . . after, but I didn't," Sarah said.

"I got your card and the flowers. They were beautiful." And they were. "Thank you for remembering me." This is not how she wanted their lunch to start, but maybe it was best to get it out of the way first. Sort of like the elephant in the room. It was there and hard to ignore.

"You're welcome, Ivy. It was a sad day in the world for all those people." Sarah was always genuine and kind— not a mean bone in her body when they were in high school. Ivy could just look at her and tell she was as special now as she was then.

"Okay, let's talk about us," Sarah announced. "You need cheering up, I can tell."

Ivy laughed. "Am I that obvious? And here I thought I was putting on a good front. Seriously, I'm glad we're here." She looked around her. "I need to start enjoying life again. It's hard. I feel so guilty. Sorry, I know you do not want to hear this."

Sarah nodded. "Of course I want to hear what you have to say. It might help to talk about what's been going on. I'm fine, Ivy. You can't wipe away the past like you wipe down a chalkboard. If it were only that easy."

A young girl around eighteen or so appeared at the table. She wore jeans, a purple T-shirt that read THE BLACKBERRY CAFÉ, and a cream-colored apron with hand-painted blackberries on the pockets. "Can I get y'all something to drink?"

Ivy smiled at Sarah. The girl's accent was so heavy, it was hard to understand what she said. But they had both been born and raised in North Carolina, so they got it.

"I'll try the blackberry tea, iced," Ivy said.

"Me too," Sarah said.

As soon as the young girl stepped away from their table, Sarah laughed, and said, "Did I sound that Southern?"

"Worse," Ivy said, and they both burst out laughing.

"Seriously?" Sarah probed.

"Close, but not as bad," Ivy said.

"I have a couple of kids in my class who are hard to understand, but it's a regional thing, and it's what they're used to. I do try to make sure the students use hard consonants though, and no slang. They always roll their eyes when I explain this to them, but they're young still, and learning. I give them a break whenever I can. I've got a good class this year."

Sarah had opened the door for the real reason Ivy had suggested that they meet for lunch. "Do you remember Rebecca? Her mother was Mom's nurse?"

"Of course I do. I have one of her boys in my class. Thomas, brilliant little guy, too."

Now, how to go about telling her story? *Start at the beginning,* she thought, *the beginning.*

"Last night, I had a strange visitor," she started, then plunged ahead. "I think she's in your class. Her name is Holly Greenwood."

Sarah's face brightened more, if that was even possible. "Holly? I didn't know you knew her?"

"I didn't until last night. Apparently, she was out alone and got lost in the woods behind my place. She was very frightened when she called her father to come pick her up, and he was not the friendliest man I have ever met, either."

A shadow filled the entrance, and Ivy was stunned when she saw the very man she had been talking about filling the doorway. Sarah's eyes followed her own.

Ivy whispered, "Speak of the devil."

"Daniel Greenwood. I have had my eye on that man for months. A hunk, don't you think? I was thinking about inviting him and Holly over for Thanksgiving dinner this year. I just haven't figured out how to approach him yet."

Ivy felt like she had been kicked in the gut. She didn't know what to say, so she said nothing. Holly saw her and Sarah and practically ran over to their table.

"Hey, Ivy. Hello, Ms. Anderson. I didn't know you two were friends," Holly said, all smiles now. Where was the frightened child who'd appeared on her doorstep last night?

"We have known one another since high school," Sarah said. "We were just catching up on old times. Why don't you and your father join us. We haven't placed our orders yet."

By this time, Daniel Greenwood stood towering over their table. "Mr. Greenwood? Would you like to join us?"

A shadow of annoyance crossed his face, and his reply sounded impatient. "I guess I can. I need to talk to you, anyway, so it might as well be here."

Ivy glanced at Sarah. Her friend's face was pink with embarrassment. This guy was incredibly rude. Why Sarah would want to invite him for Thanksgiving dinner was a mystery.

Holly's voice was laced with exasperation when she said, "Dad!"

"Sorry, I mean, sure, we would like to join you two ladies."

Ivy could not keep quiet. "If it's inconvenient for you, please do not feel obligated."

She barely knew this man, and already she did not like him. Not at all. What kind of man lets an eleven-year-old child roam the woods at night?

"No, it's fine, really. Let me grab a couple chairs," he said.

"It's so cool to see you outside the classroom. Aren't you supposed to be grading our quizzes for Monday?" Holly asked.

"I finished up this morning," Sarah told her. "And do not tell anyone I told you, but you did very well. I'm super proud of you." Sarah gave Holly's hand a quick squeeze.

"Math?" Ivy asked.

"How did you know?" Sarah asked.

"We talked about it a bit last night," Ivy explained. "Holly says she prefers spelling and English." Ivy smiled at the little girl. She was going to be stunning in a few years. She could almost feel sorry for her father, but didn't.

"I was lost and saw Ivy's lights on last night. She let me use her phone," Holly explained to Sarah.

"Well, that was very kind of her, but why were you in the woods after dark?" Sarah asked, concern on her face.

Daniel Greenwood appeared with a chair in each hand. He placed them on either side of the table. He motioned for Holly to sit down; then he sat down.

At least he has manners, Ivy thought. *Or is this just an act for Sarah's sake?*

"Why don't you tell Ms. Anderson why you were out last night?" Daniel's voice was that of a stern father, and he never took his eyes from his daughter's face.

Is this his way of silencing her? He is really quite intimidating, Ivy thought. A big man, muscular, though he was handsome in a rugged, mountain man sort of way.

"I went home with Roxie and we had pizza. Then I sneaked over to Miss Carol's to practice for The Upside's annual Christmas musical. I was only supposed to be gone an hour, while Kayla and Roxie covered for me. Instead, I ended up getting lost, and that's when I saw Ivy's porch light. I followed the light, then I knocked on her door to use her phone. I'm grounded now and have to study math all weekend, plus three hours every night until I bring my B minus up to an A." After telling her story, Holly proceeded to give her dad a dirty look.

Ivy could not help but grin. Holly was a spunky little thing. Maybe she had jumped the gun. Maybe she was ornery, and her father was putting his foot down.

"The Upside? How did you get involved with that place?" Ivy asked, her curiosity suddenly piqued.

"My dad works there," Holly said.

Ivy was stunned at Holly's words.

Her father works at The Upside?

The waitress brought their blackberry teas. "Y'all gonna be eatin' at the same table? I can bring ya a drink if ya are."

"We are," Sarah told the waitress.

"I'll have an ice tea. Holly?" Her father raised his brows.

"Can I have what they're having?" she asked.

"Sure," he answered.

"So a regular ice tea an' a blackberry tea? Be right back."

"Yes, ma'am," Daniel Greenwood replied.

"Mr. Greenwood is a horticultural specialist. He designs all the landscaping for The Upside," Sarah explained.

"Is that so, Mr. Greenwood? How did you get involved with The Upside?"

He shook his head, his long hair brushing the collar of his shirt. *A well-fitting shirt,* Ivy thought.

"I studied horticulture in college."

College? Ivy had misjudged this man by his appearance. She thought he was employed by the cemetery. Not that that was a bad job, but she was glad when he'd said he worked at The Upside.

"That's interesting. I always wondered about the land-scaping there. It's beautiful. I just assumed they had . . . To tell you the truth, I'm not sure what I thought," Ivy admitted. She never really discussed her father's other business ventures. The airline was enough.

"Lawn boys?" Daniel Greenwood said. He actually smiled.

Ivy's heart lurched. *Good grief, the man is beyond good-looking when he smiles. No wonder Sarah is so interested in him.*

"No, not exactly. I just did not know. Truly." And she gave him a genuine smile in return. She had been wrong about this guy. Sarah was right. He was a hunk, probably one of those dads who had a hard time raising a daughter on his own.

The waitress returned and placed two more glasses on the table. "I can put y'all at a bigger table if you want." She said the last word like *won't.*

"This is perfect, but thanks," Sarah said.

Ivy felt a slight nudge beneath the table. Sarah wanted to be as close to Daniel Greenwood as humanly possible.

For a split second, Ivy couldn't blame her.

The young girl stood by the table and patiently took their orders, answering their questions patiently. She was a good waitress for one so young, Ivy thought.

"Now, y'all hang tight, an' I'll put this order in right away."

As soon as she stepped away from the table, they all grinned.

Chapter 21

It had been years, if ever, since Daniel had had lunch with two beautiful ladies at once, longer than he wanted to admit. And Holly was gorgeous, just like her mother, so make that three beautiful women, one much younger than the other two. He was not real thrilled when Sarah Anderson had invited him and Holly to join her and the lady from last night, because he knew that Sarah had a massive crush on him. Word traveled fast in small towns. She was sweet and attractive, and an excellent teacher, but he felt nothing even close to attraction for her.

Now, this other woman, Ivy, she was unlike any woman he'd encountered lately. Maybe even ever. There was something sad and haunting in her green eyes. They reminded him of newly sprouted seedlings, they were such a deep green. Her skin was as white as a fresh-picked gardenia.

He chuckled, realizing that he was thinking like a lovesick puppy.

"Dad, are you okay?" Holly asked. "You look weird."

"Thanks, but I'm fine. I'm just tired, I guess," he said to her, then smiled.

She shook her head. "I haven't seen you smile this much in a year."

Again they all laughed, and Sarah blushed.

He had to let her know he was not interested in her, not in the way she wanted. It was hard to date with a young daughter. He did not want Holly to get attached to any of the few women he'd dated, and she did crave a woman's attention. He'd never introduced her to them, and he wanted to keep it that way. His job was to raise her and keep her from getting hurt. Then, when she was in college or married, he'd worry about his own love life. When she spent the night with Roxie or Kayla, those were his nights to venture out as an adult man and enjoy the company of a woman. He was not dead, despite what his daughter thought.

Dead, like Laura. She had been his first true mature love, but there'd been times in their marriage that Daniel thought she was more in love with her career than with him and Holly. And this was playing a big role in the way he was raising Holly. He could not encourage a musical career in any way. It had cost him a wife and Holly a mother. He knew he was strict, but she would thank him for this when she was older, or so he told himself. Though sometimes he wondered if he was just putting a good face on his own fears and desires.

"So, Holly, how is the practicing going?" Sarah asked. "I have seen the posters everywhere, and it's going to be the best musical yet. And I cannot believe you're the star of the show."

Ivy looked at Daniel.

"Holly is not the star," he said to Sarah. "I have told her she's way too young to get involved in the music business. She spends too much time with those women at The Upside."

Holly's eyes filled with tears. "Dad! You are so mean! I *have* to perform in the musical, I just have to. My life depends on it." She let the tears fall, which Daniel thought unusual.

"We can discuss this when we get home. We're here to have lunch, okay?" he said to her, knowing his voice was stern, but when it came to all the music garbage, he had to be stern.

The twangy waitress showed up, holding a tray above her head and a stand in the other. "Yummies are here," she announced in her bright, perky voice.

She placed their plates in front of them. "You'll love the quiche. Mama used our eggs from the hens this morning. Fresh as you can get."

Ivy and Sarah had both ordered the spinach quiche.

"Thank you," Sarah said politely. "I'm sure it's delicious."

Ivy, on the other hand, wished she had ordered a rare hamburger, but quiche seemed so ladies-who-lunch–like that she had told the waitress she would have the same as Sarah. She had never been one of "those" types, not that there was anything wrong with them. It just was not who she was. And really, she thought as she sliced into her lunch, after eight years of what she had gone through, who, exactly, was she?

Unsure, but ready to start the process of discovery, she bit into the quiche, and it was indeed excellent. She would take back that rare-hamburger thought.

"Holly, eat your sandwich, okay? Now is not the time to sulk," Daniel said. He'd ordered a cheeseburger, medium rare, Ivy had noticed.

Sarah took a bite of her quiche. "This is fantastic. I think I have found my new favorite restaurant. How's your cheeseburger, Daniel?"

He had a mouthful of food, so he nodded up and down, and muttered something that sounded like, "Good."

"I didn't know you were a singer," Ivy said to make polite conversation.

Holly looked at her dad. "I'm not." She crossed her arms over her chest.

"Holly, that's enough. Ivy is trying to be polite to you," Daniel admonished.

"I'm sorry, I guess this is a touchy subject," Ivy offered, looking at Holly. The girl rolled her eyes, but directed her gaze to her father. Ivy got what she was trying to convey.

"It is. Dad hates music. Hates me singing. Hates everything," Holly said. She took a bite of her club sandwich and sent glaring daggers at her father.

"This was a bad idea. We should have stayed home. You can't act like this in public. If you want me to stop treating you like a little kid, you need to stop acting like one."

All eyes went to Daniel.

He shook his head. "I did not mean that the way it came out." He inhaled and exhaled. "She's eleven, I realize that, much too young to begin a singing career. I want her to stay a kid as long as possible."

"Your father means he does not want you to grow up too soon," Sarah explained to Holly. "Am I right, Daniel?" She smiled at him, and Ivy saw she had a speck of the spinach in her front tooth.

Ivy was trying not to laugh, but she could not help herself. She bit the insides of her cheeks, but could not keep it together. "Sarah, can you come with me to the ladies' room? Now?"

Sarah looked at her as if she had lost her mind. "Now?"

"Yes, now."

They both got up and went to the ladies' room. As soon as they closed the door, Ivy burst out laughing. "Sarah, you have a giant gob of spinach on your teeth. If you're trying to impress Mr. Greenwood, you need to rinse your mouth."

Sarah looked in the mirror. "Oh, my Gawd! How embarrassing! I don't think I can go back out there now." She cupped her hands under the water and sloshed it around in her mouth, spitting the offending piece of spinach into the sink.

"Yes, you can. We can't just stay in the bathroom while they eat."

"Of course you're right. I just feel like an idiot. It's obvious I like the guy."

It was, and Ivy did not have the heart to tell her that she was sure the feelings were not reciprocated.

"Let's finish lunch. We'll worry about that another time" was all she could say. He might like Sarah. Who was she to say? She had been out of the romance market way too long to know what the acceptable signals were now. Maybe she would Google it tonight, just for fun. Suddenly she felt overwhelmed with guilt. She had gone almost an hour without thinking about the family she had so tragically lost.

But wasn't that the point?

Back at the table, Ivy did her best to make conversation that was not offensive to anyone. "Daniel, how long have you worked at The Upside?"

"I have been there since the beginning."

"Dad's the manager," Holly said, finally out of her bad mood.

"I'm impressed," Ivy said.

"Yes, I have been to The Willows for dinner, and the grounds throughout are a treat to the eyes," Sarah gushed, then turned to Ivy. "That's one of the fine dining restaurants at The Upside."

Ivy nodded. "Yes, I have been there a few times." Did Sarah know that her father had built The Upside and still owned the restaurant and the other two there? She was not sure, but she did not want to say anything . . . just in case.

"Have you tried it yet, Daniel?" Ivy asked. She was curious, and she knew Sarah would relish the info.

"No, I have not had the pleasure, but I'm sure I'll get there eventually."

"Can you take me with you?" Holly asked. "I have never been to a fancy restaurant." She seemed to be in a better mood, her anger toward her father forgotten for the moment.

"We can do that for your twelfth birthday if you want," Daniel said, and he knew she would hold him to it. "I'll make reservations as soon as we get home."

"When is your birthday?" Ivy asked.

"It's the crappiest day ever. It's New Year's Eve."

"Holly, enough with the language," Daniel said, but he had a slight smile when he spoke.

"The biggest party of the year," Sarah added. "I think it's a perfect day to have a birthday. Wherever you go, you know there's going to be a party."

Holly seemed to be thinking, then spoke up. "That's true. I guess I never thought about it like that. Dad, can Roxie and Kayla go, too?"

"Sure, why not?" He wiped his mouth with his napkin. "We'll have a party of our own."

"Can Ms. Anderson come? Please, please, please."

Ivy saw Daniel's discomfort, but she could not help smiling.

"Absolutely," he said. "And would you like to join us as well, Ivy? The more, the merrier, I always say."

Ivy watched Sarah. One minute she thought she had a date, sort of, and in the next, she was deflated like a day-old party balloon.

"Oh no, I couldn't, really." Ivy wanted to give Sarah half a chance with Daniel.

"I insist you come along, since you were kind enough to let Holly use your phone and look after her."

She smiled. This was not going as planned.

"That'd be a great idea. Ivy, please come with us. I want you to meet Roxie and Kayla. They're my BFFs."

Ivy raised her brow in question. *"BFFs?"*

"Where have you been? You mean you don't know what a *BFF* is?" Sarah asked, apparently stunned; then she realized what she had said.

Ivy felt tears well up in her eyes. *Crud,* she thought. This was not the time or place, but she couldn't help it. She used her napkin to blot her tears. "Sorry, I have been . . . out of touch for a while." She directed her attention to Holly. "What exactly is a *BFF*? I would love to know." She gave her a big smile, just to let her know she was okay with whatever it was.

"It's *best friends forever,* and we have been friends since we were little kids," Holly explained; then she asked Ivy, "Do you have a BFF?"

Ivy smiled. "I'll let you in on a secret. Ms. Anderson and I were best friends all through high school. We had a few adventures ourselves back in the day, didn't we?" Ivy looked to Sarah for confirmation.

Sarah blushed. "We were quite the handful, and that's all I'm going to admit to," she said.

Ivy smiled again. Sarah did not want to advertise their past, and she agreed. Those were their memories, and now was not the time to share them, especially with an eleven-year-old.

Chapter 22

Surprised when Daniel picked up the lunch tab, Ivy thanked him, feeling awkward and not knowing why. It was not like he hadn't paid for Sarah's, too. He was just being polite, she guessed, even though she had questioned his behavior earlier. It wasn't like she had been out socially and had anyone to compare him to. She had no clue what one considered acceptable etiquette in today's dating world. And she was not in the dating market. Definitely not. Sarah was, and as her friend, she could help *her* by making sure Sarah had some alone time with Daniel Greenwood.

They left the café together and walked to their cars, parked behind the restaurant. "Thanks again for lunch. It was a treat, for sure," Ivy said to Daniel. "I'm not sure about New Year's Eve, though." She gave a wan smile to Holly. "I . . . Well, it's been a long time since I have celebrated New Year's Eve." There was so much more to be said, and maybe she would, another time; it was tough trying to explain her life to a child, and in front of her father. "I have been somewhat of a recluse."

"No, you are not getting out of this," Sarah informed her. "We will all celebrate Holly's birthday, together. You can meet her friends, and we'll have a great time, won't we?" Sarah said, her lovesick gaze settling on Daniel.

Ivy thought she was doing her a favor by trying to back out, but apparently she was wrong.

"Yes, please come with us, Ivy. I really would like for you to meet my friends. Right, Dad?"

Daniel shook his head and tugged at his daughter's long ponytail. "Yes, we'd enjoy your company, along with Ms. Anderson's, of course. I'm sure Holly and the girls will supply us with plenty of entertainment."

Ivy tried to catch Sarah's eye so she could give her some kind of hint or signal, but Sarah never looked her way, standing there all doe-eyed over Daniel. Really, come to think of it, it would not matter if she was there or not. The fact that it was Holly's birthday, and she had planned to invite her friends, meant that there would not be much of a chance for Sarah to establish any kind of relationship with Daniel. If that was to happen, it would happen with or without Ivy's help.

Remembering that she was going to try to live her life and move forward, she decided she would go to the birthday celebration. And maybe, by then, she would be able to arrange for the tab to be on the house without embarrassing Daniel. After all, it was her father's restaurant.

It would be entertaining, to say the least. Holly was quite a little spitfire, and Ivy had already become quite fond of the girl.

"Okay, you've convinced me. I'll go. Thanks for inviting me," she added, realizing *her* social etiquette was a bit rusty. She would ask Sarah about an appropriate gift for Holly's birthday. She would know, given the fact she spent so much time with the adorable little girl.

"We'll both look forward to it, then. Holly has to get back home now to study, don't you?" he asked his daughter.

Her face paled, but two bright patches of red dotted her cheeks. "I hate math. I'm sorry, Ms. Anderson. I can't help it. I just don't get it, and I want a tutor, but Dad won't let me have one. He's very *adamant* about that. Right?" Holly looked at her dad.

He took her hand in his. "Let's not start, okay? We've had a nice lunch. I'll let you call Roxie later. Maybe," he told her. "But studies first."

Holly's face brightened. Her face was quite expressive. "Excellent!" She beamed. "Not the study part," she added immediately. "I'll try, Ms. Anderson, I promise."

"I know this, and your test score shows so much improvement," Sarah said. "I'm very pleased with Holly's efforts. She excels in so many other areas."

Ivy knew that Sarah had said this for Daniel's benefit. Maybe he wouldn't be quite so hard on his daughter. Though after witnessing them together, Ivy was sure Daniel's parenting skills were up to par. He might be a tad too strict, but it was not her place to interfere. If Sarah suspected that Holly's home life was anything other than having a stern father who wanted what he thought was best for his daughter, surely she would have intervened by now?

"See? I told you I was studying," Holly confirmed.

"I know you're trying, kiddo. Now we'd best let Ms. Anderson and Ivy get on with their day. I'm sure they have a lot to catch up on," Daniel said. "Thanks for inviting us to join you. It's been . . . interesting."

Sarah gazed up at Daniel, but his attention was on Ivy, and Ivy had to admit that she was strangely flattered by his obvious interest. The past twenty-four hours had been eye-opening, to say the least, though just this thought brought on a renewed wave of guilt. She knew that would continue to happen if she were to move forward. She expected no less, as she was human. It would be tough, and she would do her very best to live life to its fullest.

The process had begun when she had answered her door last night. And there was no going back.

"Yes, we do. It's been a very long time," Sarah replied. "I'll see you Monday, Holly." She gave the little girl a hug, then held her hand out to Daniel. "I'll see you soon?" She said this as though it were a question.

Daniel cleared his throat. "Actually, I'd like a minute of your time, if you don't mind?"

Sarah's perfectly peach complexion glowed with longing. "Not at all. Ivy, Holly, could you give us a minute? There's nothing like the present," she said cheerfully.

"Of course. Holly, would you like to go to Baubles?" Ivy asked. "It's just down the block," Ivy said, before she remembered that fateful day so many years ago when she had planned to shop there for Elizabeth and James. To this day, she had never been inside the unique store. Now, with her new attitude, and partly in gratitude for what Holly, unknowingly, had done for her, Ivy thought it a good place to start a new friendship with Holly, even though she was sad that she had never taken her own children there to shop.

"Really? Can I go, Dad?" she asked her father.

"Sure. Meet me back here in twenty minutes, if that's okay with Ivy?"

"Absolutely," Ivy confirmed.

She reached for Holly's hand and found it to be a perfect fit in her own.

Chapter 23

The day was turning out to be way cooler than Holly had anticipated. Whatever had turned her dad into Mr. Nice Guy, she did not know, but she liked him so much more this way.

She really liked Ivy and could not wait to tell Roxie and Kayla about her. *She is the bomb!*

Holly was unsure why her dad had asked Ms. Anderson for a private chat, but she didn't really care. Holly now knew that her math grade was improving; and even though she was grounded, she had made a new friend. She wanted to tell Ivy about the Christmas musical.

As they walked down Main Street, hand in hand, Holly peered inside the windows of the shops as they passed. Some had already begun decorating for Christmas, even though it wasn't even Thanksgiving yet. Weird, but she didn't care. Maybe she would talk her dad into a real Christmas tree this year. They'd never decorated for Thanksgiving, so maybe she could push her luck and try for Christmas.

"So, was Ms. Anderson as cool as she is now when you all were in high school?" Holly asked. "She's the best teacher I have had."

Ivy laughed. "She was the most popular girl in school, so I suppose that would qualify as cool."

"I think she kinda likes my dad," Holly said as they entered Baubles.

Inside the store were a variety of unique toys, games, and items made by local artisans. Wooden puzzles, rocking horses, spinning tops, but Holly was too old for that stuff. Holly spotted a display of glittery crossbody bags and picked up an aqua-blue one, with silver sequins in the shape of a dolphin. She peered inside, then put it down and picked up a bright red hair barrette, with a matching headband. "This is pretty," she said, and placed both items back on the display rack.

"Red is my favorite color," Ivy told her. "What about yours?"

"Pink and purple. And I totally love anything that sparkles. So, do you think Ms. Anderson is crushing on my dad?"

Ivy could not help but laugh. "I don't know, I just reunited with Ms. Anderson. We did not stay in touch after high school. Why do you believe Sarah . . . Ms. Anderson . . . likes your father?"

"This is so gross, but Jen, that's Roxie's mom, said every woman in town thinks my dad's hot. I could just kinda tell because Ms. Anderson was acting goofy at lunch, like some of the fifth-grade girls do when they have boyfriends. Plus, she's always offering to help tutor me in math. At my house. It's okay, though. My dad needs a girlfriend. He's never dated since my mom died."

Ivy stopped so abruptly that Holly bumped into her. "I'm sorry. I'm a klutz."

"Trust me, I know *klutz*. I have three left feet." Ivy picked up the red barrette and headband. "Do you like these?" she asked.

"They're very pretty. I was thinking they would look nice in my hair for the Christmas musical, but Dad's pretty much set against me singing. I do not know why. He does not like music or noise. And he folds his socks really straight. Don't you think that's weird? Did you ever have a boyfriend who folded socks? I thought all boys were slobs, truly, but my dad is the neatest person I know."

Ivy burst out laughing. "I can't say I've ever had a boyfriend who folded socks." She thought of John, and his huge drawer of socks. They were thrown in a pile and picked out according to color.

"So how come you don't have a boyfriend? You're incredibly pretty and nice," Holly asked in her wide-eyed, innocent way as she walked to the end of the aisle, touching knickknacks along the way.

Ivy decided to tell the truth. There was no getting around it. Sooner or later, she would have to talk about the loss of her family with people, maybe even strangers. It was incredibly sad, but in her heart, she knew she had to start remembering the good times she had shared with John.

Swallowing the sob that rose in her throat, she said, "I was married once. My husband died. It was a very long time ago."

Holly turned to her, and before Ivy knew what was happening, the little girl embraced her. "I'm sorry, Ivy. I didn't know. Was he, like, sick or something?"

While Ivy knew she needed to force herself to speak about John's death, she wasn't sure if now was a suitable time to reveal the complete cause of her loss. She did not want to burden Holly with more grief, since she had lost her mother, too. Keeping in mind her age, she said, "No, he wasn't sick. He was in an accident."

"Like my mom. Dad said she died a very sudden and tragic death. I hate those words. It's . . . I do not know, kind of scary, I think. He hasn't ever told me the details. He thinks I'm too young. I really can't remember her, but I do have a picture. I look like her," Holly said.

"She must have been a beautiful woman, then," Ivy said, and she meant it.

"She was pretty. Dad says I have her hair and eyes," Holly offered very casually as though she were discussing a stranger.

"Speaking of, it's about time we headed back to meet your dad. I think we have gone over our twenty-minute time limit."

As they made their way out of Baubles, Ivy planned to return and get the sparkly red barrette with headband for Holly.

Why? Just because she could.

Chapter 24

Daniel had not planned on having this talk with Sarah Anderson in a parking lot, but, as she had said, there was no time like the present. "This is a bit awkward." He jammed his hands in his pockets, feeling like a schoolboy asking the most popular girl in school if she would go with him to senior prom. And worse, he knew Sarah had no clue what he was about to spurt out. "Listen, this is not easy for me to say, so I'm just going to say what I have to say. I'm really trying to focus on Holly now. She's a great kid, as you know, a little snarky, but what kid isn't?"

This was not coming out as easily as he'd thought. Sarah had stars in her eyes, no doubt about it, and he hated to, but he had to extinguish them. "I'm not really open to us—you and me—being anything more than friends." He felt like a total jerk, but it was necessary. "If I have assumed more, I feel like a major idiot."

The look on Sarah's face was enough. He did not need to hear the words.

Obviously, his words had taken her by surprise.

"No, no...I thought we...well..." Sarah took a minute to gather herself. "We can be friends. I'm good with that. Really. Maybe I have been too persistent with my offer to tutor Holly, too. She's made drastic improvements. Her latest test score shows me that she's really putting in an extra effort in a subject she dislikes and has trouble grasping."

Sarah was rambling, and it made Daniel feel like a jerk. "Good to hear. I know I'm hard on her, but I want her to succeed in all of her studies."

"Well, then, it's settled. I will not worry about tutoring Holly, and the other . . . We're . . . friends, right?" She smiled, and offered her hand. *She's a true lady,* he thought. And it made him wish that he did feel something for her, but it would be unfair to her.

He squeezed her hands. "Friends, Sarah. Truly. You know my daughter probably better than any female, and I want your relationship with her to remain as strong as it's been. She adores you, you know?"

"The feeling is mutual," Sarah added.

Daniel saw Holly and Ivy heading their way; their timing could not have been more perfect.

"Dad, I saw a really cool barrette and headband at Baubles. It's red and sparkles like Dorothy's shoes in *The Wizard of Oz.* It'd look great in my hair. For Christmas." She radiated excitement. "Can I add that to my Christmas list?"

Daniel laughed. "I suppose you can. I hope she wasn't any trouble?" he said to Ivy, who wore a huge smile. The haunted look in her eyes was still there, but there was something else that he had not seen during lunch. *Peace? Joy? Contentment?* He could not say. Whatever it was, he liked the change.

"She's a doll, and we had a nice, though quick, trip up and down the aisles. I think Baubles has something for everyone," Ivy told them. "I plan to return and do a bit of shopping myself." Ivy winked at Holly. Daniel saw that and approved.

"So I need to get going, I have a million and one things

to do," Sarah said quickly. "Holly, I'll see you on Monday. Ivy, call me later. We'll plan another lunch."

"Of course. Maybe we can make reservations for The Red Barn?"

"I'll check my calendar and call you with a date," Sarah replied. She fished through her purse for a pen and removed a business card from her wallet. "What's your number?"

Daniel watched the two women interact. They were as different as night and day. Sarah: peppy, pretty in a girl-next-door way. Bright blue eyes, shiny brown hair cut at a sharp angle, enhancing her square jaw. He was sorry he did not have feelings for her. She was pure down to the core. Ivy, on the other hand, was the complete opposite. *Woeful, maybe?* He was not sure. Slender, with the lean body of an athlete, her honey-colored hair reached the middle of her back; and unlike Sarah's, there was no style or shape to it. Just long and thick. Green eyes, and ivory skin untouched by time; he thought she was mysterious and wondered why he'd never run into her before. During lunch, she had talked about growing up and living in Pine City her entire life.

Knowing this about her made her even more intriguing. Where had she been hiding? He had not a single clue, but he was interested in finding out more about her, and maybe getting to know her in ways that he had not wanted to acknowledge wanting to know someone in a very long time.

"I'll look forward to lunch," Ivy said; then she gave Sarah a quick hug.

Sarah smiled. "Me too. See you Monday, Holly." She waved and made her way hurriedly across the parking lot to her car.

Daniel returned her wave and felt bad about hurting her. "Holly, we'd best get going. You have more studying to do. Ivy, it was nice talking to you. Maybe we'll run into each other again." His eyes met hers.

"Promise you won't forget New Year's Eve?" Holly asked Ivy.

"I promise. It was nice seeing you both," Ivy said, and she, too, gave them a half wave and walked across the parking lot to her car. Daniel was surprised to see she drove an older-model Mercedes. He was not sure it suited her, but a car was a car. He watched as she opened the door and got inside.

"Dad? Earth to Dad?" Holly blurted out. "Is something wrong?"

Daniel pulled his eyes away from Ivy as she pulled out onto Main Street.

"I was thinking. I'm just fine," he said, and meant it. "Let's go home, and if you study for one hour, you can call Roxie."

"Woo-hoo!" Holly shouted. "Thanks."

"Sure thing, kid," he said, and he yanked on her ponytail again.

The ride home was a blur. Daniel could not stop thinking about Ivy. It amazed him they'd never run into one another, but there was something else about her. Another version of her? Someone she reminded him of? Maybe a woman he'd passed on the street? Whatever it was, he could not get her out of his head.

Holly was seated at the table, immersed in her math book, writing numbers in her notebook. He really needed to back off with this math thing, but he had to focus on his long-term goal for his daughter, keep it front and center.

He did not want her to pursue a career in music.

Daniel spent the next half hour in his den, reworking one of the designs for his upcoming work on The Bright Side condo project. He was having trouble concentrating. His thoughts kept returning to Ivy.

She had definitely made an impression on him. Why her

and not Sarah, who would welcome him into her life with open arms? He was not looking for a relationship. Holly's future was uppermost in his life plan. Yes, he'd been with a few women since Laura's death, but there had never been any deep emotional attachment to any of them. Something told him Ivy was not the kind of woman who'd involve herself in a physical relationship, just for the pleasure of it. No, she was the kind of woman who would love deeply and expect the same in return.

Chapter 25

Ivy found a parking spot right in front of Baubles. Before anyone else had the chance to scoop up that cute barrette and headband, she wanted to make sure it was still there, so she immediately headed for the store after lunch. Inside, she was greeted by a young woman. "Anything I can help you with, just let me know," the salesperson said kindly.

"Thanks," Ivy said. She knew what she was there for. She walked over to the display where the barrette and headband sparkled. Smiling, she took both off the rack. This was not a birthday gift for Holly, just a gift for the sake of giving. And it was still too soon for a Christmas gift. She would ask Sarah how to go about giving Holly the gift. She did not want to offend Daniel, who truly seemed to love and care for his daughter. Strict, yes, but Ivy's opinion of him had been wrong. He was definitely not abusing his daughter. Holly was eleven and so in need of a female role model. Sure that Sarah filled this role, Ivy was anxious to find out what she and Daniel had discussed. Hopefully, he'd invited her out. This would be perfect for all three of them.

As she stepped away from the display rack, she spotted

a large square of folded notebook paper on the floor. She picked it up, bringing it to the register with her. She put the items on the counter. "I found this on the floor," she said, and slid the folded paper across the counter to the young girl.

The girl took the paper and opened it. Her facial expression went from mild interest to disbelief. "This is not good," she said, and positioned the note so Ivy could read it.

> *Dear Mrs. Pellegrino:*
> *I need to find out what happened to my mother. Dad does not allow me to talk about her. I am very afraid that he might have done something to her. Like killed her and put her body somewhere. . . .*

Stunned, Ivy took the paper and read it a second time. "I was just here with the girl who wrote this."

"I remember."

"I'll take care of it. Let me pay for this," she said as she picked up the note and put it in her purse. She quickly took care of her purchase and returned to her car.

Had Holly planned for someone other than Mrs. Pellegrino to find her note? If so, why didn't she just give it to her when they had walked to Baubles earlier? Or she could have easily passed it to Sarah? Or did it simply fall out of her pocket? That aside, were the allegations actually true? Was Daniel Greenwood truly hiding his wife's cause of death from Holly? Was he keeping his daughter from discovering what had really happened to her mother? Ivy did not have any answers, but she knew where to begin her search. Without giving it a second thought, she dialed Sarah's cell phone number.

"Hello?"

"Sarah, it's Ivy. I need to see you right away. Can you meet me? Your place, mine, anywhere that's convenient."

"I suppose I could. Is everything okay? Did something happen after I left?"

"Yes, and I need you to see something."

"Then come over to the house, Mom's old place on Hickory Lane."

Ivy remembered the house from her many visits as a teenager. "I'm on my way." She hung up and headed over. Ten minutes later, she drove through the newly installed security gates. *Times are changing,* she thought as she shut off the engine.

Sarah's home looked the same as it had when they were in high school. Redbrick, black shutters, and white columns, it was a beautiful place. If she remembered correctly, it was filled with antiques and priceless art, likely the reason for the gates.

Sarah opened the door before Ivy could knock.

"You've been crying." Ivy stated the obvious. "Has something happened to your mother?" Sarah's mother continued to live with her, but Sarah had told Ivy that her mother was in and out of the hospital all the time. Each time her mother was admitted, Sarah was not sure if she would come home.

"Oh, Mom's fine. She's taking a nap now. I'm just a crybaby," Sarah explained.

"Bull! You're not a crybaby. Never have been. What happened?" Ivy asked. The entrance looked exactly as it had during her many visits as a teenager. The kitchen had been updated with new cabinets, granite countertops, and new appliances, but everything else felt familiar.

"You first. I'll make some tea," Sarah said, then proceeded to take glasses from the cupboard and fill them with ice.

"After lunch, I went back to that store, Baubles. Holly had admired a barrette set while we were looking around, and I decided to go back and buy it for her. They're handmade, one of a kind, at least I did not see any others, so I find this piece of notebook paper on the floor and take it to the girl at the register. She read it, then gave it to me to read." Ivy took the note out of her purse and handed it to Sarah.

Sarah filled the glasses with tea before taking the note. She scanned it; then her mouth moved, but no words were spoken.

"Speechless," Ivy stated.

"I simply cannot believe this. It's impossible."

Ivy sat down at the large oak table, and Sarah sat across from her. "How do you know?"

Sarah took a drink of her tea, then said, "Ivy, I hate to bring up the past again, but I must. Holly's mother, Laura, was killed in the same plane crash that your family was in. I can't believe Daniel would keep something like that from her. And I can't understand why Holly would write something like this. It's not like her to be so . . . dramatic."

Ivy felt as though she had been sucker punched.

"What?" Sarah asked. "You didn't know?"

Ivy shook her head. "Of course not, why would I? I never met either of them until last night, when Holly knocked on my door."

"I'm sorry, I just assumed. It was all over the news," Sarah said apologetically. "The names of the passengers."

"I was totally nonfunctional at the time," Ivy reminded her.

"I'm sorry, Ivy. I'm not thinking straight," Sarah said.

Ivy did a quick calculation. Holly would have been around the same age as Elizabeth and James when her mother died. No wonder she craved female attention. Was her note just a way of gaining her father's attention? Surely, the woman the letter was addressed to would contact Daniel Greenwood?

"Do you know this Mrs. Pellegrino?" Ivy asked.

"Sure, Jen Pellegrino, she's Roxie's mother. I do not know why Holly would do this, unless she's really mad at Daniel."

"Does she get along with him?"

"Pretty much. He's very strict, and like any eleven-, almost twelve-year-old, Holly resents him for that alone, but that's typical for her age. I'll talk with her Monday. I'm sure the note is nothing more than an angry daughter trying to get even with her dad."

Ivy hoped Sarah was right.

"Are you going to tell me why you were crying?" Ivy asked. "You were upset when I called."

"If you must know, Daniel Greenwood just wanted to let me know that he was not interested in me and that we could only be friends, and that Holly really cared about me, and he wanted that to continue." Sarah's eyes filled with tears. "I'm not crying from the rejection—I was crying from the pure and utter humiliation! I think, no, *thought* Daniel was a nice guy, so I was interested. It wasn't like I invited him for a sleepover. I'm not sure if I can ever look him in the face again. I was so mortified, I just stood there in the parking lot and agreed with him. I do not think I have ever been so embarrassed."

At that very moment, Ivy decided for the second time that she did not like Daniel Greenwood, not even a little bit.

Chapter 26

Ivy did not want to put Sarah on the spot, so she said, "I'll call Daniel myself and tell him about this note."

"It's really not your place," Sarah said. "I'll talk to Holly on Monday and set up a parent-teacher conference with Daniel. I'll also have to alert the school's counselor. It's the normal protocol for something like this."

"This did not happen at school, Sarah. Even I know you're not responsible for what your students do when they're out of the school's jurisdiction. I was a student once, I remember. I know things have changed some since I was in elementary school, but I'm not *that* old."

Sarah nodded. "You're right, but I feel an obligation to Holly. She's a good girl, and I'm sure this note was written in a moment of anger. Otherwise, if these things were true, which I know for a fact they're not, I would be obligated to report him to the authorities if I suspected there was any kind of abuse, verbal or emotional."

"The least I can do is take the note to Daniel," Ivy persisted. "That way, you won't have to look at him. Can't you have a conference over the phone?"

Sarah wiped the condensation from her glass with a

napkin. "I can, though it's not your responsibility. Besides, I'll have to face him sooner or later."

"Shouldn't he know about this note now, rather than later?" Ivy asked again. Even if its contents were just the words of an angry little girl, he still needed to know—if anything, just so he could explain her mother's death to Holly. And it was certainly necessary for him to do that as soon as possible. Just look at the result already of his not having done so.

"Yes, you're right. I wish he would explain to Holly what happened to her mother. Poor child, she's so needy right now," Sarah said. "So if you want to take the note to Daniel, go ahead. Tell him you found it."

"I can do that now, if you'll give me his address," Ivy offered.

Sarah got up and opened a couple of drawers before she found a pen and a slip of paper. She wrote down the number. "He's likely to ground Holly until she's a senior citizen, once he sees this. Though, with luck, this could be the opening he needs in order to tell Holly what happened to her mother. I'm so sorry that you have to go through this."

Ivy was, too, but today was a fresh start, a new beginning, and it had been anything but dull. Since she had found the note, Ivy felt obligated to give it to Daniel, despite her mixed feelings about him. It would also give her an excuse to give Holly her gift when she arrived.

"I'll drop it off on my way home."

"If you insist, though I can take care of this on Monday. It's been an eye-opening day, to say the least," Sarah observed dryly.

"I'll call you later," Ivy said. She took her glass to the sink and rinsed it. Confronting Daniel and Holly could be therapeutic for her, and for Holly. She hoped it was positive for everyone involved.

"Yes, do. I'm anxious to hear Daniel's explanation for keeping Laura's cause of death to himself. I can't believe Holly has not found this out on her own yet."

"It's not a topic easily talked about, trust me on that. He has his reasons, I'm sure, though that is not really an excuse." Ivy thought about her words. They aptly applied to her as well. She had kept James's and Elizabeth's rooms locked up all these years for her own protection. Maybe Daniel Greenwood simply wanted to protect his daughter?

"It's not, but talk with him if you can. You two have a lot in common, so maybe it will help you both," Sarah said, forever thinking of others.

"I'll touch base later," Ivy said. She gave her friend a quick hug and, together, they walked to the front door.

As soon as Ivy left Sarah's house, Ivy's hands began to tremble. They shook more and more, the closer to Daniel's house she got. She scanned the address again when she turned down a long drive that led to a two-story house painted a pale yellow, with dark green shutters. Though it was late fall, the grass was still a bright summer green, the shrubs were well tended, and Ivy saw tubs filled with annuals in the colors of autumn. Deep golds, browns, burgundies, and reds. Knowing Daniel's profession, she had expected nothing less. She took the bag from Baubles, along with the note, got out of the car, and walked down a beautiful stone path leading to the front door.

She knocked lightly and waited, her heart hammering in her chest. The door opened, and Ivy smiled. Holly had answered, and she did not look like an unhappy, abused child.

"Hi, Ivy," Holly said, and stood aside so she could open the door all the way.

"Is your dad home?" Ivy asked. She did not want to come inside, unless he was there.

"Yep, he's in his den. He practically lives there. I'll go get him. Come on in," Holly said.

Ivy stood inside the entrance, surprised to see pots of greenery, vases with bright blooms placed strategically on shelves, tall topiaries flanking both sides of the entryway. From what she saw, the inside of the house was as meticulous as the outside. Then she remembered Holly telling her that Daniel folded his socks, and she could not help but smile.

"Ivy," Daniel said, startling her.

Here goes. "I came by to give this to Holly." She held out the paper bag. "Just a little something," she added.

Holly, who stood beside her dad, took the bag, peered inside, and squealed with delight. "Thank you so much! I was afraid someone would buy them before Dad had a chance to. I'm going to put them on, I'll be right back," Holly said, then quickly gave Ivy a hug before racing down a long hallway.

"Come inside, please," he said. "I was about to pour myself a cup of coffee."

Ivy did not say anything as she followed him to the kitchen. Windows overlooked the lawn in back, which was as neatly manicured as the front lawn. Baskets of hanging flowers swayed in the late-afternoon breeze. Definitely not what she had expected. Daniel motioned for her to sit down. A math book and papers were spread across the tabletop. Ivy smiled.

"Holly is still studying, I take it," she said as Daniel slid her papers and book aside and placed a cup of coffee in front of Ivy.

"She just finished. She's all excited because I told her she could call Roxie," Daniel explained as he took the seat across from her.

After Ivy showed him the note she found, she was sure Daniel would not be allowing Holly to use the phone, but it is what it is, and he needed to see this. "I saw how much she admired the barrette set, and bought it for her. I hope you don't mind, but that's not my main reason for coming over."

"Is this about Sarah? I know you're friends with her. She's a supernice woman, a great teacher, but I—"

"It's not about Sarah. It's Holly." She took the note from her purse and handed it to him. She watched as he read it.

His dark brows slanted in a frown. "Where did you get this?" he asked her.

"I found it on the floor at Baubles when I returned to get Holly's gift. I thought you needed to see this."

Daniel nodded. "I do, and thank you for coming all the way over here to give me the note." He drew in a deep breath and let it out slowly. He peered around the corner before he continued. "Of course this isn't true. You would not be here if you thought I was some sort of . . . crazy psycho."

"No, I wouldn't," Ivy stated, but remained silent. She wanted to give him a chance to explain, if he chose to do so, even though this was not her problem, and he really did not owe her an explanation.

"Glad this didn't scare you away," he said. "It's a bit complicated for me and Holly."

"Why is that? I know it's none of my business, and you can tell me to back off," Ivy said.

"No, you're fine. Really. I need to talk about Holly's mother."

"Don't you think Holly should be part of this conversation? I know what happened, Daniel. It's beyond horrific, but she needs to know."

His jaw clenched, and his eyes narrowed. "Do you really know? One day, you're a family, and in a matter of minutes, everything you have planned, worked for, hoped for, is crushed. You cannot begin to imagine how tough it's been. Raising a child who wants to follow in her mother's footsteps.

"Had Laura taken a different career path, she would be here now, and we would not be discussing why Holly is writing notes about her crazy home life. The details of which, in the main, are completely untrue."

Running footsteps put a stop to her response before it began.

Holly had taken her hair out of a ponytail. Her long, golden, shimmery, and bronzed hair reached her waist; the sparkly barrette and headband highlighted her already beautiful head of hair. "I love it!" she exclaimed, then hurried over to give Ivy a hug. "Thank you so much for this." Holly touched the headband.

"You're welcome. I wasn't sure they'd still be there, so I took the liberty of purchasing them before someone else beat me to it," Ivy said, and that was true.

"Holly, why don't you take your books to your room, and come back and sit with us. There is something we need to talk about."

Chapter 27

Daniel knew that this day was coming, and he dreaded it. Now he had to face the facts. Holly needed to know what had happened to Laura. His telling her she had died suddenly and in a tragic manner was true, and those words had stuck in his daughter's mind. It was up to him to explain exactly what he'd meant when he used those words.

She had an active imagination, true. But if she really thought him to be the crazy person she described in her note, he had to dispel the idea that he was holding her captive, and Holly certainly needed to know there were consequences when accusations like those in her note were made. Fortunately for him, he knew they were not true, as did anyone who knew him at all.

"Am I in trouble?" Holly asked as soon as she returned to the kitchen.

"Have a seat," Daniel said. "We need to have a talk."

Holly looked at Ivy. "Now? With company?"

"Ivy is welcome to hear what I'm about to say. That is, if she wants." Daniel looked over at Ivy.

She shrugged, opening her eyes a bit wider, but said nothing. He gave a slight nod.

Daniel took the note from his back pocket and gave it to Holly. "Ivy found this on the floor at the store."

Holly turned red, then white, when she saw her note. Tears filled her eyes and rolled down her face like two silvery rivers. "I'm sorry," she said in a whisper.

"No, Holly, I am sorry," Daniel said.

She looked at him, waiting for an explanation. "If I had told you the truth a long time ago, you would not be writing notes like this. It's my fault. You know I would never hurt you in any way, right?"

Holly's red-barretted head bobbed up and down.

"I have always wanted what's best for you, and maybe I'm a bit too strict sometimes." He held up his hand. "Don't say anything. I know I am strict most of the time." He glanced at Ivy, who waited patiently for his explanation. She looked slightly uncomfortable. This was a family matter, he knew, but for some odd reason, he needed Ivy to hear his explanation, too.

"You were so young when your mother died. You already know that. Your mother was a wonderful woman, and she loved you very much, no doubt about it, but she also loved her career." Daniel paused, unsure if his words were coming out as they should, but he went on. "She had gone to Charlotte to audition for a Broadway musical."

Holly's eyes doubled in size. "What?"

"She had received a callback from a famous producer, but she had to go to Charlotte for the final audition. So she went to Charlotte."

"And she never came back? She didn't want me? And you just pretended she died so you wouldn't hurt my feelings?" Holly asked, her voice high-pitched.

"No, Holly."

"Just tell her what happened, Daniel," Ivy suggested.

"You're right, Ivy. Laura booked a flight to Charlotte,

went on her audition, and was on the return flight home when the plane crashed."

A heavy silence hung in the air.

Tears gushed down Ivy's face, for she knew firsthand what Daniel had experienced.

"Oh, my God!" Holly said, breaking the ominous silence.

Daniel nodded.

"Why didn't you tell me?" Holly asked, her face displaying myriad expressions.

"I don't know. I suppose, in my own way, I was trying to protect you."

"Dad, is this why you won't let me have a computer?" Holly asked.

Ivy gave him a little half smile.

"No."

"So what did she do? Was she an actress?" Holly asked, her curiosity aroused.

Daniel cleared his throat. "Your mother was a singer. She had a beautiful voice."

Holly's jaw literally fell open. She stared at him, but she did not say a word.

"I need to go," Ivy said. "I told my father I'd stop over." She stood to leave, and Daniel touched her arm. "Thanks, Ivy, for, you know"—he looked at the note— "bringing this to my attention. And for thinking of Holly. It means a lot. To both of us."

"It does?" Holly asked in typical eleven-year-old fashion.

Ivy laughed, and so did he. He had not felt much genuine laughter in a very, very long time. He liked the way it made him feel. He liked the way his daughter looked at him when he laughed. And he liked the way he felt when Ivy was near him.

"Yes, it does," he finally answered, never taking his eyes from Ivy. "More than you know."

"Oh," Holly said, smiling. "So how did it happen?"

His daughter's question brought the past back full force, putting a halt to any thoughts he currently had of asking Ivy to stay for dinner.

"I really do need to go," Ivy said. "Holly, I'll look forward to your party, and maybe I'll see you before then?" she told Holly as she walked toward the door.

"Can she, Dad?"

"Of course she can." Daniel paused and decided there was no time like the present, words that had been preached to him on more than one occasion by his good friend and coworker, Jay Johnson. "Would you like to go to Ollie's with us tonight? For pizza?" Daniel asked before he could call back the words.

Ivy stopped and turned to look at him. He knew his face was coloring; he just wasn't sure if it was red or white. Either way, he was toast.

"Ollie's, huh?" Ivy asked. "Pizza."

"You have never been to Ollie's?" Holly asked. "They have the best pizza in Pine City. And subs, too, right Dad?"

Ivy seemed to be considering his invitation. "Only on one condition."

"Okay. And what would that be?" he asked, a bit tense.

"That Holly wears her hair down and keeps her sparkles on," Ivy said teasingly.

"Holly?" Daniel looked at his daughter. "Your call."

"Are you kidding? Of course I'll keep my sparkles on! Eating out twice in one day? OMG, I cannot wait to tell this to Roxie. Can I call her now?"

Shifting the mood from morose to excited in a matter of seconds, Daniel gave up. "You can call. Ten minutes, and not a minute more. Got it?" he said as Holly practically flew out of her chair.

"Yes, you can set the timer, and does this mean you're

going with us, Ivy? I will even wear a dress, if you want," Holly said.

"Yes, and no, you do not have to wear a dress."

"Woo-hoo!" Holly shouted. Before she ran out of the kitchen to call Roxie, she gave Ivy a hug; then she gave her dad the biggest, brightest smile he'd seen on her face in a very long time. His chest swelled with love for this beautiful little girl who was his daughter. And he had to admit, if only to himself, he was just a little bit too excited about going to Ollie's for pizza.

Chapter 28

In a hundred years, Ivy could never have predicted the events of the first day of her new life. If anyone had told her as little as forty-eight hours ago that she would be going out to dinner with a man and his daughter, she would have told them they were crazy.

Her thoughts were all over the place as she drove to her dad's house. She had completely forgotten exactly why she was going to his house, though he'd be glad to see her out and about, no matter her reason. Fifteen minutes later, she parked her Mercedes next to her father's red Corvette. *When did this happen? Maybe it isn't his,* she thought as she got out of the car, taking the keys with her. Out of habit, her father always kept the doors locked. He'd once told her it was habit from when her mother was ill. If, God forbid, someone tried to get into the house, her mother would at least be able to call the police. His reasoning was that if someone tried to force the door, she would know that it could not be him. To this day, Lila and Rebecca still had keys to the house, even though Lila had moved to Raleigh years ago and no longer needed them. It had not made much sense then, and it still didn't, but she understood habits and how hard they were to break.

She slipped her key into the lock, turned the knob, and called out. "Dad! It's me. You decent?" She smiled at the image her words brought forth.

"In the kitchen," he said.

Despite his great wealth, her father had never updated the kitchen. The same white side-by-side refrigerator, the stove with those next-to-impossible-to-cook-with electric burners, and the dishwasher that had broken years ago were exactly as before. A small parlor-style table, with three wrought-iron chairs, remained by the window that looked out on the mountains, in all their brilliant fall colors. Not many changes in the kitchen.

Her father wore a pair of faded jeans and a Duke sweatshirt, along with a floral-patterned apron. She was briefly reminded of the waitress at The Blackberry Café. The image made her laugh out loud.

Her dad turned to her. "Ivy Fine, you look"—he gave her a quick once-over—"happy as a lark. It's good to see you out and about," he added, giving her a peck on the cheek.

"And you look, well, silly," she said, smiling. "What's with the apron? And what smells so good? I did not know you still cooked for yourself. I thought you went to all those fine restaurants you own."

"Thanks for the compliment. This was your mom's apron, as you well know. I guess I'm a bit of a sentimental old fool, still wearing it. I'm making beef Wellington. It's quite an undertaking."

"I'm impressed. A big deal for just one person," Ivy remarked.

"Margaret's coming over for dinner. She's picking up her car."

"So that explains the red car parked outside. I thought it was a bit too sporty for you. Where is your car?"

"We traded cars. Hers was due for an oil change at the

dealership, and she had a doctor's appointment, so we traded for the day. I had a bit of time on my hands, so I took the car in and waited."

Ivy nodded, but did not say anything. Margaret was a great lady, but every time her name was brought up, Ivy was reminded that it was her son, Mark, who was piloting the plane whose crash had taken her family's lives. But had it really been Mark's fault? Though the NTSB had determined the crash to be the result of pilot error, it had never been proven, and the error that had presumably caused the crash still remained a mystery.

"So I had lunch with Sarah Anderson today," Ivy said, opening the refrigerator and taking out a can of soda. "I didn't know she was teaching fifth grade here in Pine City. I didn't even know that she was back in town."

"Yes, she moved back several years ago. Her mother was ill, still is, as far as I know. It's a good thing, your going out today. You look good, Ivy. Better than I have seen you in quite a while."

She took a drink of her soda. "I'm not sure if I should be offended or complimented. You saw me yesterday, remember? Surely, I cannot have changed all that much."

He stirred something on the stove, which smelled delightful. "It's the attitude. Something's changed." He turned his back to her, added some spices to the concoction on the stove, turned the burner down, then faced her. "You look as if a weight has been lifted off your shoulders. You want to talk about it?" He motioned for her to take a seat at the parlor table. They'd had many talks at this table, and Ivy was warmed to know that her father was still on that page. She sat in what was once *her* chair and took a long pull from her soda.

"I guess your visit opened my eyes," she said.

"So, out of the blue, you called Sarah and made a lunch

date?" he asked, his tone clearly disbelieving. "I'm glad, though. For whatever reason," he slyly added. He knew her well.

"There was more to it, but you already know that. This little girl showed up at my house last night. Apparently, she had gotten lost in the woods, and she used my phone to call her dad. You might know him. Daniel Greenwood." Ivy watched him for a reaction.

"Of course I know him. He's a master with anything that grows. He works . . . Rather, he runs the horticultural end of The Upside, and all my grounds. The restaurants, all of my properties. So you met him?"

"I did." No way would she give him more information. *He's going to work for it. Just like the old days.* She smiled at the memory.

"What?" he asked.

"I was just thinking about . . . the old days. Nothing specific," she said. "So what's your take on Daniel Green-wood?"

"What do you want to know?"

Ivy finished her drink and crushed the can, then threw it across the kitchen into the garbage can. She chuckled. "It's good to know I haven't lost my aim," she said.

"Daniel Greenwood is a private guy, that much I know. He has an excellent reputation, hard worker. I can't say I know him well, but what I do know is all positive. Why are you asking me these questions? And why now?"

Why was she? She was not sure herself. Maybe she was searching for the voice of approval. If her father thought Daniel Greenwood a decent man, then it would be fine to spend an evening with him and Holly.

"I was curious, that's all," she replied. "Actually, that's not the only reason." *Here goes,* she thought. "I'm going to Ollie's with him and his daughter. Tonight. For pizza." Ivy waited for the onslaught of guilt, but only felt a touch

of sadness that James and Elizabeth had not had the pleasure of Ollie's pizza.

The look on her father's face was worth a million bucks
times ten.

"I'm not going to ask how this came about"—he shook
his head left to right—"but if it's the reason for the sudden
change, I'm beyond thrilled for you." He took her hand
and gave her a quick pat, just like he used to do when she
was a kid. This pat always indicated their chats were over,
but now, she knew otherwise. The delightful scent coming
from the pot gave off a tinge of a burned smell.

"Good gravy!" her father said as he picked up the pot
and carried it to the sink. "No, not good gravy. See, this is
what happens every time I try to make this recipe. I need
to stop watching the Food Network late at night." He
dumped the contents down the garbage disposal, then
rinsed out the pot. "I'll have to start over. Good thing I
have extra ingredients. I always buy double, and often
triple, just in case something like this happens."

"I need to go. Sorry about your gravy," Ivy said, standing to give him a quick peck on the cheek.

"Enjoy yourself, Ivy. It's time," her father said.

She nodded, not bothering to say anything.

As she backed her car out of the drive, it suddenly hit
her that she was actually going on a date! And with the
man Sarah had set her heart on. Sort of.

This is for Holly, she told herself as she drove home.
The child needed female companionship, and her father
was simply part of the package. At least that was what she
tried to convince herself of.

She parked her car and hurried inside, so she could get
ready. It had been so very long since she cared about her
appearance that the thought felt strange, almost foreign to
her. Inside, the house was dark, and everything smelled of

old coffee. She went to the kitchen. She had forgotten to turn the coffeemaker off; she had been in a bit of a daze when she had left for her lunch date.

Venturing out to lunch with a friend had not been a part of the routine she had established for herself. She took the carafe of thick coffee, ran cool water in the pot, then added a bit of dish detergent.

"Later," she said, followed by, "Now I'm talking to my coffeemaker!" She rolled her eyes, but inwardly she was thrilled that she could joke about such nonsense.

Before she could change her mind, she opened the drapes in the living room, then ran upstairs and opened her bedroom drapes. She looked at her bed. A pile of messy sheets twisted every which way. Quickly she made the bed, straightened the items on her night table, then went to her closet in search of something to wear.

Her clothes were top-of-the-line. Chanel, Prada, Stella McCartney, were just a few of the labels. Though they were almost a decade old, she knew they were still stylish. However, she was not going to the Oscars. She was going to Ollie's for pizza. She snickered at the thought of wearing a designer dress to a pizza joint. She had lost a lot of weight in the past eight years. All of her slacks were too baggy, and her blouses hung from her shoulders. But, thanks to Rebecca, who was slender, and always thought of Ivy before she took a trunkload of last season's clothes to a local consignment shop, Rebecca would choose a few items that Ivy could wear. Other than these clothes, she had not acquired anything new in years, other than the undergarments she ordered online. Thankfully, she found a pair of Ann Taylor jeans in a small size, then slipped them on and walked across the room to stand in front of the mirror. The fit was perfect, not too loose and not tight. She pulled them off and walked across the room, wearing her T-shirt and undies. And that was when she was hit by pangs of guilt.

"What am I thinking?" she asked aloud. "How can I do this? How can I act as though I am just a normal woman going out for pizza with a friend?"

She sat down on the bed. Tears blurred her vision, but she let them fall. She was making a big deal out of nothing, she thought as she wiped her nose on the hem of her shirt. She had to eat, didn't she? And was it wrong to share a meal with others?

She didn't think so.

For once, she was going to do what was expected of her by her father. If she bawled her eyes out later, well, she would have puffy eyes and a stopped-up nose.

And with that thought in mind, she headed for the shower.

Chapter 29

For the third time, Daniel checked his reflection in the mirror. He needed a haircut, and it wouldn't hurt his feelings if he lost ten pounds. His dark Levi's were ironed to perfection, a skill he'd learned when Holly had started school. No more pleated skirts straight out of the dryer for his daughter, once she had started first grade. Though glad he no longer had to bother with the pre-K uniform, he'd continued to iron some of his clothes, which led to his becoming somewhat of a neat freak. As the years passed, he'd had way too much free time on his hands, hence the overkill with the laundry and folding his socks, which, come to think of it, was sort of odd. Holly teased him about his habits, deservedly so, he guessed, at least by most manly standards.

Checking to make sure that all the buttons were properly matched with the correct buttonhole, he made fast work of tucking his khaki-colored shirt in his jeans. He wore the same brown leather belt he'd had since his college days.

"Dad?" Holly called, and tapped on his door. "Hurry up, or we'll be late."

He smiled. "I'm good to go," he said, and stepped out

of the room to find that his daughter had also taken extra care with her appearance. She was dressed in a red jumper with black leggings, and the red UGG boots she had received for Christmas last year, along with the hair accessories Ivy gave her earlier in the day. Her cheeks were flushed. She looked adorable, he thought.

"Oh, my God, you have on *way too much* cologne." Holly pinched her nose, even though she was grinning. "Ivy will think you're trying to impress her."

He was, but he wouldn't say this to Holly. "It's a new brand I thought I'd try out. On you. Apparently, it's a bit strong," Daniel told Holly. "And whatever you do, do not mention this to Ivy." Hating to add this last bit, he felt he had no choice, since Holly sometimes forgot to filter her words before they escaped her pretty mouth.

"I won't," his daughter agreed.

"Then let's not waste another minute." Daniel gathered up his truck keys from the bowl he kept on a table in the entryway.

Though it was only half past six, the autumn air was sharp and crisp as they stepped out of the house. "It's going to be a rough winter," Daniel said.

"How do you know?" Holly asked while she waited for him to open her door.

Once he was in the driver's seat, he cranked the engine over. "Just feel it in my bones. There's a scent in the air, like a giant snowball heading our way, and my nose is a radar," he joked.

"Dad, I do not want to be mean or anything, I know I'm in massive trouble for that note." She paused. "I'm sorry I wrote that stuff, but all that aside, I am not three. I do not believe that your nose is a radar or that a giant snowball is heading our way. I *used* to believe that a zillion years ago. Just so you know."

Daniel hadn't a clue where his daughter's conversation

was leading, but he let her talk. He had not felt so at ease with Holly in a very long time. Instead of worrying about every little thing she did, he found it was nice to simply let her be herself, say what she wanted without fear of being punished. Though he would not admit it to her, he knew he'd gone overboard big-time with the math, but he would do anything in his power to steer Holly away from the career that had destroyed their future. Of course, though she was much too young to see the significance now, she would later. He was positive.

"Do you like Ivy?" Holly asked.

Daniel chuckled. "She seems nice enough. Why do you ask?"

Holly fiddled with her seat belt. "Because you're being, like, super nice."

He laughed even harder. "Am I really that bad?"

"No, you're much worse, but it's okay. I understand. You're sad and lonely. You need a girlfriend, a grown-up to talk to. You need to stop spending so much time looking at your garden books, too." Holly made this announcement as though she were a relationship advisor, like one of those online dating commercials that swore they would find the right partner *if* you joined them. He certainly did not need guidance in *that* department. Though to Holly's credit, she was not aware that he'd dated a few women. He did not feel the need to add this to their adult conversation. Again, when she was in college, married, or, perhaps, a great-grandmother, he would talk with her about such things.

"I like my garden books. Like you like your Harry Potter books," he said, and reached over to pat her. "I'm glad you like reading."

"Then why don't you tell me this stuff when I'm home? I always feel like I have to sneak to read. Especially now, and I haven't finished *Deathly Hallows*, and I have to return it to the library this week. I can't even check it out again because I have already gone past my limit. They only allow you to check a book out so many times, especially the popular ones. If I had a computer, I could just download the books from the library. They have an app for that, too, in case you didn't know."

Daniel was getting an earful from Holly and loving every minute of it. He made a sharp left, then another left turn, and pulled into the parking lot at Ollie's. Saturday nights were always packed, and tonight was no different. He should have picked someplace nicer, a place where he could actually make a dinner reservation. Ivy probably thought he was ignorant of the finer things in life.

"I didn't know that," he said as he scanned the parking lot. Finding a space at the very end, he parked the truck, then turned to Holly. "You look really pretty tonight, just like your mom." As soon as the words were out, he wanted to take them back. Not the pretty part, but the mom part.

"You really loved Mom, huh?" Holly asked as she unhooked her seat belt.

"I really did. She was very special to me." There were times during their marriage that *he'd* wondered if she thought he was as special as he'd thought her to be. There was always that little nagging doubt that if she were to be given a choice between him and her career, her career would win first place. He hated having those thoughts. It'd been such a long time ago, but he had a daughter to think of, and he did not ever want her to have to choose between her family and a career, though he was of the mind that one could have both if one was willing to make sacrifices.

"Dad, for the third time, let's go in. It's getting cold out here."

He was so focused on his thoughts, he had not heard her at all. "Sorry, come on, let's go put our name on the waiting list."

Inside Ollie's, Daniel gave the hostess his name and told her there would be three in his party. She peered behind him as though looking for a third person. "It'll be a few minutes," she said.

Daniel nodded and stepped aside. His stomach was in knots. He had not been this nervous over a date since . . . ever.

Chapter 30

Ivy added a touch of cherry-red lipstick and made a face in the mirror. Surely, there was an expiration date on lipstick. Ivy looked at her reflection. The color was fine, just old. She took the jar of Vaseline she used for chapped lips and dabbed a bit in the center of her mouth. Closing her lips to spread the shine, she had a sudden flash of Elizabeth watching her while she put her makeup on. Sad, but in a new way, a way she had yet to decipher, there were no tears, no closing down the memory. Instead, she allowed herself to remember how she had dabbed pink lipstick on Elizabeth's little rosebud-shaped mouth, then dusted her nose with face powder. Her daughter loved it when they "played makeup," and so had she. She held back a sob, and her throat tightened. Taking a deep breath, she released it, slowly allowing herself to relax, allowing the memory to unfold without a physical reaction. She closed her eyes and remembered.

"How's come I can't go with you and Daddy?" Elizabeth asked. *"I want to dress up, too."*

Ivy sat at her vanity table, adding the finishing touches

to her makeup. "You will someday, when you're older, I promise."

"But when is someday?"

She laughed at her three-year-old daughter. "It will be here sooner than you think," Ivy explained. And it would. There would be school proms, dates, and, most likely, a wedding day. All in good time, Ivy thought as she reached for her tube of soft pink lipstick.

"Come a bit closer," Ivy instructed her daughter.

She took the lipstick, dotting it on Elizabeth's puckered little mouth. Then she took her powder puff and dusted her daughter's nose. "Now let's have a look." She had pulled Elizabeth on her lap so that she could see her handiwork.

"Oh, I'm pretty, Mommy! Just like you," Elizabeth said, then turned around in her lap to hug her.

"You're much prettier," Ivy said, and hugged her daughter a little bit closer.

"Will you teach me to do this when I'm big like you?"

"I wouldn't miss it for the world," Ivy said, then set Elizabeth down.

Had she known that would've been her only opportunity to instruct her daughter on how to use makeup, she would have gladly stayed home and continued the lesson.

Ivy glanced at the clock on her bedside table. If she did not get a move on, she would be late, and she had always detested tardiness in any form.

Now would be a good time to return to her habit of days long past. Pushing all negative thoughts aside, she went through her sweaters until she found one that was halfway decent. A red cashmere, with long sleeves and a turtleneck. She pulled it over her head, then looked in the mirror again. Satisfied that her outfit was presentable, she brushed her hair, letting it fall across her shoulders and down her back. She needed a trim and a color, but for now, this was it. Satisfied, she slipped into her black suede boots and went downstairs. With a quick glance around to make sure she had not left on any lights or appliances, which should not be running, she found her keys and headed out the back door.

Butterflies danced in her stomach, a feeling she had not experienced in so long that it surprised her. She chuckled. "This is *not* a date," she said aloud as she pulled onto the main road. *And it isn't, is it?* Dates did not bring their children along. Or maybe they did?

It had been a very, very long time, and she would be the first one to admit, she had no clue what one considered acceptable in today's world. It did not matter, she thought. For whatever reason, she was having pizza with a man and his daughter, a little girl whom she just happened to think was adorable.

Ten minutes later, she was searching the parking lot for a spot. She had not actually dined inside Ollie's since . . . *ever*!

As many pizzas as she had ordered throughout the years, she had never been inside. Amazing, she decided, after locating a parking slot between two large trucks. Turning off the ignition, she closed her eyes and took a few deep breaths. This was her day of new beginnings. She wanted to live; she needed to find a new normal in her life and forget her old ways. If having pizza on a chilly autumn Saturday night with a man and his daughter was to be a part of her new normal, then it was time to accept these facts and do her best to live in the moment.

She tossed her keys in her purse and headed for the entrance. As soon as she stepped inside, the scent of fresh-baked bread, garlic, and something else she could not put a name to teased her senses. It was warm, maybe a bit too warm, she thought as she searched the tables for Daniel and Holly. Chatter from the diners, clinks of flatware, and an occasional burst of laughter livened up Ollie's more than she had expected. Actually, she was not sure what she had expected, and reminded herself, again, that this was a new start for her.

"Ivy!" came a voice from her left. "Over here."

She turned and saw Daniel and Holly seated beside an older couple on a long bench against the window. She gave a quick wave of acknowledgment and headed their way.

"I didn't know Ollie's drew in such a crowd," she said to Daniel and Holly. Daniel stood up and pointed to his empty seat. "Please have a seat. They said it would be a few minutes."

Ivy sat next to Holly. "Thanks. I love your boots," Ivy said. And she did.

"Me too. Dad gave them to me for Christmas last year," Holly said, stretching her black-tighted legs out so Ivy could get a full view of her boots.

"Well, all I can say is that's a very cool gift, and I love the color." She patted the little girl's back. She was thin, but not so much that it alarmed her. Most likely, she was going to be tall, just like her father.

"Me too, but pink and purple are my faves. Not sure if they make pink or purple boots, but how cool would that be if they did?" Holly asked.

Daniel shook his head. "She likes boots. What can I say?"

Ivy nodded. "Of course she does. What girl doesn't?" Small talk, but Ivy did not feel quite as awkward as she had at The Blackberry Café. Hard to believe that had only been a few hours ago. Which explained the reason why she was not that hungry.

"So what are your favorite toppings?" Holly asked.

"Good question." She thought for a few seconds, and replied, "I like everything, minus anchovies, which I do like in a Caesar salad. . . . So whatever you choose, I'll love."

"As long as there are no anchovies?" Daniel added.

She felt a wash of color rise to her cheeks. Glad the place was a bit on the dim side, she nodded. "What about you?" she asked.

"Same. I like anything."

The hostess called, "Greenwood, party of three," and they all followed her to a booth at the back of the restaurant, near the kitchen door. In the old days, Ivy would have asked for a booth away from the kitchen, but now decided it was a good idea to have a bit of traffic coming and going. The last thing she needed was a cozy little corner. Though one could not get too cozy with a little girl in the picture. Why she was having these thoughts completely perplexed her.

Daniel and Holly sat on the side nearest to the kitchen, and Ivy faced them. A low hanging light above their table reflected the golds and deep browns in Daniel's hair. Sarah was right. He was good-looking in the extreme. She took a deep breath, then picked up the menu, hoping to hide the blush staining her cheeks. A warm glow flowed through her. Right at this very moment, she was content. No past. No future. Just the moment.

An older woman, tall and thin, with steel-gray hair styled in a pageboy, came to the table. "Hey, Daniel. Holly. What's the occasion? I have not seen you two twice in one week since I do not know when." She looked at Ivy while she said this.

"Luck," Holly offered, and they all laughed.

"You want a few minutes to look at the menu tonight, or will it be the usual?" the woman asked.

"Give us a few minutes, Geraldine," Daniel said, adding, "Since we have a guest tonight."

"Sure thing, you just wave your hand when you're ready to order. You want a draft beer now, while you look over the menu?"

"Not tonight, we'll each have a Sprite. Ivy?"

"Sprite is fine for me, too."

When she had poured her alcohol down the drain, she was sure she would have some kind of craving. Luckily, she had not, nor had she missed it. In fact, the thought of it made her sick. To think that she had spent all these years in a drunken stupor amazed her. Unsure if her health had been affected, she made a mental note to go see her doctor for a full checkup. Her father, as always, had been right. She was still young, and she did have a future. Though she seriously doubted she would ever have more children, she did want to live out the rest of her days clearheaded, without the lingering aftereffects of alcohol.

"Then three Sprites it is," Geraldine said.

"She's the owner," Daniel explained. "Ollie's wife."

Ivy nodded. "I've never been here, can you believe it? I have ordered delivery from them numerous times over the years, but tonight's my first visit." She needed Daniel to know this for some reason that she herself was not even sure of. Maybe she wanted him to know she had no memories of being here with anyone from her past?

"Wow, that's really super weird, Ivy. Everyone who lives in Pine City has been to Ollie's," Holly informed her.

"Well, I agree that it's high time I had the pleasure, and, voilà, here I am," Ivy said. "I know they have the best pizza ever."

Geraldine brought three tall glasses of ice with three cold cans of Sprite. "Y'all ready to order?"

"Ivy? You choose," Daniel said.

"Let's have what Holly usually has. I'd like to be surprised."

"Good choice," Geraldine said. "The kid's got good taste."

"Thanks," Ivy said. She pulled the metal top of the can back. A slight fizzing sound bubbled up; then ice crackled as she filled the glass with soda.

"So what's your job, Ivy, or do you even have one? I am going to be a singer, but I guess you already know that," Holly said, her words bursting with enthusiasm.

Leave it to a child to cut through the flesh and go straight for the bone, Ivy thought. She would have asked the same question at her age. "That's a good question. I went to college, Duke, where I majored in business. I worked for my father until a few years ago." Was that even an answer? She did not think so, but it was all she was willing to share at this point. She could not speak about the plane crash, especially now that she knew that Daniel had lost his wife in the very crash that took her family from her. Though she knew she was being unrealistic, she felt responsible for his loss. Silly, but true.

"Holly, I think Ivy would rather talk about something besides work. Am I right?" Daniel asked her.

"No, it's fine. Really." She was not being 100 percent truthful. It was not fine. She cleared her throat. "I worked for an airline many years ago." There. It was out in the open.

"Cool," Holly said, then apparently remembered what her dad told her earlier about her mother. "I mean, *not cool.* You know *cool,* like you could travel, *cool,*" Holly said, trying to dig herself out of the verbal hole, but the more she said, the deeper she fell into the darkness of her words.

Ivy knew it was up to her to make this right. Honesty was always the best policy. "I did not travel much. And it was a cool job for a while. I enjoyed my work, loved the freedom I had, and bringing home a paycheck was nice, too." Lame as ever, but she had never rehearsed how she would explain her circumstances to a stranger if asked.

She did not want to burden Holly with any more thoughts of sadness.

In order to change the subject, she asked, "So tell me about this annual Christmas musical? How in the world did you get involved in such a big project?" During lunch, Sarah had explained to her just how big a deal The Upside's Christmas musical was.

Holly looked at her dad. "I don't think I'm going to be allowed to sing this year."

Ivy raised her brow, trying to hide her confusion from Holly. "Why is that?" she asked. Was there more to this father-and-daughter team that she did not know? Were they ill? She hoped not. She could not handle another tragedy happening to those she cared about. Though it had only been a day, Ivy felt as though Daniel and his daughter were in her life for a reason.

Maybe Holly getting lost was meant to be?

Chapter 31

"It's the happiest I have seen her since the accident," George explained to Margaret. "That child's visit had a positive effect on her. I think it's what's brought about this new change in her."

"I'm happy to hear that. As we both know, I have stood in her shoes, and it's the most horrifying news a parent will ever hear, but we have to live our lives. I know Mark would have wanted me to move on," Margaret explained.

They'd had this same conversation many times, and each time, George saw the hurt and loss etched in Margaret's face. At sixty-five, she was a very attractive woman, but there was a sadness about her that he knew would never go away. He saw this in Ivy, too; each time, his heart broke a little bit more for her. And for Margaret. While he'd lost his wife and two grandchildren, he had not lost a child, and that was the worst loss possible.

"You know I hate what you've had to go through," George offered. "I wish I could make all the negativity in your life disappear, but I am a realist."

Margaret smiled, her eyes crinkling at the corners. "Yes, you are, and I, for one, am glad. I do not know where I would be if not for you."

After all the years he'd been with Margaret, he had the grace to blush when she complimented him. "You'd be just fine without me, we both know better."

"Who would possibly make beef Wellington for me, and on a Saturday night?" Margaret took a sip of the wine she had brought over.

"I'm sure there's more than one willing gentleman out there who would not mind giving you a go," George said, then laughed. "Oh, that does not sound very nice, does it? You know what I meant."

"I do."

More than once, he'd wanted to ask Margaret to move in with him. Now that he was moving to his new home at The Upside, he wondered if she would give in if he were to ask her to marry him? He adored her, and he knew the feeling was mutual. They shared most of their lives together. Why not share them under the same roof? He had not told her about selling his house or the airline. This was part of the reason he'd invited her over tonight. Normally, he would take her out to a special restaurant of her choosing. She loved The Willows, and he did, too, but he did not want to frequent a place he owned too often, because he did not want his manager to feel as though he were checking up on him. Margaret had agreed when he'd explained this to her.

Margaret knew him better than anyone, even more than Elizabeth had. He was in love with her, and he knew that the feelings were reciprocated. When he asked her to be his wife, he wanted it to be special. Not in his kitchen, sitting at the old parlor table. A plan began to take shape. He smiled.

"Why the big smile?" Margaret asked. "You look like you're up to something. Did you take the Corvette on a wild drive across the parkway today? Are the police going to keep my little red 'vette on their radar now? If so, I will have to tell them you're the speed demon, not I."

George shook his head and laughed. "No worries there. I had the oil changed, went to the supermarket, and here I am."

"I hope so," Margaret said, her eyes sparkling with mischief.

"I do have something I would like to share with you," he said. "Would you like another glass of wine first?" he asked, reaching for the bottle. She nodded, and he poured them each another glass.

"What's the big mystery? I know that look. You have something up your sleeve," Margaret stated.

George cleared his throat, took a sip of wine. "I have decided to sell Macintosh Air. I have had a buyer interested for a few months. I'm not sure how much longer they'll be interested, so they made me an offer, and I accepted."

Apparently, she was surprised, as all she could do was nod.

"And I'm going to put this place on the market. It's too big for a single guy. Ivy has no interest in the place. She told me it would be the perfect home for a family starting a new life. I agree with her. You know my house at The Upside has been move-in ready for quite some time. I have decided now is the time." George sighed. "What do you think?" He wanted her opinion, valued it very much. If all went according to plan, she would be sharing his home, too.

"I think it's high time. You have the restaurants, The Upside, and The Bright Side is breaking ground. You love this area, and your 'retirement' home is an architectural dream. I'm with you all the way." Margaret held her glass high in the air. "Let's make a toast."

He clinked his glass to hers.

"To the brightest, biggest, and best holiday season ever!" Margaret said, then added, "And it's about time you moved on. I mean this in a positive way."

"Of course you do, I know that. I have enough to occupy me, that's for sure. I am not going to mind getting rid of that airline. Maybe I should have done it years ago. It might have helped Ivy to move forward."

"I do not know about that. You made the airline a success, and I know after the crash, you worked harder to make it so. After all the lawsuits, and media coverage, you did not give up. I've always admired you for that," Margaret said.

"That means a lot to hear you say that. I have often wondered if Ivy resented me for hanging on to the company. She seemed totally at ease when I told her I was selling out. It's like a dark cloud hanging over all our shoulders, or at least that's what I have begun to believe.

"She met Daniel Greenwood today. Apparently, his daughter is the star of the Christmas musical Carol Bishop and her cronies are working on. I have not heard her sing, but the talk is she will bring tears to your eyes."

"Oh, George, that's exciting! I don't know him, but I see his work throughout The Upside. He's very talented and dedicated. Do you think Ivy's interested in him?"

"I hope so. He's a fine man. A bit stiff, though. His wife was killed in that plane crash, too. I'm not sure if he's told this to Ivy or if she's shared her tragedy with him. My gut tells me those two are perfect for each other. It might take a bit of work on Daniel's part, though. You know how guilty Ivy's always felt. If he can get through to her, and help her ease some of that guilt, it would be a miracle."

"It's almost Christmastime. And miracles always happen during Christmas," Margaret said.

With that, an idea began to really take shape, and George planned to make this holiday season one of his best ever.

Chapter 32

"That was one of the best pizzas I have had in . . . forever," Ivy said to Holly. "It's my new favorite, too."

"Are you just saying that to be nice? Because if you are, you don't have to. It's cool if you don't. Really," Holly added as they waited for Geraldine to bring the check.

"I'm serious. Black olives, pepperoni, along with all that hot, gooey cheese. What's *not* to like?" Ivy said, a huge grin on her face. She had not felt this at ease in a very long time. She knew this little girl was put in her life for a reason. She did not yet know what it was, but something told her that Holly would play a very important role in her future.

Daniel took the check from Geraldine and placed a few bills on the table. "Are you girls game for an ice cream?" He slid out of the booth. "All that salty stuff has me craving something sweet."

"Dad! You *never* eat sweet stuff. I do not know what's happening to you, but whatever it is, I am totally cool with it," Holly said, her clear blue eyes twinkling as bright as a star.

"Ivy?"

This was certainly turning out to be a much better evening than she had anticipated. She could not remember the last time she had had ice cream. Yes, she suddenly recalled making banana splits for James and Elizabeth. Between them, they'd eaten the entire jar of maraschino cherries, and both wound up with stomachaches. Of course, she had allowed this, and felt horrible, but both had loved topping their banana splits with all those cherries. Tears filled her eyes, and she let them flow. She needed to remember her family, the happy times, and there were many.

"Are you all right?" Daniel asked as he steered her toward the exit.

Taking a deep breath, she nodded. She took a used tissue from her purse and blotted her eyes. "Memories," she said in explanation.

Daniel did not ask her to elaborate, and she was grateful.

"Let's get that ice cream," Ivy said as they walked to their cars. "I'm assuming you want to go to Double Dips, unless there's another ice-cream parlor in Pine City?" She had been housebound for so long, she really was not sure.

"Yep, that's the place. Would you like to ride with us? I can bring you back to your car when we're finished?" Daniel asked.

Ivy was surprised by the question. Did this mean he enjoyed being with her, or was he simply asking as a gesture of kindness? Or for Holly's benefit?

"I would love to," she said before she started overthinking the offer. "Lead the way."

Daniel led her to an older-model pickup truck. It appeared to be a silver-gray color, but it was hard to tell with the sun down. He opened the passenger door, Holly jumped in, and Ivy hefted herself up, then sat next to Holly. A totally different view from this high off the ground. She liked it. Maybe she would buy a new SUV or a truck. She was due for a new vehicle. Something fun. Maybe this was why people drove these larger vehicles—they ruled the road and could see what was in front of them.

Daniel started the truck, put it in reverse, then backed out of his parking place and piled onto the main road.

"Ivy, just so you know, Dad does not usually eat anything sweet. I think you have put some kind of spell on him, in a good way, of course." Holly grinned, and Ivy patted her black-tighted leg.

"Thanks, I think. I'm not sure I have anything to do with your dad, but we're all enjoying the evening, and that's a kind of magic all in itself, don't you think?"

"It really is. Because Dad is usually very boring and mean," Holly explained, then cupped both hands over her mouth when she realized what she had said. "I mean—"

"She's right," Daniel said. "Except the *mean* part. I think you could replace that with *strict*."

"Whatever," Holly said. "You want to hear something?" She turned her attention on Ivy.

"Yes, I do," Ivy responded. She liked this little sprite more with each passing minute. Would Elizabeth have been so sweet and friendly, had she lived to be Holly's age? Sadly, that was something she would never know.

Holly started singing, softly at first, so low she could barely hear her. Then she began to sing louder.

"Silent night, holy night. All is calm, all is bright. . . ."

Ivy leaned as close to her as she could without actually getting in her face. Her mouth opened, but she did not say a word. Instead, she listened to a child who sounded years older; yet she sang so clearly, and purely, that tears came to Ivy's eyes. In all her years, she had never heard "Silent Night" sung so . . . heartfelt, each word a gift as Holly continued to sing. Ivy was stunned. No, shocked. This child was nothing less than a musical prodigy!

"Enough, Holly," Daniel finally said.

They parked in front of Double Dips. The silence in the

cab was deafening. Ivy finally understood what that expression meant. At a complete loss for words, she simply stared at this child, who appeared to be just like any other eleven-year-old. Until she sang. *Magical, uplifting.* Those words did not even begin to describe the feelings the child projected as she sang the popular Christmas carol.

Ivy had goose bumps.

"What?" Holly said as she slid across the seat so she could get out on the driver's side. Ivy was still too stunned to move. Shaking her head, hoping to return to the moment, she got out of the truck and followed Daniel and Holly inside.

No wonder she was the star of The Upside's Christmas musical.

She had the talent to be so much more. In the world of music, she could be whatever she wanted to be. An opera singer? The star of Broadway musicals? Who knew what else? She had that kind of talent.

All Ivy knew was that this little girl from a small town in the Appalachian Mountains would someday woo the world with her voice. Until then, she would . . . Ivy did not know what she should say.

Or do.

Inside the ice-cream parlor, Ivy's thoughts were all over the place. Holly's voice, definitely the most beautiful singing she had ever heard.

Ever.

"Ivy, what's your favorite flavor?"

Again she had to force herself to be in the moment. "That's a good question." She peeked at the giant tubs of ice cream in the display. "Mint chocolate chip."

"That's mine, too!" Holly said excitedly.

"Three double-scoop cones of the mint chocolate chip," Daniel said to the young boy who worked there. "Holly, find a table, and I'll bring the ice cream."

Ivy watched the father and daughter. Where was his re-action to his daughter's talent? Did he not know that a voice like hers, in one so very young, was virtually un-heard of? A once-in-a-lifetime phenomenon?

Ivy was now on a mission. She planned to meet Miss Carol; then she would do everything in her power to make sure that Holly did not lose her leading role in this year's Christmas musical.

Chapter 33

As soon as Ivy was inside her house, she rummaged through her purse and pulled out her cell phone. Scrolling through her contact list, she found Sarah's number and hit the SEND button. She glanced at the clock on the stove. It was a little after ten. She was probably up. It was Saturday night. No one went to bed early on Saturday nights.

"Hello," Sarah said, sounding fully awake.

"Hey, Sarah, it's Ivy. I hope I'm not interrupting anything," she said.

"Just reruns of *The Golden Girls*. Pretty sad, huh?" Sarah stated. "I need to get a life."

"You have a great life, Sarah. All those kids in your class love you, and I heard this from a very reliable source."

"And might I ask who that would be?"

Ivy saw no reason to keep her night with Daniel and Holly a secret. "Holly Greenwood told me. She idolizes you. I had pizza with her and Daniel tonight. At Ollie's, then we went for ice cream. Which is part of the reason I'm calling." She did not want to sound gossipy or come off as a busybody, but there was no one else she could ask.

"Okay," Sarah said. "What's up?"

"Have you ever heard Holly sing?"

"It's quite a shock the first time you hear her, isn't it? She's amazing, isn't she?"

"I'm still reeling. She sang 'Silent Night.' Not only does she have the most beautiful voice I have ever heard, but I have never heard it sung with so much heart and passion. It was an experience, to say the least. I wondered if you knew how I can get in contact with Miss Carol."

"She's the director of the Christmas musical, isn't she?" Sarah asked. "I don't have her telephone number, but I'm sure your father could find it for you."

Ivy hadn't even given her father a thought. Of course he would know how to contact her. "I'll call him tomorrow. I have no idea why I didn't think of that."

"So how did you manage to wrangle Daniel Greenwood to take you out for pizza?" Sarah asked.

Ivy did not hear one ounce of jealousy in Sarah's voice, so she told her. "I brought that note to him, and I think he was shocked that Holly wrote all those silly things, but it affected him badly enough that he told her what had happened to her mother. She seemed to take the news in stride.

"I don't think she really remembers much about her mother, which is just too sad. She was a bit embarrassed about the note, though. Daniel didn't get angry. Mostly he seemed regretful about her even thinking those things, because he had never let her know what had happened to her mother. So he invited me to have pizza with them, I think because he knew this would make Holly happy. I met them at Ollie's, met Geraldine, the full deal. Then we went to Double Dips for ice cream. I left my car at Ollie's and rode with Daniel to the ice-cream shop. That's when Holly sang 'Silent Night.' I simply cannot believe how gifted she is! I simply do not understand why Daniel doesn't encourage her. It's not as if she is a supremely talented tennis player and they would have to move somewhere she could receive the training necessary to make her into a Serena Williams or something. But instead of encouraging her, he just told her to stop, said that was enough. I was surprised . . . no, flabbergasted."

"I'm probably assuming this, but I think I'm onto something here. Daniel does not want Holly to have a career in music. His wife was a singer, and I'm guessing he thinks something bad will happen if Holly chooses the same path," Sarah suggested.

Ivy considered this. "What a waste of talent. This is going to sound crazy—and maybe it is—but it's what I feel. I need to do whatever I can to make sure Holly gets to sing in that musical. I do not know why. Dad's invited me to go each year for the past three years, but I never have. Now I feel . . . I have to go, and I have to make sure Holly performs. Does that make me sound crazy or what? Especially given the fact that I just met them."

"Pine City is a small town, Ivy. Most of the residents are decent, hardworking people. We look after one another, you know how it is? I think it's perfectly reasonable for you to pursue this. Daniel needs to move on and allow his daughter to enjoy being a young girl, and he needs to let the world hear her sing. So, no, you do not sound crazy at all. In fact, I think this is the best news I have heard all week. Hey, if you have a . . . thing or a crush on Daniel, it's fine with me. I am *so* over him. He was such a jerk, embarrassed me to death. I still cannot think of that scene this afternoon without feeling mortified, so trust me, he is off my list of potential men to date. Pine City, I am sure, still has a few other eligible bachelors."

Ivy laughed. "I'm sure you'll find the right guy. Remember what they say, it usually happens when you least expect it." She knew firsthand. Though she was not really sure if Daniel Greenwood had invited her out because she was there and had witnessed a private family matter, or simply because he wanted to get to know her better. Time would tell, but for now, she had to do everything in her power to see that Holly got to sing in the musical.

"So, are you telling me you and Daniel might be an item?" Sarah asked. "It's fine, really. I do think he's a hunk, but there's no harm in that." She laughed.

Ivy was clueless. "I have no idea what's in the future for Daniel or for me. I just feel compelled to make sure Holly performs in that musical. I feel like this is . . . a new beginning for me." She did, and though her sadness over the loss of her family would remain in her heart forever, she knew John would have wanted her to move on. While James and Elizabeth were much too young for her to form an opinion about what they would have wanted, she felt sure they, too, would want their mommy to be happy. As young as they were, they'd understood what *happy* and *sad* meant.

"Ivy, this is a blessing in disguise. I feel it in my bones. I'll help you in any way I can, and do not hesitate to ask if you need me," Sarah offered.

Ivy recalled how close they'd been in high school and knew Sarah's words were sincere.

"I will, I promise."

"Think of this as an early Christmas gift," Sarah said. "It's time to kick off the holiday season, anyway. I'd planned to invite Daniel and Holly for Thanksgiving dinner, sort of a jump start to Christmas, you know how it is? Maybe you could come, bring your dad, anyone you like." Sarah's voice was so upbeat and cheery, Ivy could not help but feel her friend's enthusiasm. "Think of this as your first gift, you know, like the one your dad always gave you a few weeks before Christmas. Remember those days?" Sarah asked.

Ivy had not thought about them in years, but she remembered exactly how she had felt. So antsy, knowing what she had put on her Christmas list. In high school, she would always make a lengthy list of clothes, gadgets, shoes, and boots.

She remembered her first computer. Dad had given it to her right after Thanksgiving. It was big and bulky, and he'd given her a membership to an Internet service that required using a phone line. At the time, a computer was not something one found in everyone's home, as it was now, but she had had that on her list, and Dad had come through.

"I do," Ivy responded fondly. She had insisted on *not* celebrating any holiday since losing her family. Now was as good a time as any to rectify her lack of Christmas spirit and start celebrating the sacred day. Though she had only experienced Christmas three times with the twins, some motherly instinct kicked in, telling her they would want her to celebrate this holiday, as well as Easter and Thanksgiving. Those were the holidays that they'd been old enough to have somewhat of an understanding of, so she would honor their memory by promising to celebrate as though they were here alongside her, if only in spirit and in her heart. "Those were some of the best times, for sure," Ivy concluded. "I'll let you know about Thanksgiving."

"Please do, as it's . . . *this Thursday!* I am so behind. I should start baking now. I do not know where my head has been," Sarah said, sounding a bit dismayed at getting a late start on her Thanksgiving prep, but Ivy knew she would pull it off. She had plenty of time.

"You'll be fine, I remember how organized you are," Ivy said. "I'll see if Dad has plans for the holiday and get back to you. If we decide to join you, I'll let you know ASAP."

"Sounds good to me," Sarah said. "Call your dad now, get Carol's number, and let's do what we can to ensure Holly gets to perform in the musical."

"Thanks for listening to me," Ivy offered. "It's been a long time since I've felt as positive as I do now. I'm so glad we had lunch today."

"Same here, and let's make it a habit, okay?"

"Absolutely," Ivy said. "I'll talk with you later."

After they said their good-byes, Ivy's thoughts were all over the place. What to do, how to do it, and *could* she persuade Daniel to allow Holly to share her gift with Pine City and, maybe, the world?

Feeling she had a purpose, a reason to look forward, a germ of an idea lingered in the back of her mind. But before she allowed herself to toss the idea to the winds, Ivy found her purse and removed one of the keys.

This key would unlock memories that she had kept hidden away for so very long. Maybe it was time to release them, allow herself to feel, and know that whatever emotions she felt, they would propel her forward to a future where new and happy memories could be made as well.

Chapter 34

"I had a great time tonight," Holly said. "I totally like Ivy, don't you, Dad? She's very pretty, too. Do you think she's pretty?"

Daniel shook his head. He'd anticipated these questions and thought he'd prepared himself, but found he was struggling to answer his daughter.

"I'm glad you enjoyed yourself. I did, too. We need to do this more often."

"Dad, why are you suddenly so cool? I don't get you. And I know I'll probably get in trouble for asking this. Did you get hit on the head by something?" Holly asked this in all of her eleven-year-old seriousness.

He laughed. "Probably seems that way, huh? But to answer your question, no, I did not get hit in the head." Maybe in another sense he had, but he would contemplate that some other time.

"So why the ice cream and stuff?"

"Sit down." Daniel motioned to a chair in the dining room. "I think I need to explain some things to you."

"I hope this is not gonna take long, because I still have three pages of math to study," Holly said as she plopped down onto a chair.

"You can leave the math for tomorrow. I think you have studied enough for one day." He pulled out the chair opposite hers.

"Cool," Holly said.

Daniel had noticed her excessive use of the word *cool* and was amazed that her generation used it, as it had been his generation's slang word of appreciation for anything and everything as well. What was it about words and styles? *Recycling to the next generation,* he supposed.

"Dad, are you gonna tell me whatever it is you said you were going to? I'm kind of tired."

Daniel focused his attention on Holly. "Sorry, I got lost there for a minute. Okay, I was going to explain . . . things." How did one explain a loss of this magnitude to an eleven-year-old? In terms she would understand, of course. Keep it simple. He took a deep breath, letting it out slowly. "It's been just you and me for most of your life, as you well know."

Holly rolled her eyes. Normally, he would have given her his *father look,* but now was not the time. All kids rolled their eyes when their parents were talking to them. That's just the way things were. He recalled doing that himself on more than one occasion. And, usually, getting a lecture about it. Again . . . here was another habit passed on from generation to generation.

"I have kept a very important part of your past from you, Holly. I have no excuse other than I wanted to save you from . . . *grieving,* but I know now you were much too young when your mother's . . . accident changed our lives. I should have explained the manner of her death to you before, and I should have done so without a stranger as a witness. That was stupid of me, and if I took you by surprise, I really am sorry. I know my timing is off the charts now, but I can't let tonight's revelation pass without an explanation."

He watched his daughter, saw how focused and purposefully she listened while he spoke. Maybe she was just a teeny bit wiser than he'd given her credit for?

"I'm totally cool with it, Dad. I really do not remember much about Mom. I have a picture of her, and sometimes when I look at it, I think she's smiling at me, but I know that's just stuff for crazy people and little kids. I really am okay with not having a mom."

Is she?

"I'm not okay with it, Holly. There isn't anything I can do to change our family circumstances, but I would if I could, trust me."

"So date Ivy. That would change our *'family circumstances.'*" Holly made air quotes when she said the last two words. "It's not like she's married or has a boyfriend."

Daniel wanted to ask how she had gained all this knowledge about Ivy's personal life, but it was not the time. He let it pass. "I want you to be the best you can be, you know that, right? And I'll support you . . ." He stopped when he realized he would *not* support whatever she chose to do with her life. He'd lucked out and caught himself before he had the chance to finish the sentence.

"*No matter what?*" Holly finished for him. "Because if that's what you were going to say, then you should let me practice with Miss Carol, so I can be the best I can be in the musical. I will not stop singing, Dad. I cannot stop singing. And you cannot ask me to. You might as well ask me to cut off my arm or my leg.

"Maybe you can stop listening, but I will not stop singing. It's in my blood. You said Mom was a singer, right?" She placed both hands on the table, then leaned forward. "I want to sing like her, for her memory, or whatever. I think that's how I could best remember her even though I, like, don't."

"Holly, it's much more complicated than that."

"How?" she asked. Certainly a reasonable question.

Daniel considered her simple question. Exactly *how* complicated was it? A nagging thought nudged him in the back of his mind: *It's only as complicated as you choose to make it.*

Had he spent the better part of the past eight years making Holly's and his life more complicated than it needed to be? He had loved Laura dearly. He reserved a special place in his heart for her in life and for his memory of the life they had shared together. Deep down, he knew Laura's profession was not the cause of her death. He'd always believed that if Laura had not been involved in the theater, and singing, all that went along with her career, that she would be here with them now. Nothing would change the facts, and though it hurt to admit this, even if only to himself, Holly should not be punished for this enormous talent given to her by her mother. In denying his daughter's natural gift, he realized he was denying his past, Laura's past, and, quite possibly, Holly's future.

Holly yawned, stretching her arms out in front of her. "So, are you finished? I am, like, really, really sleepy."

He stood up and leaned over his daughter, kissing the top of her head. "I think I have said enough. Go on to bed, and we'll talk more in the morning."

"Okay. Night, Dad. I really had a good time tonight," Holly said, then gave him a quick hug. She headed off to her bedroom. "I really like Ivy, too. Just so you know."

He did, too. And he liked Ivy way more than he wanted to admit to Holly, or even to himself.

"Night," he said as he pushed both dining-room chairs beneath the table and turned off the lights. As he headed to his den, his thoughts were all over the place. He'd been content to live his life just the way he had been living it for the past eight years; then Holly sneaks off, and he does a complete 180. He sat down at his desk, opened the top drawer, and removed a key to unlock the right-hand drawer. It had been years since he had opened the drawer and actually read through its contents, but it was time.

Stacks of newspaper clippings highlighted the horrid crash that changed his life. Laura's name had been mentioned in several articles. Had she not been on her way home from auditioning for Paul Larson, he doubted her name would have been mentioned in any other context other than the flight's manifest, just another unlucky soul to board the doomed flight. The flamboyant Paul Larson told *The Charlotte Observer* that he had decided to choose Laura to star in the musical she had auditioned for. He never knew if that was true, or if this was just the Broadway producer's way of garnering publicity for his upcoming musical. It did not matter, not really. It changed nothing. The musical continued to play on Broadway to this very day and had won several Tony Awards. No doubt this would have been the highlight of Laura's career if Paul Larson's claims were true. He supposed he would never know.

As he skimmed through the articles, a name caught his eye. More than once he'd briefly passed over the name, but now it seemed significant. He located the article with the flight's manifest.

Ivy Fine. Mrs. John Fine. Formerly Ivy *Macintosh*.

He read the piece again, his heart racing so fast, he thought it would explode from his chest. There had to be a mistake; this was merely a coincidence.

Daniel crossed his fingers and unlocked the left-hand drawer, which held his laptop computer. If his daughter knew he possessed the technology she had been asking for since third grade, she would never forgive him. Putting that thought aside, he booted the computer up, logged on to the Internet, and began his search.

Chapter 35

Before she could change her mind, Ivy inserted the key into the lock. Expecting the lock to be rusty or difficult to unlock, when the doorknob turned easily, for a split second, she thought she had made a terrible mistake. When the knob turned gently in her grip, she gasped. By entering one of the rooms she had kept off-limits for the past eight years, Ivy was taking the next step of joining the world again. She knew that if she was to ever come to terms with her past, she had to confront her memories of the two little children who would forever be in her heart, always.

Tears filled her eyes as she stepped into the room. Inhaling, she smelled something in the air, a lingering scent of . . . *baby lotion*? She used the sleeve of her sweater to blot her eyes. Looking around the room that she had not entered since the accident, she took in the single bed. It was covered with a faded pink comforter; the other twin bed, with its plain blue blanket pulled up to the top, waited next door.

"Bink bank," she said out loud. James's name for his twin's favorite pink blanket. Ivy walked over to the bed, and smoothed the wrinkles from the precious covering. She brought the pillow to her face and inhaled, expecting to breathe in the clean scent of the organic shampoo she had used on both children. Musty and dank, it smelled only of a long-closed room.

Holding the pillow, she sat on Elizabeth's bed, where Mr. Tibbles, her teddy bear, usually rested, but Ivy did not want to think about the bear now. Hugging Elizabeth's pillow and breathing in its scent, she could swear she smelled her favorite perfume, just a hint. And then she remembered that the last night she had put Elizabeth to bed, they had played makeup after her bath. Ivy had let her spritz herself with *"Mommy's big-girl spray"* before putting her to bed. She had forgotten about that night until just now. The tragedy had pushed aside this special memory, and Ivy cried at the injustice of what had happened to her sweet, innocent children. And John, too. She returned the pillow to its place at the head of Elizabeth's bed.

Standing in the center of the room, she slowly turned around, taking in eight years of . . . *a room.*

As she continued to spin around the room, she thought how this was simply a room in a house that was no longer a home, that had not been a home since the fatal crash.

She stopped and closed her eyes until the room stopped spinning. There were two chests in the room, a pink one and a blue one. She hadn't gotten around to moving James's dresser and his toy chest into his big-boy room. She opened the top drawer of the blue chest, expecting to find his clothes neatly folded, as they'd been the last time she had opened the drawer.

It was empty.

She opened the next drawer and the one below. Both were empty.

Flying across the room to Elizabeth's pink chest, she opened all the drawers and, again, found nothing. Not a trace.

Who had removed the clothes that belonged in these

drawers? She whirled around the room, realizing all the toys, books, and games that belonged to her daughter were no longer tossed around the room. Elizabeth's Dora the Explorer dolls had been removed from the shelf above her bed. Her miniature table and two matching chairs were gone as well. All of James's books were gone, too. His ant farm, the plastic containers of Legos, were nothing but a memory.

She wanted to . . . She was not sure what she should do. All of this, or, to be more precise, the lack of her children's possessions, stunned her. What had she expected? She was not sure. Ivy had no memory of anyone's clearing out their rooms, but she had not been in any shape to recall exactly who came and went the first couple of years after their deaths.

Her father, perhaps? Or Rebecca, most likely, had cleared out their rooms, leaving nothing more than the barest reminders of the two who'd spent such a short time in them. While she wanted to feel anger at whoever made the decision to remove all traces of her children from their bedrooms, she found she could not. Had she discovered that their toys and games had been removed a few years ago, she felt sure she could have mustered the proper emotion, be it anger, sadness, or grief, but now, all she felt was relief. So many years she had dreaded this confrontation with the past, feared the emotions it would stir up. Whoever chose to remove James's and Elizabeth's toys and clothes had only done so to spare her the horrid task that no parent should ever have to undertake and the accompanying emotions that no parent should ever have to endure.

Feeling sad, but incredibly relieved, she went over to the single window opposite the bed and pulled the curtains aside. She remembered when she had instructed the deliverymen to place the bed on the wall away from the window. Then her thoughts had been on chilly breezes seeping through the window, bringing on a stuffy nose and a sore throat. How simple her worries had been then, she thought as she struggled to open the window.

Using both arms and what strength she possessed, she was able to push the double-framed window up. The night air sent a chill through her. Briefly she thought her decision to keep the children's beds away from the windows in their rooms had been a wise one.

Ivy lowered the window just enough to air out the room's mustiness without turning the upstairs into a meat locker. She stood in the center of the bedroom, seeking the proper emotion, but all she felt was a deep-rooted sadness in her heart at the loss of two bright futures for children whom she and John had created and loved deeply. Still loved. That would never change. A mother always loved her children, no matter what.

She did. Now that her alcoholic fog was completely gone, she was not about to take one more minute of life for granted. Life was so very short, as she well knew. It was more than a disservice to her family's memory to cower inside this house in a drunken stupor, getting plastered in order to get through each day. That was in the past, and if she wanted to live in the here and now, it would have to stay in the past.

With the knowledge that James and Elizabeth would always be remembered and loved by her, she walked out of her daughter's room, but left the door partially open. She gripped the key in her hand, but knew she would never have to use it again. She would open up James's room tomorrow morning. The doors to her past would finally be open, and now it was time to unlock the possibilities of what her future held.

Holly Greenwood's magical voice came to mind. Recalling her talk with Sarah, and her desire to do whatever she could to make sure the young girl sang in The Upside's annual Christmas musical, she knew, *felt,* deep in her heart that helping this child realize her deepest wish was a gift that had been handed to her, and there was no way she was going to turn her back on this unexpected present.

Downstairs, she filled the teakettle with water and placed it on a burner to heat up. While waiting for the water to boil, she scrubbed the thick globs of burned coffee from the pot she had left to soak yesterday. When the kettle whistled, she removed it from the stove and poured the boiling water over her chamomile tea bag. She added a spoonful of honey and stirred the golden sweetness before heading to the living room. Normally, she would have spent the rest of the evening drinking and binge watching whatever her program of choice was, but now she simply wanted quiet, time to think, time to plan a future, something that she had all but forgotten existed.

Chapter 36

"I'm surprised you would even speak to me after the way I treated you yesterday," Daniel said into the phone. "Holly and I would love to come to your place for Thanksgiving dinner."

"You can bring a guest, if you like. And as many as you want, too," Sarah said. "I'm in a giving mood today."

Daniel could not help but laugh. How Sarah Anderson had summoned up the courage to call and invite them to her home for Thanksgiving dinner was a mystery, and one he could not solve, but she had reached out to him, and no way was he going to turn her down. Then there was the fact that he had heard what a fantastic cook she was. It would be nice, really. No more fake turkey and instant mashed potatoes. "I'm honored. Truly. It's been ages since someone cooked for us," he said into the phone.

"Oh, it's my pleasure," Sarah said. "To cook, I mean."

He knew exactly what she meant, and instantly had a killer of an idea assault his empty brain.

"Thanks, I have . . . a friend who I am sure would appreciate a homemade Thanksgiving dinner."

"The more, the merrier. Now, if I do not get busy, we'll

all have to settle for one of those plastic turkey dinners. Give Holly a hug from me."

"Sure thing," Daniel said, then placed the phone back in its cradle. He walked down the hall to the kitchen to pour himself another cup of coffee. It was after nine, and he decided to let Holly sleep in, given all the effort she had put into studying yesterday, not to mention he had kept her up late last night. Or late for a child. Apparently, she had not set her alarm clock.

He'd spent the better part of the night online reading article after article on Macintosh Air, its owner, and anything he could find connected to the family. What he had discovered blew his mind, and he was not 100 percent sure his findings were what he believed them to be, but he definitely planned to find out. As soon as he deemed it was not too early to make a social phone call, he returned to the phone and dialed the number he'd already memorized.

"Hello," came a sleepy female voice.

"Did I wake you up?"

"Daniel?"

"The one and only," he said, grinning. She recognized his voice already. That made him happy.

"Is Holly all right?" she asked, alarm in her voice.

He could have kicked himself for scaring her. "Yes, she's still asleep. Is this a bad time? I can call back later."

"No, it's fine. I was just getting out of the shower," she indicated.

An image of her getting out of the shower sent a thrill up and down his spine. It felt odd to have these sorts of feelings about a woman he barely knew.

He had not rehearsed what he would say when he spoke to her, but he just could not blurt his questions out. They were way too serious. So how did he go about asking her if what he'd read was true? "I thought you and I could, uh . . . go out for breakfast. I wanted to catch you before you ate." He sounded like a high-school boy and was a bit embarrassed by the fact.

"You sure do eat a lot," Ivy joked. "Will Holly be coming along?"

Did this mean yes? "She's asleep. I didn't want to wake her."

"Well, I am up now," came his daughter's voice from behind him.

"Forget I said that. Holly is awake now, and if she would like, of course, she can come with us."

"Where?" Holly asked as she danced down the hall to the kitchen.

Daniel held up a hand. Realizing Holly could not see behind her, he spoke into the phone. "Can you hold on for one second?"

"Sure."

He laid the phone down and hurried to the kitchen. Holly was busy fixing herself a bowl of cereal, just like she did every single day. Sad that he never bothered making her a proper meal, he decided he was going to spend the rest of his life making it up to her. "You want to go with me and Ivy to have breakfast?"

Holly turned around and stared at him. "You really have gone cuckoo. But yes, I will go. This cereal is stale. Do I have time for a shower?"

He thought of Ivy and her shower. "Of course you do, but make it fast, okay?" He smiled, then hurried back to the phone.

"Yes, Holly wants to go." Daniel just realized Ivy had not said that she would actually go.

"Do you want to meet at The Blackberry Café? I saw where they served breakfast on the weekends."

"Yes, that's perfect. Is half an hour too soon?"

"If you can make it forty-five minutes, you have a date,"

Ivy said. "My hair is sopping wet, and I do not want to go outside without drying it first."

A date? Is that what she thought his invitation was? Dates were for evenings and did not involve talking about tragedies. Or did they? It had been so many years since he'd cared about another female's ideas, he was not sure what her words meant. Maybe it was just that. A word. He was reading way too much into this.

"I'll see you there" was all he said before hanging up. He went to his room and changed into a chambray shirt and a pair of khaki slacks. He always wore jeans, but it was Sunday. He did not want to appear to be more heathenish than he was.

He combed his hair. Sometime in the near future, he planned to get a haircut. Reaching for the new bottle of cologne he'd used last night, he stopped. Holly said he'd used too much. He'd go without, as he'd taken a shower in the wee hours of the morning. One last glance in the mirror before closing his bedroom door. He had not slept in his bed, so he had not needed to bother making it up. And if he did not make up his bed, who cared? His OCD habits were starting to get on his nerves.

"Woo-hoo! You look like a . . . man," Holly said, stating the obvious. "I mean not my-dad-kind-of man. I did not know you even had normal clothes."

"There are a lot of things you do not know about your dear old dad, but you'll find out soon enough." Daniel looked at his daughter. "And you do not look like the eleven-year-old I sent to bed last night. You look like you're . . . almost twelve." He laughed, and Holly did, too.

Holly wore a pair of jeans with a red sweatshirt, her long hair pulled in a high ponytail. Daniel almost said she was the spitting image of her mother, but he did not. It would not mean anything to her, at least he didn't think so. Maybe someday, when she was older, he would let her look at her mother's professional photos. She was sure to see the resemblance.

"I'm almost twelve. You mean I could probably pass for thirteen, right?" Holly asked.

"No, that's not what I meant, kiddo. I mean you look really pretty in that red sweatshirt. Now let's get a move on, so we're not late."

Once they were inside the truck, he turned on the heat to take away the chill from inside. He backed down the drive and headed for The Blackberry Café. He checked the clock on the dash. Right on time.

"Dad, can I ask you a question?"

"Of course," he said.

"You're really not acting like the dad I know. The mean one. Sorry, but it's true. I can't remember us ever talking as much as we have in the past two days. Are you trying to be, like, super cool and nice because something bad is gonna happen to you? I am old enough, you know. You can tell me if you're sick or something."

Daniel physically had to force his foot to remain on the accelerator and not slam on the brakes in the middle of the road. Did his daughter really think so little of him? Of course she only based her opinions on his actions in the past, and past behavior always indicated future behavior. He was not acting like himself. He knew this very well, but how to explain?

Taking a deep breath and easing off the gas, he reached across the seat for her hand. "I guess I am acting kind of different, huh?"

"Beyond weird, if you want to know the truth." She squeezed his hand.

"This is not easy for me, Holly. I know I have not been the most attentive father. I have not made much of an effort to involve myself in the daily details of your life, and I have not allowed you to have a peep into mine, and I want to change that. Starting now. I do not want you eating stale cereal for breakfast every day. I do not want you to be afraid to voice your opinion. Most of all, I want you to . . . I want you to be *proud of me.*" His eyes watered when he said those last few words. He did want her to be proud of him. It was normal for girls to think their fathers were . . . the pie in the sky. At least he hoped. Holly would be a teenager in the blink of an eye. He knew the years ahead would be hard on both of them. If he did not have an easy, comfortable relationship with her now, before those teen years, he never would. The words weren't coming out as smoothly as he would have liked, but he felt like Holly got the gist of what he was trying to tell her.

"Dad, I am, like, super proud of you. Miss Carol thinks you're the best horticulturist in the world, and I do, too. I see all that grass and bushes, and stuff. I know what it looks like in the back of one of the trucks, and I see what happens when you plant them. You are kinda old-fashioned, though. I really think you need to think about a computer and the Internet. I'm gonna need one, once I'm in high school, and all. Just so you know.

"And, Dad, can you please, just this once, let me practice for the musical? It's, like, the most important thing in the world to me now. More than a computer or a cell phone. I do want one, though. Roxie and Kayla are asking their parents for cell phones for Christmas this year. Or I'll take one for my birthday. That would be so cool."

Now probably was not the best time to tell her he'd had a computer for several years, that his work required using one. It was the reason he locked himself in his den every evening. He did not want her to see that he owned one. Why? He knew why, and now that he'd told her about Laura, he saw no harm in revealing his little secret.

"Holly, I have had a computer for a number of years. I do not know why I have kept it such a secret, but we have Internet, and there's a laptop in my desk."

Holly scooted to the edge of the seat, then turned to look at him. "Are you for real? Like, telling the whole truth? You're not just saying this to make me, like, feel good or anything? Because if you are, Dad, this is a very uncool thing to do. I really hope you're being truthful."

He pulled into the parking lot behind the restaurant, shut the engine off, and turned to his daughter. "I am being totally honest with you. I'll even show you my Mac-Book later." He wanted to laugh when he saw her eyes almost double in size.

A light tap on the window took their attention away from their conversation.

"It's chilly out here," Ivy said when Daniel opened his door to get out of the truck. Holly jumped out and ran around the front of the truck.

"Ivy, you are not going to believe the stuff my dad has been hiding from me. I am, like, in major shock. I can't wait to call Roxie and Kayla. Unreal. Let's go inside. I am positively starving."

Ivy smiled at Daniel, and the ice around his heart melted. It did not matter one little bit that the temperature was close to freezing.

Chapter 37

Ivy had been a bit taken aback by Daniel's early-morning phone call and invitation, but seeing how happy the father and daughter were right now, she could not help but feel a bit on the jolly side herself.

They were seated at the same table as yesterday. It seemed like a very long time ago, but it had only been a few hours. The same young girl who had waited on them yesterday delivered menus to the table.

"Hey, y'all are gettin' to be regulars now. We have a breakfast special, and it's rockin' good eatin' today. Homemade buttermilk biscuits, with sausage gravy, and three freshly laid eggs on the side. I had some myself, and I'm tellin' ya, I'm gonna have to walk ten miles just to feel good about myself again."

Ivy laughed. "That sounds delicious. I have not had a buttermilk biscuit in years. I'll take the eggs soft scrambled, with a cup of coffee."

"Make that two specials," Daniel said, then turned to his daughter. "Holly?"

"No way am I eating that much food! I'll have the Belgian waffle, with orange juice."

"I'll just put your order in and be right back with y'all's drinks."

"She's really got the Southern twang down, huh?" Daniel observed.

"Indeed," Ivy replied. She thought the young girl might be adding more emphasis on the *y'all, gettin'*, and *eatin'* herself. It made her smile. And for that alone, she would sit and listen to her talk all day. Smiles and laughter had definitely been lacking in her life the last eight years. *Not anymore,* she vowed.

The young woman returned with their drinks, plus a basket of biscuits. "Momma said to bring y'all these, as they're right out of the oven. Here's homemade blackberry jam, too." She placed three bread plates on the table, along with a crock of butter.

"I'm going to have just one," Ivy said, reaching for the basket. "With the jam. Where in the world do they find blackberries this time of year?" she asked as she slathered her biscuit with butter and jam.

"I would guess with a name like The Blackberry Café, they have their sources," Daniel said as he took a biscuit from the basket. "Holly?"

"I guess I'll try one because that waitress was, like, super cool to bring them."

Daniel passed the basket over to his daughter.

Ivy bit into the biscuit, butter dripping down her chin. "These are divine," she said, then wiped the butter from her lips and chin. Daniel watched her, and instead of making her uncomfortable, she felt a warm glow flow through her. This had not happened in forever. She was not going to overanalyze her feelings, not now. She wanted to speak with him about Holly's performance, but not in front of Holly. She had not yet called her father this morning to get Carol Bishop's phone number, but she might not have to if she could corner Daniel before they finished. It was all she could do not to ask him exactly why he'd called her so early on a Sunday morning, as she was sure it was to ask her to be more than just a dining companion.

"I have never been out to eat this many times in my life," Holly said. "Dad doesn't usually go out, right?"

He grinned. "Right, which is going to change. I have been too dedicated to my work. I need to stop and smell the roses. Pun intended." He reached for Holly's hand.

Ivy laughed. "I totally understand. I have been"—she wanted to say *in mourning,* but that sounded so antiquated, even though it was true—"lost for a while," she completed her sentence.

"I know, Ivy," Daniel said, his gaze intent on her own.

"About loss? Yes, I suppose you do, and I'm so sorry for your loss."

"I am so sorry for *your* loss." His words held a much deeper meaning than that of a casual acquaintance. His words were so . . . *personal.*

"You do," she said, instantly convinced he knew about John, James, and Elizabeth. For some unknown reason, she was glad that she had not had to explain this. "You know that my father owns Macintosh Air, too?"

Daniel's eyes sparked with what she thought was a flash of anger, then . . . *sympathy?* "I wasn't absolutely positive, but you have just confirmed it for me."

Was he angry? Did he blame her for his wife's death, even indirectly? As she had blamed Mark for the death of her family? The exact sequence of events leading to the crash had never been determined; yet when pilot error was deemed to be responsible, she had never even considered anything other than that. Her father had never accepted the National Transportation Safety Board's decision, but she had refused to listen to his theory of a possible terrorist incident.

The waitress brought their food to the table, making a

big show of placing the plates just so. "Y'all eat up, and I'll be back with more coffee." The restaurant was starting to fill up with eager diners, so she did not linger at their table this time.

For the next ten minutes, they ate their breakfast, and the young girl, returning with the coffee, told them that if they needed her, "Just give a holler and call for Tanya."

Ivy nodded and drained the last bit of coffee. "There is more, but I'm sure you know this," she said, focusing on Holly. This was not a discussion she wanted to have in front of her.

"Yes, I do. And we're okay, Ivy. With everything. It's a tragedy, but it happened, and I'm finally trying to"—he nodded at Holly—"get on with life."

Holly had been watching them as she ate her waffle. Ivy decided she was extremely smart and was simply watching them to see how their stilted conversation played out. She liked this little girl more with each passing minute.

"So I finally learn we have the Internet, a MacBook, and Dad sneaks and uses the Internet at night. Right?"

Daniel shook his head and wiped his mouth with his napkin before placing it on the table. "I'm not a big fan of allowing children to live online. However"—he looked at Holly, a huge grin on his face—"being that you're almost twelve, I'm going to allow you to use the computer now, so you'll know how to use one by the time you're in high school."

"Which is not *that* far off," Holly stated. "And I already know how to use a computer. We have computer lab at school."

Tanya swirled over to their table, leaving the check. Ivy reached for it, and before she knew what was happening, Daniel placed his hand on top of hers. "No, I invited you. It's my treat."

He'd paid for pizza and ice cream last night. "You do not have to buy my breakfast."

"Yes, I do. I'm old-fashioned that way. A lady never pays for her meals when she dines with me."

"Like *that's* ever happened," Holly interjected.

His hand remained on top of Ivy's. "Then thank you." Ivy felt as if a jolt of electrical current were racing up and down the length of her arm. She wanted to pull away, but she did not want to let on that she was feeling all the sensuous, delightful sensations that had been nonexistent for so very long.

"Can I have a word with you?" she asked. While her heart was hammering in her chest like a bird's fluttering wing, she had not forgotten what she wanted to discuss with him.

"Holly, why don't you pick out an apron and a jar of jam." He stood up and removed a few bills from his wallet. "Here, and you can take care of the check, too."

"Cool," Holly said as she fanned the bills out. "I know this is your way of getting rid of me. But it's cool."

Ivy could not help but laugh. "You are one smart cookie. If you do not mind, I just need to speak to your dad for a minute."

"Take as long as you like," Holly said. "I'm gonna look at the cookbooks."

Ivy gave Holly a pat on the shoulder as the little girl walked away. "Thanks, I'll just be a minute." Ivy headed for the door, with Daniel following close behind.

In front of the restaurant, a large group of diners were waiting to be seated. Ivy walked to the edge of the parking lot. "Is this why you wanted to have breakfast? To tell me you know what happened to my family?"

There, she had said it. She needed to clear the air; then she would tell him what she had planned to say.

"Partly, but if I'm honest, and I always try to be, I wanted to see you again."

"Really?" she said, her voice not much more than a whisper.

"Yes. Really." Daniel took her hand in his. "If I'm being too forward, you'll tell me?"

She laughed out loud. "You are a Southern gentleman, no doubt. And yes, I will tell you." His gaze settled on hers. Anticipation seized her, and she was filled with a new sense of urgency as he watched her. She wanted to tear her eyes from his, but she could not. Would not. If this was part of her new beginning, she would accept it right now and live in this moment. He continued to hold her hand in his very warm one.

"You wanted to talk with me about something Holly should not hear?" Daniel asked, reminding her why they were standing in the parking lot.

"Yes, I do." She cleared her throat and gently removed her hand from his. She could not focus if he continued to touch her. "I wish you would let Holly sing in the Christmas musical. I know I'm probably sticking my nose where it does not belong, so you do not have to tell me, but when I heard her sing last night, I could not imagine her not sharing her gift with the residents of Pine City. She's a prodigy, Daniel. Right now, she is better than virtually anyone you can hear singing on the radio today. You know this, right?"

He inhaled and crammed his hands in his pockets. "She's extremely talented, as was her mother. Actually, Holly is much more talented than her mother ever was. Though Laura did not start her career until she was much older than Holly. Laura was on her way home from an audition when she died."

Ivy nodded, but did not speak.

"I have spent the last eight years trying to keep Holly

focused on getting an education and planning for a career in anything but music. It's been hard on her. I have not allowed music in my house since her mother died."

Ivy opened her mouth, but she stopped before she blurted out something she would regret. Daniel needed to talk, and she was going to let him. They didn't have a lot of time. Holly was bound to come rushing around the corner any minute.

"It's bad, huh?" he asked.

She nodded. "It is."

"I guess, no, I *know* I'm trying to protect myself from . . . losing her to a musical career too soon. She's young, but talented enough to have one now, I am aware of that. I guess I want to protect her as long as I'm able."

"And you think if you allow her to participate in a small-town musical, she'll have an instant career?"

He shrugged his wide shoulders. "I do not know that for certain, but I have never wanted to take the chance."

"What about what Holly wants? Given her talent, it's almost a disgrace *not* to share it with the community, especially at Christmas." Wasn't she one to give advice?

Daniel nodded, slowly, and chewed his lip. He took a deep breath, slowly letting it out, his nostrils flaring. "You're right, Ivy. I'm going to have to loosen the reins, aren't I?"

"I think you already have."

Holly came running around the corner, a bag in one hand and wadded-up bills in the other. "Here's your change, Dad." She held the crumpled bills out to him. "Are you okay? You look, like, weird or something. Ivy?"

Ivy did not say a word.

Daniel focused his attention on Holly. "Look, I know you're supposed to study math today, but I have a better idea."

"You want to take me out for pizza again tonight?" Holly asked.

"I think it's time I took you to Miss Carol's. So you can practice."

Holly looked at Ivy, and Ivy felt tears of happiness fill her eyes.

"Dad, are you serious?"

"I am."

Ivy knew she was witnessing a moment between a father and daughter that would profoundly change their lives. All of their lives, because she knew that hers was changing, too.

Chapter 38

Sarah could not recall ever having so many people over for Thanksgiving dinner. She was loving every minute of this gathering of friends, old and new.

In the kitchen, her mother was sitting at the table arranging the cookies, which they'd baked the night before, on a bright red tray. "You're glowing, dear," Clara stated.

"I am, for sure," Sarah said. "And it has nothing to do with this turkey in the oven or all of this." She pointed to a pot filled with steaming-hot buttered homemade mashed potatoes, stuffing, green beans, and seven pies lined up on the counter. She had more than enough food to feed an army of hungry young men, not to mention her actual guests. Sweet potatoes, cranberry salad, a fresh spinach salad, turkey gravy, and yeast rolls were just a few of the dishes on the menu. As always, she had cooked too much, but that was okay. There would be plenty of leftovers for her guests to take home with them.

While she had dreaded facing Daniel Greenwood after their lunch last Saturday, Sarah was beyond thrilled when he brought his friend and coworker, Jay Johnson, over to meet her. He was beyond handsome, she thought. He had dark blond hair and dark eyes, and he reminded her of a

Greek god. He was tall and built like an oak tree. She had noticed this, and ever since being introduced, she had been running around the kitchen like a schoolgirl with her first crush. He had looked at her with something more than polite interest and kept coming to the kitchen to see if he could help. "No, you guys just enjoy the football game. I have everything under control."

Ivy and Holly were busy setting the dining-room table with Sarah's mother's best china. Margaret and George were bustling about making drinks for everyone. Sarah Anderson was in her element, with a houseful of happy people to feed.

Christmas carols played softy in the background, delightful smells penetrated throughout the house, and an occasional shout from the den let Sarah know she had made a good call when she had invited Ivy and her family for Thanksgiving dinner.

Ivy had looked like a new person when she had arrived this morning. She wore a dark green sweater, with black leggings and black boots. Her hair was styled in loose waves, and her green eyes sparkled. She had added just the right amount of makeup, and Sarah remembered the times when they used to spend hours going through all the glossy magazines, trying to learn the latest fad in makeup. Ivy had mastered her look today, and Sarah was sure it was not from cosmetics alone.

Daniel, Holly, and Jay had arrived a few minutes later. When she realized that Daniel's friend had not tagged along for just a home-cooked meal, she was absolutely certain that this holiday season was going to start off as one of her best ones ever.

"We're finished in the dining room. Let me help get these goodies out while they're still hot. You're sweating," Ivy observed.

"It's a bit . . . steamy in here, in case you haven't noticed," Sarah said as she lifted the roasting pan from the top of the stove and carried it over to the sink. "I'm going to be washing dishes all night, but who cares? Are you sure you're okay with all the extra people? I know I didn't tell you when I invited you and your dad, but I wanted it to be a surprise."

"Actually, I think it's the best holiday gathering I have attended since"—Ivy stopped, but she knew that if she was to move forward, she needed to be able to verbalize her family—"the last one I spent at home with John and the kids. It's all good, Sarah. Really."

"I'm relieved, but I had a feeling this is just what you needed. Me too, for that matter," Sarah said as she squirted liquid detergent in the roasting pan, then filled it with water. "I am going to let this thing soak for a while." She rinsed her hands and dried them on a tea towel covered in pictures of cartoon-like turkeys with the words GOBBLE GOBBLE written above their heads in little circles with down-pointing arrow-like extensions.

"I'm looking forward to gaining five pounds today. I plan to have a slice of each of those pies, too," Ivy added as she reached for the mashed potatoes. "Let's get this show on the road. I am starving, and something tells me those two guys are going to be as well."

"Mom, can you bring the rolls?"

"I'm not that far gone, young lady. Of course I can," Clara Anderson said. She was a bit wobbly, but still was able to walk without assistance.

Fifteen minutes later, they were all seated around the table in the dining room. "I'd like to thank you all for coming today. It means more than you know," Sarah said. She smiled and saw that Jay Johnson was also smiling. "I'd like to say grace."

They all bowed their heads as Sarah recited all she was

thankful for. After several utterances of "Amen," the food was served, the conversation was light, and everyone seemed to have picked up on the air of general good cheer that the day deserved. When they'd finished the turkey and all of the seemingly endless side dishes, Sarah, Ivy, and Holly cleared the plates and returned with pies, one red velvet cake Margaret had brought, and three trays of sugar cookies, plus a huge bowl of whipped cream for the pumpkin pie.

When they were halfway through dessert, George tapped his glass with his fork. "If I could have your attention for a minute, I have something I would like to share with you all."

All eyes were on him, and he stood, then cleared his throat. "I have an announcement I'd like to make. Ivy, I have asked Margaret to marry me, and though it was touch and go for a bit, I finally persuaded her to accept my proposal."

Everyone was silent for a split second; then they started offering congratulations all at once. When the talk died down, Ivy spoke. "Dad, this is the best news I have heard in years. Margaret, I'm thrilled for you. Truly. I think we should make a toast to the happy couple."

"Absolutely," Sarah said, and raced to the kitchen for one of her special bottles of champagne, along with several crystal flutes, all of which she placed on a tray.

"Let me," Jay said as he took the champagne from her and expertly popped the cork.

Sarah knew she was blushing and simply did not care. Jay filled the flutes, except one, and Sarah raced back to the kitchen for the sparkling white grape juice she had purchased for Holly.

With champagne flutes held high, Ivy made a toast. "To my father, who never gave up on me, and to Margaret, who never gave up on my father." She paused. "And to Holly, who knocked on my door and changed my life."

"Cheers!" they all said, and clinked their glasses together.

This Thanksgiving, all those at the Anderson home had been given many blessings, and each and every one of them knew that on this day, their lives were changing, and it was all for the better.

Chapter 39

Though she knew it would bring back painful memories, she also knew that it was time. After the crash, at some point, Rebecca had taken down Holly's Christmas tree and packed up all the ornaments. She also must have been responsible for removing James's and Elizabeth's things from their rooms, even if Ivy had no memory of doing it or arranging to have it done.

Just as she used to do over eight years ago, Ivy called Baker's Tree Farm and asked them to deliver the biggest Fraser fir they had, minus the lights.

She had spent most of the morning dragging the large crates of decorations from the attic to the living room, where she planned to spend the day sorting through them. She had made a cup of coffee with her new Keurig coffeemaker and brought the drink with her to the living room.

The last few days had been a whirlwind. Her father's announcement and the sudden changes in her day-to-day life were still a bit of a shock, but in a good way.

She recalled her conversation with Margaret during dinner last night.

* * *

"I want to move forward as much as you do, Ivy. I under-stand your loss. More than most," Margaret had told her.

Ivy had agreed that she did. "I have been so focused on my own grief, I never gave much thought to what you were going through. I am so sorry, Margaret. I . . . Well, you know what it's like. I do not think there is anything else I can say, except welcome to the family."

Their words had been brief but consoling. Ivy discovered that she and Margaret had much more in common, other than their shared tragedy. Margaret adored her father, and they discussed a wedding date. Ivy found herself getting caught up in Margaret's excitement, despite all the sorrow that had plagued them both for so long.

Centering her attention on the large crates, she placed her cup on the coffee table. She brushed off the dust, then pulled the lid aside and placed it on the floor. One by one, she unwrapped ornament after ornament. Tears pooled, and she let them. This was not easy, but it was absolutely necessary. All the reminders of that day came rushing back with full force, but she continued to plunge through the boxes, determined to move forward.

Two hours later, she had unpacked all of the basic decorations. She had saved the final box for last, as she knew that this box held the most treasured of her ornaments.

She removed the delicate wrapping from the first ornament. A set of silver Christmas bells with the words OUR FIRST CHRISTMAS and the date of her and John's wedding engraved on the back brought back so many memories of her wedding day and the day they'd bought this ornament. While sad, it was not so sad that she couldn't smile at the memory.

Also in the box were several collectable ornaments she

had thought were simply fun and cute at the time she had purchased them. Sleighs with smiling reindeer, snowmen with colorful scarves, and a variety of bears wearing bright red hats were just a few of the ornaments she unpacked.

Knowing she was saving her most treasured for last, she took the small box and removed its lid. The ornament inside was covered with Bubble Wrap and tissue paper. The tears that she had managed to keep at bay flowed freely as she viewed the small crystal angel etched in gold trim, which was now barely visible, with its soft, faded blue eyes, and the small chip on its left wing, a gift from her mother. She would not be hanging this on the tree this year.

It was time to pass this angel on to another little girl who'd lost a mother she did not remember; yet Ivy knew Holly would understand the sentimental meaning behind the little angel and would no doubt treasure it as Ivy had all these years.

A sharp knock on the door startled her. She put the delicate angel back in its box and placed it on the sofa. Hurrying to get the door, she stopped when she saw it was a young man from Baker's with a giant Fraser fir. She opened the door as wide as possible to allow him entrance.

Fresh pine filled the entrance, along with sharp, cold air. The temperatures had dropped since Thanksgiving. Forecasters were predicting a white Christmas this year.

"Where would you like me to set this up, ma'am?" the young man asked.

"In here," she said, and led him to the den. This year, she was not going to place her tree in the formal living room, as she found the room lacking in warmth and a bit cold. In the den, she would view the tree daily, since she was planning to enjoy every minute of the holiday season this year, unlike Christmases past.

The young man cut the plastic binding from the tree,

sending the tightly wrapped branches springing out in every direction. "Sorry, this is one of our bigger trees this year."

"No apologies needed. This is just the kind of tree I asked for. You do have a stand, right?" When she had called Baker's, she had asked for a tree stand, and as many strands of lights as possible, and had to remind them not to put them on the tree this time as they had before.

"Yes, ma'am. And a bunch of lights, too. They're in the truck. I'll be right back," he said as he made his way to the front door, which Ivy had left open when he brought the tree in.

A few minutes later, the giant tree was in its stand, the huge branches dropping to the sides like welcoming arms. The den smelled like the tree farm, and Ivy was so excited about her plans for the evening that she did not hear when the young man addressed her.

"Again, if there's nothing else," he said. "I'll be on my way."

"Sorry, yes, this is perfect." She had tucked a hundred-dollar bill in her pocket and took it out and gave it to the young man. "Merry Christmas, and thanks so much."

His eyes sparked with delight. "Thank you," he said, clearly delighted at her generosity, and Ivy led him to the front door.

"If you're sure you do not need help stringing those lights, I'll be on my way then."

"I'm sure."

He waved, and she stood on the front deck and watched as he drove down the long drive until she could no longer see the big truck's taillights. Then she went back inside and made herself a fresh cup of coffee.

For the next two hours, Ivy crawled up and down the small stepladder, winding the lights in and out, up and down the tree's many branches. When she was finished, she placed the cord by the wall plug, but she did not want to turn the lights on until the tree was completely decorated, and that would not happen until later tonight, at which time she was planning to host her very first Christmas-tree-lighting party.

She had invited Daniel and Holly, and, of course, her father and Margaret. Holly was bringing Kayla and Roxie along, and Ivy could not wait to meet them. She had invited Sarah and Jay, who had already gone on one date since Thanksgiving. Of course Clara Anderson was also invited, but she had told Ivy that she had best stay home, as she did not want to fall and break a hip. Ivy had understood and promised to take lots of pictures for her to look at in the comfort of her home.

Ivy had also invited Carol Bishop, who promised to bring Maxine Hammond, who had a special guest she wanted to bring. She also included Carol's friends, Barbara Winters and Helen Romeril. The gathering was also going to celebrate the kickoff of the annual Christmas musical, which was now only one week away.

She had not seen too much of Daniel or Holly since Thanksgiving, as the two were spending their evenings rehearsing for the big event. She spoke to Daniel daily over the phone, had had dinner at Ollie's the night before last, and had seen that the change in his outlook, where Holly's future as a musician was concerned, was a complete about-face.

Yes, she thought as she stood back to admire her beautiful Fraser fir, this was going to be a night to remember, the first of many, she hoped.

Chapter 40

Before going downstairs again, Ivy checked out her appearance in the full-length mirror at the back of her walk-in closet.

She wore the black skinny jeans she had bought on Amazon three days before, with a red, green, and black cashmere sweater she had had for as long as she could remember. Someone once told her that cashmere never went out of style, and she agreed completely. Her black half-boots would do until she went to Asheville for some serious shoe shopping. She pulled her hair back into a low ponytail and wore a pair of silver hoop earrings. Long overdue for a new hairstyle, she would have to take care of that, too, but for now, this was as good as she was going to get. Adding just a touch of red lipstick to stain her lips, she headed downstairs to check with Tanya and her mother, Darlene, who had made most of the hors d'oeuvres for tonight's gathering.

"Wow, you look stunnin'," Tanya said when Ivy entered the kitchen.

Ivy smiled. "Thank you. It smells wonderful in here."

"Thanks," Darlene said. "It's the buttermilk biscuits you

requested. With the ham and sliced tomatoes to be added when you're ready to serve. We have it under control, Mrs. Fine," Darlene said.

"Ivy, please."

"Ivy it is. The sweet-potato biscuits are finished, and I have the pork and slaw ready to serve as soon as the guests arrive. I left three jars of the blackberry jam in the refrigerator, if you need them, and I made a few deviled eggs, too. They'll go good with the ham biscuits."

Ivy had chosen a menu that reflected her Southern roots, but did not really require a knife and fork for the most part: Cuban sliders, along with the ham biscuits, and sweet-potato pork rounds topped with the pork and slaw. Ivy did not want to go overboard, but she wanted a variety of tastes. Sarah was making her famous mushroom puffs for those who did not want anything too heavy. Margaret, who Ivy was beginning to learn was quite the baker, was bringing a pumpkin espresso tiramisu cake, along with red velvet cupcakes.

Ivy placed several bowls of roasted pecans, cheese straws she had purchased at The Bakery, and small bowls of olives and pickles on the island, where they had set up a makeshift buffet. She had also put together a fresh fruit salad, which was still chilling in the refrigerator.

Plates, napkins, and any utensils one might need were placed in a basket at the beginning of her buffet line. She could have had any one of her dad's three restaurants at The Upside step in and cater this, but she had fallen in love with the biscuits at The Blackberry Café, not to mention its owner, Darlene and her daughter, Tanya. They were a hit in Pine City, and Ivy predicted a great deal of success for the little restaurant.

"I do not remember when it has ever smelled so good in this kitchen," Ivy said as she removed another serving platter from the cupboard. She had made sugar cookies last night, and they'd actually turned out pretty decently. She had sprinkled them with red and green sugar, and was reminded of the few times she had gotten to bake with James and Elizabeth. The kitchen had looked as if a natural disaster had taken place, but she had had so much fun watching serious James as she had showed him how to measure the flour and sugar. Elizabeth, on the other hand, had not been able to keep her little fingers out of the sticky-sweet mess. She felt beyond sad, but she knew that she would always feel the loss of her family, no matter how much time passed. They were lodged in her heart forever. If when she remembered the short time they'd shared, tears poured, then so be it.

The doorbell rang, and Ivy's heart raced as she went to let her guests inside.

"Dad, Margaret, you two look"—Ivy eyed their matching red sweaters, with a felt Christmas tree in the center— "very festive. Come in, and I'll put these yummy-smelling desserts in the kitchen." She took a giant plastic cake carrier from Margaret, and her father followed her to the kitchen with a matching cupcake carrier.

"Smells delicious," Margaret stated as she removed the top of the cake carrier container to reveal the three-layered tiramisu cake. Her father did the same with the cupcakes and placed them at the end of the buffet.

"If you're sure you do not want us to stick around and serve, we'd best get out of here and let you enjoy your evening," Darlene said as she covered a pan of biscuits with a tea towel.

"We're fine serving ourselves. I just wish you and Tanya would join us, there's certainly enough food," Ivy added.

"I would, but we have an early morning, so you all enjoy the food, and you let me know what the folks say about the food."

Darlene and Tanya said their good-byes and departed.

"This probably isn't the time, Ivy, but I wanted to tell you before anyone else arrives. The airline is sold. One hundred percent—lock, stock, and barrel. And I know this is fast, but I'm pretty sure I have a buyer for the house," George explained. "To tell you the truth, I am more than a bit relieved to hand off the airlines after the holidays. I did ask that any of my family and friends be allowed to fly for free, and it's in the contract. Just in case. So what are your thoughts?"

"It's a good move on your part, and I'm okay with selling the house. Actually, I have been thinking about putting this place on the market, too. It's more room than I need. Lots of good memories here, and I'll miss them, but I need to move forward, too."

"I told you she was a smart woman," Margaret said as she poured a glass of springwater for herself. "You know, I have an idea, and, George, since I am now your future wife, I think you need to listen up."

George laughed, then wrapped his arm around Margaret's waist. "See? What did I tell you? She's bossing me around already."

"Good for her," Ivy said. "So what's your idea?" She turned her attention to Margaret.

"All that land just south of where you're breaking ground on The Bright Side, what if you were to build a family community? One close enough to The Upside for those who have family members living there, but far enough away so we do not feel as if we are being checked up on."

"That's a fantastic idea, Margaret. At least I think so. What about it, Dad?" Ivy asked.

"Actually, it's something I have had in the back of my mind for a few years. It's a good idea, and it would certainly bring more young couples to Pine City. I think this future wife of mine is onto something, but tonight let's just enjoy the moment. We can talk shop after the holidays. That okay with you, girls?"

Ivy had never seen her father this happy. He looked ten years younger, and she was so very pleased that he'd asked Margaret to marry him. While she had had nothing but negative thoughts where Mark was concerned, she knew it was time to put those to rest as well. On behalf of the airline, Ivy had formally requested that the investigation into the crash be closed.

"It's fine with me," Ivy said, then jumped when she heard a loud rap on the door.

She hurried to the door, and again her heart rate increased when she saw Daniel and Holly standing outside along with Kayla and Roxie. She opened the door. "Come in and get out of the cold," she said. Ivy had butterflies in her stomach, and it was all she could come up with.

She closed the door behind them and proceeded to lead them into the kitchen. "Dad and Margaret are in here," she said. "Follow me."

In the kitchen, after everyone went through the usual niceties, Ivy sneaked a look at Daniel. He was wearing dark jeans and a forest-green pullover, with a chambray shirt underneath. Black boots added an inch or so to his height.

Holly, on the other hand, was dressed to the nines. She wore a burgundy maxi dress, her gold hair twisted in some kind of braid that Ivy had no name for, and was wearing the headband that Ivy had given her. "You look awesome, Holly, and I love the braid," Ivy told her. "What's it called?"

"It's a fishtail braid. Dad actually helped, can you believe that? I can do yours sometime, if you want," Holly said. "It's what's trending now. You know, like what's cool."

They all laughed, the doorbell rang, and Ivy announced, "Let the party begin."

Chapter 41

Ivy's guests clustered around the tree, and when everyone was in place, she said, "Holly, would you do the honors?" She gave her the extension to plug into the outlet.

"Sure!"

She leaned down and pushed the plug into the outlet. The twelve-foot Fraser fir lit up with hundreds of tiny golden lights. There were "oohs" and "ahs"; then Ivy stood back and viewed their handiwork.

"This is the prettiest tree I have ever seen," Holly said. "Don't you think so, Dad?"

"It is definitely a *cool* tree," he agreed, and pulled his daughter close to his side.

"Dad," Holly said, suddenly a bit shy when he'd used her favorite word.

"It is a *cool* tree, for sure," Ivy chimed in, and catching Daniel's gaze on her, she almost jumped out of her skin when he winked at her. She returned a half smile, then focused on her other guests, with whom she had not had much time to mingle.

"I have heard so much about you the past few days, I feel as if I already know you, Ivy. It was so kind of you to invite us over. I do owe you for convincing Daniel to allow Holly to sing in our little musical," Carol Bishop said.

"I have been wanting to meet you ever since I heard you were instrumental in working with Holly. She has the most amazing voice I have ever heard, and especially for one so young."

"Maybe we can get her to sing a few Christmas carols tonight. Maxine will be so disappointed that she and her friend Paul could not make it tonight. He was dying to hear Holly sing."

"Oh, well, I think that's up to Holly, but I'll ask her. Excuse me, I'll go find her," Ivy said, then went in search of Holly.

Holly was in the kitchen, sitting in a chair and eating a red velvet cupcake.

"Are they as good as they look?" Ivy asked, and reached for one herself.

"Better," Holly replied.

"Miss Carol wanted me to ask you if you minded singing a few Christmas carols, to liven up the party a bit."

"If it's okay with Dad," she said, and licked cream cheese frosting from her fingers.

"If what's okay with your dad?" Daniel said. "Am I missing something?"

"Ivy wanted to know if it's okay if I sang a few carols."

"Do you want to?" he asked.

"I *always* want to sing, Dad, you know that. Let me go wash my hands first."

Holly left the kitchen, and this was the first time that Ivy and Daniel had been alone all evening.

"Nice party," Daniel said.

"Thanks. I think it's turning out to be a good time for

everyone," Ivy said, feeling awkward being alone with Daniel.

"Yep."

"Yep?" Ivy shot back.

He grinned, and once again, her heart flip-flopped.

"It's a good tree-trimming party. First one I have been to."

"Me too," Ivy said. "So I hear you have been taking Holly to practice at Miss Carol's."

"I have," Daniel said. "Carol is an amazing teacher, and Holly adores her. And she adores you, too."

"Really?" Ivy said, though she was not surprised at all, because she was totally in love with the little girl whose appearance at her door that night had brought about all these changes in her life.

"Really. And her dad does, too," Daniel added.

Ivy's pulse increased.

"Does what?" Ivy could not help it. She wanted to hear him say the words. Whatever they were.

Daniel shook his head. "You're embarrassing me, you know that? And I'm not one who embarrasses easily."

Ivy raised her brow, ready for a challenge. "I see. Are you too embarrassed to tell me what . . . I do not know, whatever! Or what?" Ivy sounded like Holly, and she laughed.

"If you really must know, I told you Holly adores you. And it seems I do, too," Daniel said, and he did not seem the least bit embarrassed by his words. "Is that what you wanted to hear?"

"Yes, it is," she said, being completely honest. Is this what *rushing into a relationship* meant? Though they were not even close to having a relationship at this point, but it could happen. If it does, she would be living in the moment, moving along with her life.

"So, are you telling me that you *adore me,* too?" Daniel asked.

A shudder passed through her. Moving forward with living in the moment, she replied, "I'm not sure if I would use the word *adore,* but maybe something along those lines would capture it."

"Then it's settled. We want to get to know each other, and we're not talking like BFFs or pizza pals, right?"

Ivy burst out laughing. "Yes, something like that." Ivy glanced at the clock on the stove. "I'm going to check on Holly. I'll be right back." Ivy did not bother waiting for a reply, but knew he was right behind her as she made her way upstairs. Possibly the downstairs bathroom was occupied, and Holly was searching upstairs for another bathroom.

When she reached the top of the stairs, she stopped. Daniel was so close to her, she could smell his fresh manly scent. Spicy and woodsy. Sexy, too. Before she knew what was happening, he turned her so that she faced him; then he placed his hands on either side of her face, brushing a gentle kiss across her forehead; then his lips touched her own.

It was the most sensuous, yet somehow chaste, kiss she had ever had, and it was not even what she would have considered a real kiss.

"To being more than friends," Daniel said before putting a bit of distance between them.

Ivy's emotions were all over the place. Thinking she should feel a sense of betrayal to John's memory, she was surprised when she didn't. It had been such a long time since Ivy had felt desired, and she had desired in return. Gathering herself as best as she could, she took a deep, shaky breath, and said, "I'll check the master bath."

"I'll look downstairs," Daniel said, knowing that the moment had passed. For now.

Ivy went into her room and peered around, but there was no sign of Holly. The door to the bath was open; yet she tapped on the door, just in case she had forgotten to close it. No answer, so she went inside. No sign of Holly.

Figuring she was downstairs, Ivy turned and headed back in that direction. As she passed James's room, which she had kept locked for all those years, she saw Holly standing by the window, singing softly. Though Ivy could not understand the words, just hearing that voice sent shivers up and down her spine. She stepped into the room, and Holly must have sensed her presence because she stopped singing.

"I'm sorry, I just needed a few minutes alone to practice. I hope I'm not in trouble for coming in here. It didn't look like you were using the room."

"It's fine, let's sit down." The room was cast in shadows, and the only light came from the master bedroom across the hall. She motioned for Holly to sit on James's bed.

Together, as they sat in the quiet room, Ivy placed an arm around Holly and began to speak. "This bedroom belonged to my son a long time ago. I had twins, Elizabeth and James, the lights of my life. They were three when they died in the same crash as your mother. I miss them every day, and I'll never stop loving them." Tears rolled down Ivy's face. "But the night you knocked on my door made me realize that life was for the living, and you seemed so lost, that for the first time since the accident, I did not think about all I had lost when I lay in bed that night. I thought about you, instead." Ivy wiped the tears from her face.

"I'm not sure what to say, but you like me, right?" Holly asked.

"Oh, sweetie, I love you! You have given me my life back. I just needed you to know this. I was not sure if you knew about my family, but I wanted you to hear it from me. When I saw you in James's room, I felt I had to tell you. I hope I have not scared you off or ruined your evening."

Holly turned and hugged her so hard, it almost took Ivy's breath away. "I love you, too, Ivy. I'm glad you had kids, and if you want, you can tell me about them. I always wanted a brother or sister."

Ivy smiled and hugged her back. "We will talk, but you have a bunch of people downstairs who want to hear you sing. Are you up to it?"

Holly jumped off the bed. "More than you'll ever know."

Downstairs, Ivy's guests were in the den, laughing and enjoying the festivities, as simple as those festivities were.

"I found a young lady who has offered to entertain us with a few Christmas carols. I do not have a piano, or any instruments, but I think she's okay without them. Holly?" Ivy said, and stood beside her.

Holly stood in front of the Christmas tree, lights twinkling like thousands of halos, and began to sing.

> "*O holy night, the stars are brightly shining,*
> *It is the night of our dear Savior's birth,*
> *Long lay the world, in sin and error pining . . .*"

When she finished, the applause was plentiful, and tears flowed freely.

She was a musical prodigy beyond anything any of them had ever heard.

Epilogue

The annual Christmas musical was sold out, and the residents of Pine City who were unable to get a seat would be rewarded with a taped replay tomorrow afternoon in the high-school gymnasium.

Ivy sat in the front row, with Daniel on her left and Kayla and Roxie to her right, along with their parents, whom she had been introduced to the night before at the big event at Maxine's. She had held a small gathering of the performers at her house and introduced them to her friend Paul, who must have been someone very important. Ivy knew that Holly had some special connection with the older woman, but if Holly wanted her to know, she was sure she would tell her when the time was right.

Her father and Margaret sat at the end of the first row. Ivy kept searching the room until she saw who she was hoping would be there as a couple, Sarah and Jay. She gave a slight wave, and Sarah waved back, her smile as wide as the stage in front of them.

For the next hour and a half, they listened to local talent sing and play instruments. Some danced, and a group of children from Pine City's second-grade class wore red-and-white-striped pajamas as they performed a song about

Mommy kissing Santa. The audience clapped and whistled, but when Carol took center stage to introduce tonight's star performer, a hush fell over the audience. You could hear a pin drop, it was so quiet.

"Some of you here tonight know our next performer, and those who do not are going to wish they did. For the past several weeks, I have had the utmost pleasure to work with this young lady, who is a gifted singer. On behalf of the residents of The Upside, it is my great pleasure to introduce Miss Holly Greenwood."

Carol walked off the stage to polite applause, the lights in the auditorium grew dim, and once again, silence fell over the audience. The buildup to this event had been the talk of Pine City for weeks, and now the residents were in for the biggest treat of the night, for many, perhaps, the biggest treat of their lives to date.

Slowly the curtain rose. Lights shaped like hundreds of twinkling stars sparkled against the deep blue backdrop. In the center of the stage was another, smaller stage, which slowly rose above the main stage.

In its center stood Holly, dressed in a long silver dress with hundreds of shiny sequins that sparkled like an angel. Her hair hung in loose waves, and she wore a shiny red barrette in her hair.

A small orchestra behind her began to play. Holly held her head down, then looked out into the audience and began to sing.

Her voice was that of someone much older, practiced, gifted, and assured. She started off with "Silent Night," hitting high notes, and each word sounded as though it were being caressed as it came from her heart. The lights on the stage brightened with the next song, and tears fell down Holly's face as she sang "The Little Drummer Boy," followed with "The First Noel." Her performance of "Angels We Have Heard on High" received a standing ovation.

"I would like to dedicate this next song to my friend Ivy Fine and my dad, Daniel Greenwood, who I love with all my heart."

For the next several minutes, Holly sang "O Holy Night," as this was her favorite song.

Ivy and Daniel held hands tightly, and tears continued to flow as Holly sang to them, to the audience, and to anyone fortunate enough to witness a star in the making.

When she finished, she received a ten-minute standing ovation, which was unheard of, according to the whispers throughout the audience.

When the rest of the performers returned to the stage, they, too, were given a standing ovation.

"I need to see her," said the man who was Maxine's guest. He dragged Maxine along with him.

Before the man could go backstage, Daniel reached for Ivy's hand and followed him in search of his daughter.

When Daniel spied Holly, he walked through the crowd, and they parted as he made his way to his daughter. "That is the most touching music I have ever heard. You sound like an angel." He hugged her, and she smiled.

"Thanks, Dad, it's all I have ever wanted to do. I just feel it here"—she motioned to her heart—"when I sing."

"And I'll never stop you again, Holly. I love you so much, kiddo, and I'm beyond proud of you tonight. You had the audience hypnotized."

"I have never heard such a voice, well, maybe once, but it was many, many years ago, and it was not nearly as perfect as this young lady's." Maxine's friend barged through the crowd and found his way to Holly.

"When you're a little older, young lady, I'm going to make you a star. Here is my card. Maxine tells me you practice with Carol. Keep practicing, and when you're a few years older, you come and see me, okay?" He whirled about and departed as fast as he had entered. The man spoke so fast, they could barely understand what he was saying.

"Who was that?" Daniel asked Maxine, who had not been able to keep up with her friend.

"That's the most famous producer on Broadway, the one and only Paul Larson," Maxine said as she raced past them.

"Do you know him, Dad?" Holly asked.

"He was the man who was going to make your mother a star. I think we have a few more years to practice, but when the timing is right, and you're a bit older, and if you still want to sing, we will go to New York and look up Mr. Larson."

Holly screamed with delight, and by this time, all those who knew her were backstage offering her their congratulations. Roxie and Kayla hugged her and kissed her, and as though this were just another *cool* thing, they wandered off to mingle with their friends.

"How about you and me making a bit of music of our own?" Daniel said, pulling Ivy into his arms.

"I'm game if you are," Ivy said.

Slowly as if he had all the time in the world, not caring that dozens of people were watching, his lips touched hers, sending shock waves through both of them.

When they looked into one another's eyes, a round of applause cheered them on. Daniel's mouth swooped down to crush Ivy's lips against his own.

This was most assuredly going to be a very very very merry Christmas.